And They All Died Screaming

Dan West

ISBN 978-1-312-49863-1

The author would like to thank Sarita Redalia,
Chris Feroz, and Rick Popko for their help on this book

Cover art and illustrations by Dan West

Also by Dan West:

The House That Dripped Gore
Dan West's Homemade Embalming Fluid
Dan West's Web of Lies

For Chris Feroz

Chapter 1

The charred ruins of the horrible Hull mansion loomed black and rotting on its desolate patch of New England forestland, looking all the more ominous behind the heavily chained wrought iron fence that surrounded it. Whether the fence had been chained shut to keep something outside or inside of the property was a matter of some debate. Whispers of the "Demon of Dorchester" had been spreading across New England since the house caught fire in February of 1975.

These were, by no means, the first rumors of a bloodthirsty demon to circulate in the area, and I, for one, was certainly not going to discourage the tales. I knew firsthand of the otherworldly horrors that haunted the halls of Hull House. I was there that day, three years ago, when the mansion lit up like a disco inferno; the day that eleven members of the Order of Yarlock the Great Deceiver met their terrible ends; the day that the detestable Edgar Belmont exploded like an Edgar Belmont-shaped piñata stuffed full of candy shaped like human intestines.

That day was the last time I'd seen Dr. Bernard Harvey alive—the last time, save for his recurring role in my persistent night terrors, always beckoning me back to the mansion and the hellish catacombs below.

Death recently came a-calling again at Hull House—even in its current state of ruin, the house still managed to work its poisonous magic. It was like a gigantic roach motel that drew humans instead of roaches, which, I guess, technically would just make it like a normal motel, so perhaps that's not the best comparison. Was it like a gargantuan hornets' nest? Or was it more like a squirming snake pit? A phantasmagoric toilet bowl clogged with sinister, otherworldly bowel movements?

Whatever the most adequate analogy, the house was just like something that was like a big haunted house that lured its victims inside, where they then died horrible deaths. That's the clearest picture I can give you of the ghastly hellhole that sat on that fog-shrouded minefield of terror.

According to 19-year-old Jamie Lynn Faraday, the only living witness of the most recent bloodbath to take place at the mansion, a group of rambunctious college kids thought it would be fun to spend Halloween night in the house smoking dope and drinking beer and telling spooky stories about the demon. Eight young people went into Hull House on Halloween night, October 31st, 1978. One came out alive, blood-caked and babbling tales of monsters and madness. To the uninitiated it might have all sounded like the plot of a stereotypical, cheap, drive-in horror movie, but I knew better—what it *really* sounded like was the setup for a new, spine tingling, edge-of-your-seat thrill ride from a dynamic new voice in horror fiction (a welcome departure from an ill-advised foray into romance novels published under the questionable title: *Juicy Black Love Gumbo*). In the wake of such a terrible tragedy, I could no longer avoid the fact that the horrors of Hull House were far from over. Though I was loath to admit it, it appeared that my sex-drenched three-year hiatus at the luxurious Poontang Palace was going to have to be put on hiatus-hiatus, putting the kibosh on my nude concertina lessons.

Miss Faraday was currently being held under observation at the Danvers State Mental Hospital.

I'd recently paid the unfortunate young lady a visit at Danvers to discuss the tragedy and to get any details that the girl could remember about what took place that terrible night; I was accompanied by Detective Morton Solomon of the New York City Police Department. Detective Solomon had previously investigated

8

an attempt on my life carried out by two members of the Order of Yarlock the Great Deceiver and was more than happy to help me conduct my private investigation in any way he could.

The detective and I thought it might be wise to keep the nature of our visit a secret and Solomon was able to sell Miss Faraday's doctors on the ruse that the Hull House massacre might be linked to a series of brutal hobo explosions in New York City that were being perpetrated by a male assailant wearing a Nazi uniform and a pair of women's pantyhose pulled over his head. The story was an effective, if odd, choice for a subterfuge and we were granted a visit with Miss Faraday.

The traumatized teen was petite and pretty, but appeared rather skittish, given her uncombed blonde hair and the dark circles beneath her wary, blue eyes. At first the young woman was nearly catatonic during our discussion, but she did her best to relate the horrifying events with as much detail as she could recall.

Apparently the trip had been the brainchild of a 19-year-old prankster named, Ronald Dickey, a class clown renown for such over-the-top antics as donning a red clown nose for his woodworking class's yearbook photo and wearing a t-shirt with a cartoon tuxedo front printed on the chest to his high school's senior prom. He'd once even sat on a whoopee cushion during a visiting narcotics officer's lecture on the dangers of drug use. Yeah, the kid was a real cut-up. Now he was just really cut up ... into several pieces.

Aside from Miss Faraday and Ronald Dickey, there were seven other teenagers present at the house: Linda Carpenter, Brad Waters, Debra Blair, Robert Neil, P.J. Hill and Sam Warner. The party started innocently enough: shortly after sundown the group began smoking marijuana and telling ghost stories by candlelight in the mansion's front parlor. Then the ever-wacky Ronald Dickey suggested that they should explore the charred, cobweb shrouded ruins of the house. Using a few flashlights and candles to guide them on their terrible trek, the tenacious, tough-talking teenagers tread the treacherous terrain, tiptoeing through tenebrous territory, thoroughly thrilled that their trickster tour guide told them terrifying tales to traumatize them.

Faraday seemed to have been the only person present that was not amused by Mr. Dickey's tiresome antics. "Ronald was clowning around as usual, talking in this stupid Boris Karloff voice as he led us around the house. Everyone kept egging him on and laughing. I was terrified, but everyone else was cracking jokes like it was all just some Scooby-Doo cartoon or something." The young woman paused, and with trembling hands, lit what would be the first of a seemingly endless chain of Marlboro cigarettes. She exhaled a thick cloud of smoke, looking prematurely old, as she stared down at the table between us. I could certainly sympathize. I had more than a few battle scars of my own thanks to that accursed hellhole, but my empathy for the teenager was outweighed by my need for details about the horrors she'd witnessed that night.

"Please continue, Miss Faraday. I think you'll find us quite a bit more receptive to believing your story than the police or the doctors here have been."

"Ronald was leading us around with this candelabra he'd found, like he was Vincent Price or something. At first everyone thought that he'd somehow come to the house beforehand and set up a bunch of elaborate jokes to scare us like in a carnival spook house. Everybody thought that because of what happened to Brad. See, we were all dressed in costumes and Brad was dressed as Superman and when we were upstairs looking around, all of a sudden Brad suddenly floats off the ground and soars down the hall, just like he really was Superman. We thought that Brad and Ronald had worked out some kind of wire rig or something. But then Brad kept soaring down the hallway and crashed right through this big stained glass window at the end. At that point he didn't seem so much like Superman, he just seemed like a bloody, dead guy in a Halloween costume that fell out of a window and broke his neck. Robert insisted that it was all just some kind of prank and kept yelling down at Brad to cut it out. But Brad just lay there like a marionette with its strings cut as this big pool of blood formed around his head.

"When we all told Ronald that the joke wasn't funny, he said it was no joke and he looked like he was genuinely about to panic. At that point we knew it wasn't an act, so we all ran downstairs to see if we could help Brad. That was when this creepy guy stepped out of nowhere and scared the shit out of Ronald and everybody screamed ... And when I say this guy scared the shit out of Ronald, I mean that literally."

Detective Solomon paused from jotting his notes on a legal pad and lit a cigarette of his own. "Mr. Dickey experienced an unexpected anal discharge?"

"It sounded like someone blowing soup through a tuba."

I took a photograph of Dr. Harvey from the breast pocket of my coat and placed it on the table before the young woman. "Was *this* the man that caused Ronald Dickey to produce a thunderous elimination of feces from his digestive tract through his rectum?"

Faraday ground out her cigarette in a cheap metal ashtray and took the picture from the table for closer examination. "Him? No way. That's not the guy."

She tossed the picture back onto the table indifferently. I was shocked by her nonplussed reaction to seeing the face of the man I was certain to be her friends' killer.

"No? You seem pretty sure about that. You want to have a second look at that picture to be certain?"

She glanced at the photograph once more. "That's not him."

I was dumbfounded, but not entirely without a contingency plan. I removed an envelope from my side coat pocket that contained a collection of photographs of members of the Hull family: Leland, Isabella, Victor, Anastasia and Harrison. I removed the photographs from the envelope and laid them across the table in front of the teenager. "These are the former tenants of the Hull mansion."

The young woman started slightly and then took the picture of Leland Hull from the photo lineup. Her eyes widened in terror and she quickly dropped the photograph facedown on the table as if it had singed her fingertips. "That's him!" she said, awkwardly fumbling for another cigarette. "That is definitely the man that caused Ronald to experience an unexpected passing of stools through the anus!"

Dread crept over me as I considered the prospect. Leland was the only member of the Hull family who had failed to put in an appearance during my previous ordeal at the mansion. I'd hoped (against my better judgment) that his spirit was actually at rest, unlike those of the rest of the family. "You're certain that this was the man you saw on Halloween night?"

"Positive."

I stood up from the table and began to pace, despite having to support my weight on a cane due to the November chill in the air wreaking havoc on the old bullet wound in my thigh. "Miss Faraday, I'm not actually a detective."

"You're not real detectives?"

"Detective Solomon is a real detective ... I'm a parapsychologist."

"An ass doctor? No wonder you were asking about Ronald's anus. But why would *you* want to know about what happened at the house that night?"

"No ... I'm not a *proctologist*. I'm a parapsychologist ... a ghost hunter."

"Oh ... yeah, I always get those two mixed up."

"Yes, some people mix them up on purpose just to irritate us."

"Well, this guy was no ghost, I can assure of that. I'm not sure he was really human, but he sure as hell wasn't a ghost."

Solomon eyed the teenager, trying his best to keep the cynicism to a minimum. "What do you mean, you're not sure he was really human?"

"Nothing ... it's crazy," Faraday mumbled.

"Please go on," I pleaded. "What happened after this man approached you?"

The young woman stared at me, tight-lipped. Sizing us up as she tapped her cigarette on the metal ashtray. She took a deep breath and continued. "The guy was absolutely terrifying. I can still see his eyes. Those horrible black eyes ... like a spider's eyes ... or like one of those great white sharks ... if it had spider eyes. All black with no whites at all. He asked what the hell we were doing there, creeping around in the dark. We told him that we thought the house was abandoned and that we were just there because it was Halloween night and the place was supposed to be haunted.

"Then P.J. started screaming that our friend had had a terrible flying accident because he was stoned and thought that he could fly like Superman. She told him that we needed to get to a phone so that we could call an ambulance." Faraday ground out her cigarette and immediately replaced it with another. "Brad didn't need an ambulance ... more like a hearse; but P.J. was just in complete denial. She was madly in love with the poor jerk."

Hoping that my gimpy Sherlock Holmes act was adequate enough to veil the true depth of my mounting horror, I braved another fantastic inquiry. "How did the man look aside from the odd, black eyeballs? Did he look like a normal, man-shaped, man-person? It's just that there are all of those rumors about the Demon of Dorchester."

"It's true," Faraday whispered, gazing blankly down at the table with a shell-shocked stare. "I saw him change ... after they took my friends."

"After *who* took your friends?" Solomon said.

"The black-eyed man said something about rats in a maze and the cold, insectile brutality of the universe and then yelled, 'Take them below!' That was when these people just came charging at us out of nowhere. They were all deformed, like those freaks in the carnival sideshows, and were all wearing these red robes with hoods. They smelled terrible ... like rotting meat. They all rushed out of the shadows and grabbed everyone, but in the confusion I managed to get free. Because it was Halloween, I'd come dressed as Little Dead Riding Hood and my hooded, red cape and weird make-up made me look like I was one of the fishy-smelling mutants. It was just by coincidence that I was able to get away. When they didn't grab me, I realized what had happened and just started acting like one of them—grunting and talking in broken English and clawing at my friends. I even bit Ronald on the arm for effect.

"While the mutant people were distracted with my friends, I took off down the hallway to try to hide from them. It was weird because it seemed like I was being guided in the darkness by some kind of force, or spirit or something. Then I tripped over some of the burned debris as I was running and fell through this wall. And when I say that I fell through the wall, I don't mean like one of the Three Stooges. I mean I fell forward and through this holographic image of a fake wall and into some kind of laboratory. It was fully lit, even though the house didn't seem to have electricity and it was lined with rows of shelves full of equipment and cabinets full of hundreds of these weird specimen jars with these monstrous looking creatures inside of them. There were a lot of charts and notes lying around, and there were several microscopes and a big shelf filled with all kinds of books. It all looked like something out of a Frankenstein movie."

By then I was hanging on the chain-smoking teenager's every word like an exceptionally handsome booger clinging to the nostril of a snotty-nosed giant. "Do you remember where this hidden room was located in the house?"

"Yes. It was on the ground floor down a long hallway past the dining room. It was off the left side of the hallway. There was a lot of rubble everywhere and everything around it was burned."

If my memory served me correctly, the room that Faraday described was the location of what had been the mansion's profane chapel, where the terrible rites of the Order of Yarlock the Great Deceiver were conducted time and time again by the members of the vile cult—certainly fertile ground on which to sow the seeds of a fresh crop of horrors.

"I could hear everyone screaming off in the distance as they were being dragged away. I was too scared to move. And then the scary man with the black eyes stepped through the holographic wall. He was laughing like a madman. I just hid in the shadows watching him.

Then he stripped off his robe and I could see that his skin was literally crawling."

Detective Solomon ground out his cigarette butt in the metal ashtray. "How do you mean, crawling?"

"I mean it was alive ... it was crawling like there were snakes and worms squirming underneath it. Then his whole body started to change." Faraday stared off into space with her dark-rimmed eyes hinting of remembered horrors.

Solomon leaned forward in his chair. "Into what?"

Faraday snapped out of her daze and met Solomon's eyes with a weary candor in her own. "Into some kind of monster."

I turned about face and took a clumsy, limping step toward the teenager, trying my best not to appear too desperate for details. "What did you see, Miss Faraday? I need to know what's lurking in the halls of that house."

"It looked like an eight-foot long tapeworm with scorpion's claws having anal sex with an inside out Komodo dragon that had a baboon's ass lined with shark teeth for a face and king cobras for hair. Out of its side was growing a giant housefly-type of insect that looked like it was shitting a retarded abominable snowman's head out of its asshole."

Solomon shot me a look that was equal parts astonishment, skepticism and concern for the teenager's mental state. I signaled for him to remain patient and continue going along with our line of questioning. He shrugged and turned back to his notepad, on which he was sketching a rendition of the creature that Faraday had been describing.

I gazed over his shoulder, examining the drawing with dread. Leland Hull certainly had changed since his resurrection from the dead, but into what was anyone's guess.

Suddenly Faraday's voice broke the awkward silence. "Are you going there to try and kill it?"

I looked into the girl's eyes with surprise. Was that actually my intention?

The teenager lit another cigarette and sized me up with her unnervingly prudent gaze. "You know what I think, Mr. parapsychologist?"

"What's that, Miss Faraday?"

"I think there's a whole lot you're not telling about why you're so interested in what happened in that house on Halloween night."

"How did you manage to escape from Hull House alive, Jamie Lynn?"

"How did *you* manage to, Mr. Matheson? I assume you didn't get that bum leg from wrestling alligators."

The kid was certainly wise beyond her years. I hadn't wrestled a gator since my mid twenties, and the telltale scars on my scalp had all but healed. Here I was, limping around like Captain Ahab on the hunt for the great white whale, and Faraday could nearly smell my desperation. "Kid, if I was to give you the full-blown lowdown on my own ordeal at Hull House, they'd have me locked up in here with you, and that wouldn't do either of us any good. What's important is that I believe you and I'm going to do my best to help get you out of here."

Faraday mulled over her options for a moment and then continued her account. "After I watched the guy changing, I ran and hid inside of what I thought was a closet. It was this black compartment with a sliding door. I got inside and closed the door and suddenly the compartment started to descend through the floor. It was an elevator that went down to these caves underneath the house. The door opened and I stepped out just as the mutants were dragging my friends past the elevator. I walked along with the group, spitting on Ronald and beating on him with a stick I'd grabbed in the lab to defend myself. At one point, the mutants actually pulled me off of him when I started biting him again.

"I looked back at where we'd come from, searching for another way out, and that was when I saw the demon."

"In the catacombs?"

"It came out of the elevator. The thing had the same black eyes as the scary man and I knew it was him. He'd transformed. He looked like some kind of devil ... with big bat wings and horns. He followed behind us into the caverns, laughing—" her voice trailed off as she repeated her cigarette ritual, extinguishing one and then immediately lighting another.

If I hadn't seen any of this with my own two eyes it would have scarcely been believable. The fiery young woman actually encountered the demon in the flesh and visited the hellish, subterranean lair that Edgar Belmont had referred to as the Gateways of the Seven Legions of Darkness; sanctuary of the mutant Heldethrach offspring (no doubt the same deformed humanoids that had abducted the terrified teenagers.) It was no wonder the local authorities had carted Faraday off to the nuthouse.

The girl's eyes became wider and wilder as she continued the tale, as if she could hardly believe her own words. "We stopped at the base of these massive portholes, these gigantic windows that stretched up to the top of the cavern. I could see things inside of the portholes ... these horrible alien creatures. It was like some aquarium in Hell! The windows were like telescope lenses looking into these other worlds or something. I don't know how else to explain it."

I couldn't have described the caverns better myself, and I prompted her to continue and hold nothing back. By this time, the girl was more animated than a Screwy Squirrel cartoon, gesturing wildly as she relived the terrible events. "The whole cave kept shifting around like a puzzle ... and the demon seemed to be controlling everything by hitting notes on this huge pipe organ."

"Pipe organ?" I said.

"Yeah ... like a big Phantom of the Opera type of thing. It rose up out of the stone and the demon sat at the organ playing notes that controlled these weird mechanisms. At first there were just these platforms in front of the porthole windows, like altars or something, but the demon played some strange notes on the organ and the altars all sank into the floor and were replaced by these chairs ... like you'd find in a dentist's office—but with heavy leather straps on them."

"Sounds a bit like that movie, Marathon Man," Solomon muttered.

"Well it wasn't something that I saw in some goddamn movie, and it was a lot worse than whatever happened to Dustin Hoffman at the hands of some Nazi sadist, Detective!" Faraday grumbled, irritated by the interruption. "They strapped my friends into these restraining chairs that tilted back and pointed the tops of their heads toward the portholes and these weird arm-like mechanisms sawed completely around the tops of their skulls and lifted the bone off so that their brains were all exposed like shucked oysters. Then these disgusting umbilical tentacles with thorny mandible suckers on the end extended down from the tops of the portholes and attached to their brains. After that, more of the arm-like mechanisms sprung up and injected these strangely colored fluids into the veins in my friends' necks with hypodermic needle tubes as these other tentacles slithered down their throats. There were these crazy explosions of color from inside the portholes. It was almost beautiful ... but so horrible at the same time ... like those movies of childbirth they show in biology class."

I wasn't sure if this wild-eyed, chain-smoking ragamuffin was the luckiest kid in the world for actually having escaped from Hull House, or the unluckiest for having witnessed its unrelenting horrors, but one thing *was* certain: This traumatized 19-year old girl now officially had a more intimate knowledge of the current, sinister goings on at the place than I did.

"My friends' eyes actually started to glow with red light, and then the tentacles down their throats retracted and they started spitting up this black goo that looked like caviar. The mutants caught the stuff in these big jars as it came out.

"The demon said something about a plague ... he called it *death from Medusa's uterus* and told the freaks to take the jars up to his lab.

"At that point, this huge, swirling cloud began to form in the air in center of the cavern —it seemed to be sucking energy from each of the portholes as it grew. I could see these ghosts of demons and these twisted monsters flying out of the porthole windows and being absorbed into the cloud ... like it was made up of these evil spirits. The same thing was happening to my friends in the chairs. You could see these nightmarish images being sucked out of their minds into the cloud. It grew and grew until it was like a massive, black storm cloud—a massive storm cloud made of pure evil." Faraday ground out her cigarette butt in the ashtray and then ran her fingers through her wild hair.

As the young woman paused briefly, I impatiently snapped my fingers at Solomon, gesturing for him to pass me a cigarette from his pack. I hadn't had a smoke in five years, but the implications of Faraday's little horror epic were giving me the nicotine fit from Hell. I had seen such a phenomenon before—a malignant cloud of pure evil. It sounded completely insane, and that is precisely what the cloud consisted of ... madness and nightmares. Just the thought of it was enough to turn my blood into cherry shave ice.

Faraday soon resumed her chain smoking, lighting up what seemed like her fiftieth Marlboro of the morning. "These giant black flaps folded around the chairs like flowers closing up and completely enclosed my friends. Then they all descended into these shafts in the floor of the cavern and disappeared. That was the last I saw of them before the police showed me the crime scene photos. After my friends were gone, I just bolted across the caverns and ran for my life. I found a stairwell that led up into the basement wine cellar and managed to stumble back to the front door and get out of the house. As I was running into the courtyard to Ronald's van, Brad attacked me."

Solomon rubbed his temples, baffled. "Brad? You mean dead, Superman, fell out of the window, Brad?"

"His brains were spilling out of a big crack in his skull and his neck was obviously broken. He was clawing at me like a wild animal. It was straight out of *Night of the Living Dead*, if that movie had had super heroes in it. That's how I got all of the blood all over me. We wrestled around on the ground for a minute and then I managed to get free and run to the van. Luckily, Ronald left the keys in the ignition and I was able to start it. I floored the gas pedal and ran over Brad as I was speeding out of the courtyard. He jumped at the van and I just rolled right over him. I drove away as fast as I could, but the fog was so thick, I could barely see the road. I don't even remember the accident. I just have this foggy memory of dreaming that I was floating in the arms of a friendly genie."

"Genie? Like from a magic lamp?" Solomon said.

Faraday glanced down at the photographs on the table. "He was some glowing, green man carrying me to safety. That's about all I can remember after leaving the house. A state trooper found me the next morning. The van was flipped over on the side of the road. I was covered in blood and playing *Hail to the Chief* over and over again with a plastic nose flute. The next thing I knew, I woke up in a rubber bedroom."

After contemplating the girl's tale for a moment, I absent-mindedly stuffed the cigarette I was holding into my mouth as if it were a stick of chewing gum and, after a few bitter, gagging chomps, spat the mangled mush onto the visiting room floor. I felt I had to be square with the kid after her spilling her guts about the events that had led to the spilling of her friends' guts, and, after vomiting a small puddle of tobacco juice onto the floor, I managed to get my choking under control enough to come clean with the young lady. "Strictly off the record, Jamie Lynn—the portholes you saw in those caves were the six remaining gateways of the Seven Legions of Darkness, constructed unknown ages ago by the slaves of an evil being known as Yarlock the Great Deceiver. I destroyed the seventh porthole three years ago. The man in this photograph ... the man with the black eyes that changed into the demon ... his name is Leland Hull. He's the original owner of the mansion. He was a warlock and cult leader and a very dangerous man, from what I know about him. His own son murdered him in that house. The cloud you saw forming in the caverns is an evil force from another dimension that draws its power from the beings in the portholes."

"You know, if I wasn't currently residing in a mental hospital, I might just think that all of that sounded a little insane, Mr. Matheson." Faraday looked to Detective Solomon for corroboration. "And what's your take on all of this, Detective?"

Solomon offered his now trademark shrug once again. "All I know is that three years ago some very dangerous members of a very dangerous cult attempted to barbeque Mr. Matheson alive before he was able to uncover the truth of what the hell was going on at the Hull mansion—the psychos even shoved a marionette up his ass as a farewell gift."

I frantically signaled Solomon to eighty-six the marionette talk, but he continued to babble on like a wound up pair of chattering joke store dentures. "Real sickos! They roasted one of their own guys just to cover their tracks ... they shoved a puppet up that unlucky bastard's ass too."

Faraday winced.

"I don't know anything about any witches or demons, but a few days later, Matheson here crawled out of that house, half dead and bleeding like a stuck pig. His hair had turned as white as goddamn snow and he looked about twenty years older."

"Three years," I corrected. "Four tops."

"Like you, old Stanley was just lucky to be alive, Miss Faraday."

The young woman looked me over, nodding slowly. "No wonder he looks like that."

I cleared my throat, unsure of her meaning. "Like what, exactly?"

"I don't know ... all weird and jittery."

Solomon chuckled. "Oh, he looked like that even before Hull House got to him. Now he just looks a little bit more worse for wear."

The poor young woman's obvious fascination with my distractingly hypnotic and somewhat intimidating sensuality had caused our conversation to veer wildly off course, and I steered us back to the dreadful subject of the Halloween night massacre. "I understand that the Dorchester Police Department presented a vastly different scenario for that evening after their investigation of the mansion."

"They said they found no laboratory and no secret stairwell in the wine cellar leading to any underground caves—just a burned, spooky, old mansion full of the slaughtered remains of several, dead teenagers. They suggested that I might have been given some kind of hallucinogenic drug during the party and went crazy without having any memory of it. I guess that was the best that they could come up with under the circumstances. When the cops showed me the photos, I didn't know what else to say. That crime scene was as staged as an off Broadway production of *The Music Man.* My friends were all butchered ... chopped up into neat, little, sandwich-sized pieces and packed into a bunch of *Welcome Back Kotter* lunchboxes. There were like fifty of them! Who the hell likes *Welcome Back Kotter* that much? That show sucks!

"The coroner said my friends didn't look like much more than piles of ground up hamburger with teeth and hair added for decoration. He said that, for all intents and purposes, they *were* hamburger, but with a distinctly "humany" flavor ... I'm not sure how he made that particular distinction, but I have my suspicions."

So, the ancient evils of the Legions of Darkness were active once again and were back in business, cooking up a deadly new plague with the shapeshifting Demon of Dorchester and an army of demonic mutants in the hellish underworld beneath the haunted Hull Family mansion. All that seemed to be missing was a battalion of undead Nazis or a werewolf motorcycle gang. What this situation called for wasn't a parapsychologist but a goddamn superhero, and the only person who seemed to even remotely resemble one that I knew of had recently been chopped up into bite-sized pieces and stuffed into a couple of Welcome Back Kotter lunch boxes. From my own experience with the horrible Krelsethian gorgon coven, I could only assume that the Legions of Darkness were some kind of interdimensional axis of evil ... orchestrators of madness and death. After listening to Faraday's account, I got the sinking feeling that this situation was going to be a bit out of my depth. Short of persuading them to change their plans to opening a wild, new, subterranean roller disco and swingers' club, I was running a little short on ideas on how to proceed.

If I intended to venture back to Hull House to fight *this* battle, I'd need to go in loaded for bear. But how the hell was I supposed to handle this conundrum, and who the hell would assist me in doing whatever the hell it was that I needed to do? I reasoned that since

Batman and James Bond were currently unavailable due to their being fictional, I would need to come up with a better contingency plan. Would I hire a small army of crazed winos and equip them with handguns and football helmets? Or would I equip them with swords and wizard costumes? Axes and monster masks? And where the hell could I find a small army of crazed winos?

Before finalizing my plan of attack, I decided that a bit of reconnaissance was in order. Faraday narrowly escaped the bowels of Hull House by unwittingly camouflaging herself as a member of the demonic mutant hordes who dwell there. Perhaps by following her example I would also be able infiltrate, and subsequently escape, from those same bowels without having the ones inside of my own body savagely torn out and used as a delightfully zesty sausage casing. In lieu of a team of occult specialists, I recruited none other than Detective Solomon to accompany me on my potentially deadly undercover mission. He was conveniently available thanks to his recently being put on unpaid, administrative leave for pistol whipping a child pornographer with an antique Civil War cannon.

To create our required ghastly camouflage, the detective suggested that we enlist the services of his nephew, Herman Pinkman, an aspiring make-up effects artist who hoped to one-day break into Hollywood movies with his monstrous creations. I felt it was worth a shot, so after renting a pair of hooded, red robes from a costume company in New York, we drove to Herman's parent's house in Poughkeepsie to check out the kid's workshop. Upon entering the cramped, makeshift garage studio, I was immediately impressed with Herman's rubber latex aliens, monsters and gore effects.

I was particularly intrigued by the weird and unsettling make-up that Herman had applied to his own face to impress us before our arrival. The prosthetic, buck-toothed overbite, weak chin and bug eyes gave the lad the appearance of a pale, puffy-faced moleman. In fact, I was rather surprised when, after complimenting him on the malformed visage, the puzzled young man informed me that he wasn't actually wearing any prosthetic make-up. I may have been a bit confused about the kid's oddball looks, but there was one thing that I was absolutely certain about: the kid had talent in spades, and by the time that Solomon and I stepped out of his make-up chair, we looked so authentically horrific that the pair of us could have easily just walked out of the pages of an old EC horror comic.

Admiring Herman's handiwork in a mirror, I couldn't help but notice what looked very much like a puckered asshole in the center of my now lumpy and hydrocephalic forehead—perhaps applied out of spite for my previous comments about the strange shape of the make-up maestro's face. When I mentioned the offending prosthetic appliance, Herman simply touched up the rubber latex sphincter with a more reddish tone, saying, "Let's just bring that inflammation out a bit more."

Though the overly-sensitive effects man had literally made me look like an asshole, his make-up work was nothing short of amazing, and I paid the kid handsomely for his efforts.

Getting into character over the course of our five-hour-plus drive to Dorchester, Detective Solomon and I grumbled and babbled at each other in mush mouthed, broken English. Through our jagged, yellow, false teeth we gurgled and croaked out our plans to infiltrate the demonic humanoid hordes and get a firsthand gander at the puss-filled boil of terror that was about to spew forth from the Gateways of the Legions of Darkness.

Going undercover was old hat to Solomon. The seasoned New York cop had, over the course of his career in law enforcement, posed as everything from depraved weenie-wagging sex perverts and crazed urine-soaked derelicts to sassy transvestite prostitutes. The detective had certainly experienced his share of craziness, and I was relieved to have him at my side under such dangerous circumstances, despite his obvious cynicism concerning the forces of otherworldly evil at work at Hull House.

Upon our arrival at the property, I pulled the car over in a wooded area about a quarter of a mile from the mansion's front gate and Solomon and I covered the vehicle with stray branches and brush to conceal it from view. We then cautiously made our way toward the house.

Now, as we stood with only the wrought iron bars of the gate separating us from the terrors that lurked within the ruins of the haunted hellhole, with our heads covered in rubber latex and our coat pockets stuffed with rank-smelling meat, I could only wonder if our noble efforts would amount to nothing more than a foolhardy suicide mission.

Gazing through a pair of binoculars at the burned ruins of the mansion, I attempted to steady my trembling hands and not "pull a Ronald Dickey" when I felt my churning bowels attempting to descend into the depths of my boxer shorts. When it became apparent that I was fighting a losing battle, I hastily retreated into the nearby woods to carpet bomb the native flora with malodorous bursts of brown buckshot. I squatted in the brush, horrified by the excessively loud volume of the uncontrollable flatulence that accompanied my emergency evacuation. I might as well have announced our arrival by farting into a megaphone. I could hear Solomon frantically shushing me as I accommodated the cruel whims of four cups of black coffee and the chilidog that I'd eaten for lunch.

The house had certainly lost none of its malignant power. Just the sight of the place was enough to send me sprinting into the woods with my bowels twisted into so many knots that they felt like a set of bagpipes being given the Heimlich maneuver by a 20-foot-long boa constrictor. As I squatted in the brush, contemplating my precariously poopy predicament, I could only hope that my present situation was not an indication of what lay in store for me this time around at Hull House. If that was the case, I might just as well put my head between my legs and kiss my ass goodbye, an option rendered thoroughly undesirable thanks to the current state of my stomach.

When I finally stepped out of the brush a few moments later, Detective Solomon grabbed me, jerking me back into the woods whence I came as he ran for cover.

"Your fellow freaks heard your mating call, bugle boy. They're coming this way!"

I chanced a glance back over my shoulder and glimpsed a sea of red swarming into the front courtyard from the mansion's front door. We fled clumsily into the thick mist of the surrounding forest as the metallic jingle of the front gate's chain sounded in the distance as it was unraveled to release the oncoming hoard.

Dashing blindly into the gray haze of fog that swirled and curled about the trees in cold moist wisps, we lost all sense of direction. Thanks to my old bullet wound, I was floundering about as if my right leg had been replaced with a wet noodle with a shoe tied to the end of it.

The throaty ravings of the mutant battalion seemed to be coming at us from all sides and as we stumbled into a clearing we realized that the sensation of being surrounded by the misshapen throng was simply due to that fact that the misshapen throng had surrounded us. Trying not to panic, Detective Solomon and I remained mute, looking just as confused as our deformed pursuers, who seemed thankfully oblivious to our costumed charade.

"Where go intruder?" one of the mutants said, looking to Solomon and me for his answer.

"Me saw two chase fart maker into woods!" another said.

I feigned a revelation, pounding my fist into my palm. "Maybe intruder make fart decoy to distract us! We leave house vulnerable from no guarding!" With that, I charged into the mist, attempting to navigate the horde back to the mansion. The group followed suit, ranting and roaring as we gave chase in pursuit of the farting phantom that had seemingly outwitted us.

Screaming wildly, I led the bloodthirsty posse of grotesque goons back into Hull House, wincing at the effectiveness of my own ingenuity as we charged through the front doors. As the rabid rabble of wretched wraiths rushed about in every direction attempting to flush out the elusive intruder, I seized Solomon by the arm and pulled him down the hallway. Training the beam of the flashlight that I'd brought along the left side of the charred hallway wall, I found no evidence of the destroyed chapel or of Faraday's secret laboratory. There was nothing but a solid wall, recently built to conceal the chamber. Clever. This little cover-up would have made

Jamie Lynn's story even more impossible to believe than it had been to begin with. Now the only entrance to the lab would be through the elevator in the catacombs beneath the house.

Suddenly the eerie sound of what could only be a pipe organ echoed through the house from somewhere below us. The pandemonium around us came to an abrupt halt and the mutant search party suddenly ceased their activities, as if called to attention by the vibrating pulse of the organ's haunting chords.

"The master summons to the gateway!" one of the mutants rasped.

Despite my misgivings, it appeared that we would be paying an impromptu visit to Leland Hull after all. We joined the ranks of the freakish minions as they marched obediently in single file toward the kitchen and down the stairs into the darkness of the wine cellar. There we entered the secret passage to the stairwell that descended into the depths of the catacombs below.

Entering the great subterranean realm of the Gateways of the Seven Legions of Darkness, we were greeted by the monstrous sight of Leland Hull. He sat with his back to the crowd upon an elevated, rocky pulpit/stage, facing his gigantic pipe organ. Slimy gray tentacles protruded from the sleeves of his black robe, curling and twisting and dancing across the organ's keyboard with horrible grace. The robe jerked and pulsated like a sack full of live eels, and I could only imagine what horrors the cloak concealed. The warlock ceased his musical tinkering and spun slowly around to face his loyal subordinates. I heard a quiet gasp from beside me and turned to see Detective Solomon staring wide-eyed at the grotesque monster seated at the pipe organ.

"It's true ... all true," he whispered, sounding incredulous.

Leland rose to his feet as the grotesque chaos of his facial features squirmed and twisted and finally formed into a pale imitation of something that looked vaguely like his former self ... save, that is, for those aforementioned, horrible, black eyes.

Suddenly a deafening thunderclap exploded above our heads, coming from the vast, swirling, storm cloud of conjured evils that hovered above us in all of its awe-inspiring horror.

Leland stared up at the vile, pulsating gloom as his lips curled into a wicked grin. He returned his gaze to the crowd. "Children of the Heldethrach, our time of reckoning draws near. The Orias Nebula will carry death from Medusa's Uterus to the population as an airborne contagion. Mile by mile, town by town, the madness will spread. The humans will have two options. They may become our slaves, or they can tear each other apart as they are driven slowly insane."

The horrible nebula above us exploded with a thunderous rumbling and bolts of venous crimson lightning flashed in every direction. Then, as if on cue, from the floor of the cave arose five black pods that unfolded like rotten flower petals to reveal a quintet of humanoid figures clad in ebony spacesuits. Tendrils of steam licked the protective suits as if they'd been plucked from a boiling witch's cauldron. Sickening blobs of gelatinous yellow slime dripped from the armor as the beings released the pressurized locking mechanisms on their space helmets. Numerous air tubes popped free and the sinister guests removed their headgear. There was a strange familiarity to the visitors that I quickly placed as a vague resemblance to the five teenagers supposedly murdered and mutilated in the house on Halloween night. The alikeness was fleeting, as, seconds after removing their helmets, the beings began to mutate into grotesqueries that I am at a loss to describe. Gazing at the monsters, I was struck by a terrible sensation of déjà vu. I had seen these things before ... when, during my previous visit to Hull House, the first Orias Nebula struck my brain helmet with its horror-charged umbilical lightening. The nightmarish visions that it shot into my brain had turned my hair as white as a Ku Klux Klan rally.

Were these freakish monstrosities ambassadors of evil from the hellish realms of the Legions of Darkness? Whatever they were they made the Heldethrach minions look like a girls' school glee club. As I beheld the creatures from the pods, my head and vision began to swim as if my eyeballs were soaking in a mixture of PCP and embalming fluid.

One of the mutant minions beside me clapped with delight. "This better than cranberry cocktail Tuesdays!"

It became nearly dizzying attempting to focus on the shape shifting features of the shapeshifting creatures and I turned away, whispering to Solomon that I needed to borrow his ever-present notepad and pen. I was about to take an enormous gamble on a big long shot, but I was desperate to form some sort of battle strategy. I flipped the notebook open and with pen poised to jot my notes, I cleared my throat and raised my hand to get Leland's attention. The warlock stared at me, slightly puzzled by the interruption.

"Yes?"

"Hi, master ... Gert Sergurglar ... Heldethrach Herald Daily. Me have a few quick questions from inquiring readers for our Conspiracy Corner column. Let's say that some foolish human was going to attempt to thwart master's sinister plans ... How you think this saboteur would go about such a task?"

The crowd began to mumble with concern and confusion.

Leland frowned, obviously annoyed. "Heldethrach Herald Daily? I don't believe I've heard of that particular newspaper."

"So is that a 'no comment'? Your minions were just wondering if master make some kind of contingency plan in case of sabotage. Me am sure your guests from the Legions of Darkness would be interested if there any real danger of things going amiss with big world takeover. Let's not forget what happened to seventh porthole a few years ago."

The pod visitors looked to Leland for a response. The warlock, in turn, glared down at me and answered between clenched teeth. "Well, Mr. Serdgurglar from the Heldethrach Herald, if you are referring to Shiverdecker's theory of malignant reversal, the odds of a human saboteur surviving the horrors of the Scorpius plane and locating the Lovejoy Codex are a million to one."

I quickly copied the warlock's cryptic response on a page in Solomon's notebook and then carefully tucked the log into the breast pocket of the jacket beneath my robe. Take that axis of evil! Score one for the human race! Now I just had to reduce those odds by figuring out how the one thing would do that other thing with the stuff.

Solomon leaned close and whispered, "You get all of that?"

"Every word."

"What the hell was it?"

"No idea. But it's a piece of the puzzle, nonetheless ... and I do mean *less*. It just sounded like a bunch of gibberish to me."

"I didn't like the sound of that shrivel dick cotex thing."

Leland approached the horrible porthole visitors, his mouth broadening into a grin. "The Legions of Darkness shall walk amongst the humans spreading death and madness across the lands with unrivaled flair and pizzazz. The kind of flair and pizzazz that only the Legions of Darkness can bring to a racial extermination!"

"Think of all pretty blood and puss colors!" one of the minions shrieked.

"And all of fantastic opportunities for raping of anuses!" another shouted.

"Me am going to shove a live vampire bat up a human's ass just to see what happens!" said another.

The crowd's mania was escalating into a near frenzy. There was blood in the water and the sharks were hungry.

Suddenly, as if inspired by the excitement of his followers, Leland Hull stripped off his robe and spread his arms wide to the heavens as a pair of gigantic, bat-like wings unfurled from his shoulder blades and two, long, black horns shot up from the corners of his forehead. The demon transformed—a horrifying feat that elicited a roar of approval from the congregation that surrounded us.

As the rabid throng began to chant in a language that I recognized as the tongue of the vanquished Krelsethian witch coven, Solomon and I backed away from the mob and crept toward the area where the elevator to the hidden laboratory was located.

We found the unmarked black cylinder, which opened when I placed an open palm to the metallic surface. Solomon and I quickly stepped inside the sheer interior and found ourselves immediately aloft in the compartment, which, seconds later, deposited us in the upstairs laboratory. Ever the detective, Solomon had thought to conceal a Polaroid camera on his person and immediately began to snap photos of the complex notes and charts hung about the walls of the room. I cautiously scanned Leland's lab work, locating a collection of small glass specimen containers sitting next to a large microscope that looked elaborately alien in construction. The covered dishes each contained a small amount of gelatinous black fluid that bore a striking resemblance to caviar. *Death from Medusa's Uterus*—the plague spat forth from the horrible realms of the Legions of Darkness.

Given our particular "no win" scenario, desperate times called for desperate measures, and I gingerly wrapped one of the glass containers in a handkerchief and tucked it into the pocket of my coat. Another long shot, but I figured the threat of exposure had already assured that I would be carrying the plague out of the house one way or another. I might as well cut my losses by pilfering a lab sample for analysis, in the unlikely event that a cure could be created.

Next, I examined the collection of books stockpiled in the aspiring mass murderer's workspace. It was then that I heard my name spoken from behind me in a voice that I had not heard for three years ... the voice of Dr. Bernard Harvey.

"Matheson!"

"Doctor Harvey?" I turned to face a glowing translucent figure hovering above us. It was indeed, Dr. Harvey—or rather his disembodied spirit, looking as irritable and human as he had before his transformation into the murderous demon three years previous. It was my old professional nemesis—the prickly curmudgeon who once delighted in berating my efforts as a parapsychologist, now returned from the afterlife as a ghost. I fought off the grin that was nearly brought on by my feeling of vindication. "Doctor ... you're—" my voice trailed off, as I was unaware of exactly how to address the apparition.

"A ghost? Go ahead and gloat, Matheson. It won't make those moronic books of yours any better." The transformation into a phantasm certainly hadn't hampered the man's acerbic wit. "I see you're now sporting an asshole in the center of your forehead. Don't you think that's rather stating the obvious, Stanley?"

"We're in disguise to infiltrate the Heldethrach mutants."

"Oh, well they aren't very intelligent. I imagine you fit right in."

"But if you're now a hideous harbinger of horror from beyond the grave, what happened to your old body? You were a monstrous, bloodthirsty demon the last time I saw you. What became of your bloated, slimy and repulsive carcass, Doctor?"

"The demonic entity that entered my tanned and muscular body, transforming me into a well-toned Adonis of terror, subsequently exhumed the putrid, rotting corpse of your psychopathic great grandfather from a crypt in the catacombs."

"Leland Hull!"

"The odor of decay, shriveled leathery flesh and telltale misshapen skull made your family resemblance unmistakable."

"But why would a hulking mongoloid brute exhume the body of Leland Hull? Was it to engage in some kind of depraved homosexual necrophilia? Was that it? Did the perverted demon who had possessed you want to plunge his erect, diseased, puss-dripping member into the rotting maggot-eaten buttocks of the long-dead warlock?"

"No, you demented idiot! The demon took Hull's remains into one of the portholes! Into some horrible alternate dimension. There were beings there that performed some kind of black magic ritual that resurrected his spirit and sent it into what used to be my mouthwatering Herculean powerhouse of a body. Leland Hull's consciousness seemed to meld with that of the demonic entity and I experienced the sensation of having my spirit cast out of my own body ... like some reverse exorcism. Out with the good, in with the bad. After all of this demonic mumbo jumbo I found myself just a disembodied spirit adrift in some threshold netherworld."

Solomon took a step toward the apparition. "You saved the girl who escaped from here. After the van crashed. The glowing green man she saw."

"She was a lot more fortunate than her friends, I'm afraid. They were taken into the portholes as well," Dr. Harvey said.

"We've seen them," I said. "What's happened to them?"

"While my spirit was trapped in that other horrible world, I experienced the alien beings performing several strange operations on the demon's body ... mutilations, transfusions ... strange rites, all resulting in that twisted version of Leland Hull that you encountered in the catacombs just now. I imagine the same sort of thing was done to those unfortunate teenagers. They are no longer human. They are now possessed by the evils of the Legions of Darkness."

"How do we stop it, Doctor? How do we stop any of this?"

"Contact my colleague, Dr. Graham Whitlock, professor of metaphysics and arcane mysticism at Leon Spinks University."

As Dr. Harvey dictated, I quickly took Solomon's pen and notebook from my jacket pocket and dutifully recorded his instructions.

"Tell him that you have gathered undeniable proof that the prophecies of Shemrach Theydarian have come to pass and that he must acquire the Opus Demonium from Professor Hiller at the Theydarian Society for the Study of the Black Arts in the town of Goblin's Dong, Connecticut."

"Professor *Edwin Hiller*?"

"You know of him?"

"I've already contacted Professor Hiller about all of this. I called him, but he just dismissed me as some nutjob trying to exploit his work in one of my sensationalist books. I tried to explain to him that my books were considered *sensational*, and not *sensationalist*, but he wasn't having any of it. He called me a weasel-faced hack and hung up on me."

"He'll listen to Whitlock, Stanley. You just keep a low profile about this and let the doctor do all of the talking."

"And what are we supposed to do about this plague?" Solomon said.

"Put the specimen in the night drop box at Diseases N' Stuff. They're a discount epidemiology center for disease control in Newark, New Jersey. Make sure to include a note that says 'Attention, Dr. Cynthia Quinlan. Danger: DO NOT DROP OR ATTEMPT TO JUGGLE. Containment required. Specimen is a parasitic organism that secretes a corrosive enzyme into the tissues of the brain. Desire immediate cure for prevention of worldwide epidemic.' Make sure you leave Dr. Quinlan an emergency phone number where she can reach you."

I examined my list of notes and scribbles, including Dr. Harvey's latest instructions. "Jesus, this is quite a grocery list. It looks like plot notes for an episode of *Dr. Who.*"

"Yes, I'm sure it will all make for superb bathroom reading," Dr. Harvey said. "Now I can rest easy knowing that the fate of mankind has been placed in the hands of two men dressed like they're on their way to a Star Trek convention."

"Better in the hands of two stylishly costumed crusaders and a weird-looking talking fart cloud than in the hands of that maniac down in the catacombs, Doc." I said, tucking the notebook back into my coat pocket.

"Yes, and as much as I would like to float here for hours exchanging verbal barbs with you or maybe break something over your head for old times' sake, perhaps it's best that you and your hydrocephalic sidekick vacate the premises before that mob of mutant mongoloids makes you for a couple of imposters."

"Uh, I can't breathe under water if that's what hydrocephalic means," Solomon said.

"It's not, but duly noted," Dr. Harvey said.

"There's just one problem: us getting out of here alive, without getting killed while doing so," I said.

"Yes, a little something that I no longer have to worry about thanks to your paranormal meddling, Stanley, but if you insist on not being flayed alive, then you can simply leave by the secret revolving door."

"Revolving door?"

"Yes. It's activated by jerking down the enormous erection on the bawdy novelty statue of Michelangelo's David over on the shelf there."

I observed the statue, which was indeed endowed with a penis the size of a large kielbasa sausage. With some trepidation I approached the sculpture and reluctantly placed my hand upon the massive shlong.

There was a quick and blinding flash of light as Solomon snapped a Polaroid of me clutching the statue's eye-popping wang. "I don't think we needed a picture of that," I mumbled, seconds before tugging the penis downward and activating the revolving portion of the lab wall which rotated partially to the left, exposing an exit into the mansion's first floor, east wing hallway.

Chapter Two

_____

As we drove into the fog, leaving the hellish mansion far behind us, we attempted to keep our panic at bay by devising a strategy for dealing with the nefarious plans of the Legions of Darkness. It would be a six-hour drive to Leon Spinks University in Rochester and so we decided to check into a roadside motel for a few hours of shuteye before attempting to solicit the assistance of Harvey's old colleague, Dr. Whitlock.

Despite the nagging sensation of having an ice pick jammed into the meat of my throbbing thigh, I paced the threadbare carpet of my dingy, "no tell" motel accommodations, again supporting my weight on my trusty cane. I ran the terrible events of the evening through my mind as I waited for Solomon to return from his search for a liquor store in the vicinity. The detective needed a belt of something strong and I certainly couldn't blame him after what we'd seen in the catacombs tonight.

The low moans, banging bedpost and squeals of phony truck stop hooker ecstasy drifting through the paper-thin walls made me think of my fiancé, Charlotte Easterbrook, who was tucked safely away in the luxurious confines of the Pootang Palace high in the Hollywood Hills of California. I fought the urge to phone her.

Charlotte was completely against my returning to Hull House, and vigilantly mindful of the fact that my last visit nearly cost me my life. She had hardly fared much better, barely escaping the house with her ovaries unscathed, and I was relieved by the knowledge that she was far away from the horrors that I witnessed this night. Still, I longed to hear the soothing sound of her cleavage.

My mother, Margot Donlevy—who first opened this Pandora's kettle of worms three years ago when she obtained my services as a paranormal investigator—had attempted to convince Charlotte that my work at Hull House might not yet be complete. She scarcely needed to remind Charlotte of the endless night terrors that haunted me since my narrow escape from the mansion and suggested that my only real chance of gaining true peace of mind might lay in revisiting my personal demons, both psychological and the physical ones with the devil horns, bat wings and big, pointy teeth. Charlotte had flown into a rage and said she would not take part in my suicide. She stopped speaking to me and would only communicate through broad comedy pantomimes and honks from bicycle horn like Harpo Marx.

Margot insisted that, before I rekindled the flames of terror at the mansion, she consult with the spiritual world via the mystical oracle, a crystal ball previously used in numerous séances by my great grandmother, Isabella Hull. It was an unspoken truth that Margot had inherited the tremendous clairvoyant gifts for which the Hull family was quite renown, yet she seldom acknowledged the fact, dismissing the issue by claiming that spiritual contact gave her terrible gas.

So as not to unduly upset Charlotte, Margot and I conducted our spiritual consultation while Charlotte was out of the house shopping for a Star Wars novelty toilet plunger for her nephew's 10th birthday. The oracle's visions were nothing short of nightmarish. Following a rather disappointing Popeye cartoon and a commercial for Chesterfield cigarettes, we were shown murky visions of widespread panic and insanity and scenes of monstrous creatures ravaging their terrified human prey.

Margot seemed to go into some sort of trance as she invoked the powers of the oracle and made a series of strange faces as if she were channeling the spirit of an extremely constipated Jerry Lewis.

We gazed into the swirling green mist of the crystal ball, at visions of a world gone insane ... mankind as rabid animals. I was particularly disturbed by the sight of a lunatic who bore a striking resemblance to yours truly—even down to his having the exact same brown corduroy pants with the hole in the left front pocket and an identical tweed jacket with the leather patches on the elbows and mustard stains on the lapels. The maniac was wearing a pair of plus-sized women's underwear on his head as he ran around like a chicken with its head cut off while clutching a pair of chickens with their heads cut off. He was drenched with blood and actually foaming at the mouth. I could only gasp with shock as I witnessed the uncommonly handsome, lingerie-topped psycho being set ablaze with a flamethrower shortly before being run over by a speeding ice cream truck. Watching the slaughter, I felt as if someone had driven over my grave with an ice cream truck.

Suddenly, a girlish high-pitched shriek pierced the air, bringing Margot out of her trance. At first I didn't recognize the voice, but then realized that it sounded just like the crazy man in the crystal ball with the underwear on his head.

Margot shivered, "What happened, Stanley?"

"The visions ... can the events be changed?"

"They are visions of things that have yet come to pass ... being aware of them, we can set the wheels in motion to alter their outcome."

"Thank God. Someone very close to me is in danger of being lit on fire and run over by an ice cream truck ... if I can prevent this dashing young man's demise, perhaps I can prevent the other horrors I saw."

"Did you happen to see a terrified old woman in the oracle that was in black and white and cried out for a girl named, Dorothy?"

"No, I think that might be from *The Wizard of Oz*, Margot."

"Oh yes, that's right. Contact with the spirit world always exhausts me. I hope it was helpful, Stanley. I dread employing the powers of the oracle. I don't know why, but it always turns my pubic hair completely gray."

Margot's trance-like state during the session prevented her from remembering the images of horror that the crystal ball revealed. I felt that perhaps that might be for the best in this case. So I lied to her about what I'd seen in the mists of the crystal ball, telling her that the visions were nothing more than harmless esoteric flashes of cute dogs dressed as professional athletes attempting to negotiate lucrative sports contracts with a man wearing a John F. Kennedy mask and powdered wig. I think she knew I was lying to prevent her from worrying, but she kept her suspicions to herself.

For her part, Charlotte finally relented and expressed her concerns in something other than pantomime and horn honking. She expressed them in shrill, piercing shrieks that nearly spilt my eardrums. She warned that I was tempting fate with my endless obsession with the house and that I was travelling down the same road as my crazy ancestors whose preoccupations with the supernatural had been their downfall. When I'd tried to counter her argument by showing her the newspaper headline from *The Dorchester Gazette* that screamed: *Halloween Bloodbath at Terror Mansion!* Charlotte began to sob. I held her in my arms and explained that my intuition told me that evil forces were very much still at work at the house ... evil forces that had been gathering strength since our discovery of the Gateways of the Legions of Darkness. Something ancient and foul was at work in those catacombs and if I didn't take some sort of action to stop it, then mankind would be at its mercy ... and mercy was a concept completely foreign to the abominable entities that slithered about in those black pockets of Hell below the mansion.

In the end Charlotte gave in, albeit quite reluctantly, letting me leave for New England with the provision that I bring along my charred and battered brain helmet; the steel-plated bowler hat that had played so vital a role in my surviving the previous visit to Hull House.

Now, as I paced back and forth, I could think of almost nothing more than being back in Charlotte's arms, nude and slathered from head to toe in salad dressing—ready for a roll in our rubber "sex coffin." I walked to the bed and unlatched my small suitcase, extracting the battered bowler hat from atop the clothes that I'd absentmindedly stuffed into the suitcase before my flight. Burns from the first Orias Nebula had exposed spots of its steel under casing and singed bits of the lining around the brim of the hat. I recalled the horrors that the malignant cloud had fired into my brain like a near-fatal blast of nightmare buckshot ... horrors that turned my hair as white as the Lawrence Welk Show and my skin as pale as Moby's dick. As my mind drifted back to those flashes of hell, I was startled by a knock at the door from Solomon. I tossed the hat onto the bed as Solomon's muffled voice inquired if I had a woman in the room with me. Unusually jumpy, I'd let loose another high-pitched shriek when startled by the knock.

I unlocked the door. "It was just a horror film on television, some woman being chased by a monster. I shut it off."

"Horror movie? Christ, Stanley, haven't you had enough of that crap for the night?" Solomon pulled a pint of Jack Daniels from a paper bag, unscrewed the lid and then took a long swallow. He offered me the bottle and I gladly accepted—taking an ample, burning belt that resulted in a brief coughing fit.

Solomon plopped down in the room's single, shabby chair. "I have certainly seen some crazy shit in my time, Stanley, but tonight took the goddamned cake. You really think this Dr. Whitlock is going to believe any of this insane bullshit? I was there, and I can barely believe it. If I came to me with any of this, I would think that me was a psycho."

"Well, if Whitlock is a professor of arcane mysticism this should certainly pique his interest. Whatever it is that we've uncovered, it's about as arcane as it gets."

Solomon took another swig from the bottle, eyeing the bowler hat atop my bed. "Hat on the bed ... isn't that supposed to be bad juju?"

"You mean worse than what we already have to work with?"

"Yeah, we do seem to be pretty far up shit creek, my friend. Far enough to hear the cannibal's drums beating off in the distance."

"I just hope we're not the ones beating off in the distance thinking we can stop these maniacs."

Solomon raised an eyebrow at the muffled sounds of phony sexual euphoria emanating through the walls. "Speaking of which, it sounds like the soundtrack to an X-rated movie in here."

"Charming isn't it? About as erotic as listening to your grandparents getting it on."

Solomon took another swing of Jack Daniels. "I guess in your case that might sound even more disturbing if your grandparents were using those portholes under the house."

"You mean what Dr. Harvey said about the demon taking my great grandfather's corpse into the porthole?"

"Yeah. Why don't you tell me a bit more about exactly who the hell it is that we're dealing with here."

"Leland Barnes Hull was the man who had the house intentionally built over those portholes in 1859. He was a self-made millionaire who made the bulk of his fortune through various scams and shady real estate deals. He was also a sadist and sexual degenerate who founded the Order of Yarlock the Great Deceiver and worshipped the evil being who, according to legend, constructed the Gateways of the Seven Legions of Darkness thousands of years ago.

"He was also a self-proclaimed warlock who claimed to have telepathic communication with the dark forces of the Legions of Darkness, and claimed that he was immortal and would rise from the dead ... a claim that I used to believe was disproven when his own son, Victor split Leland's skull open to prevent him from attempting force Victor's mother, Isabella to mate with a demon that he had summoned from one of the portholes. I guess now that he actually seems to have risen from the dead I stand corrected. I thought the claims were just his delusions of grandeur. The man was quite insane. Nothing was too depraved for his appetites. He was said to have engaged in cannibalism, bestiality, human sacrifice ... even traditional Dutch clog dancing."

Solomon grimaced. "Klompendansen?!"

"Klompendansen."

"Jesus."

I limped to my suitcase, which lay open on the foot of the bed, and extracted the weighty, leather-bound volume of *Tenets of The Order of Yarlock the Great Deceiver: The Complete Works of L.B. Hull.* "Something told me I should bring this along." I passed the book to Solomon.

He set the nearly drained pint of Jack Daniels atop the battered Formica table situated next to him and examined the book's cover, then carefully opened the book, thumbing through its pages with the intense and meticulous interest of a man seasoned by more than a decade of work as a police detective. "This might be the first volume on occult mysticism that I've perused, but I wouldn't think there would be so many advertisements."

"The man was a shameless huckster and a tireless self promoter."

Solomon continued to thumb through the book with a smirk on his face. "*Flatulence-Be-Gone rectum sealant compound? Aphrodite's Soothing Breast and Buttock Liniment?*

"If you think that stuff's crazy, read some of his ranting about the Order of Yarlock the Great Deceiver."

Solomon examined a passage in the book with a confused grimace. Finally he read aloud: "*The dwellers in the great abyss now stir in the black, putrescent jelly of their demonic purgatory, where they bide their time until their days of reckoning. Those demons and witches cast into darkness, those hateful and loathsome beings that rightfully prey on the innocent and their sanctimonious shepherds. The ancient evil ones of the Seven Legions of Darkness: Krelsethian, Athvenog, Selurach, Yazalaryat, Urisyazram, Slogarath, Hemyulac.*" He leafed through the book again, stopping to examine another passage that caught his eye. "*One shall never deny oneself any pleasure of the flesh, no matter how animalistic or perverse ...* charming ... and under that passage is an advertisement for something called *a patent leather fisting mitten for the anal adventurer.*"

"Maybe we can use that against him."

"Really? This weirdo seems like the type who might enjoy a good fisting."

"No, I mean use the book against him ... not the fisting mitten. Maybe there is something buried in the text that we can use to our advantage."

"Like what?"

"I don't know. Maybe this Dr. Whitlock or Professor Hiller can get something useful out of it."

Solomon swirled the remaining swallow of whiskey around in the bottle and then quickly inhaled it. He rose to his feet and passed me the book. "One thing's for sure, my friend. I never saw this kind of action with the NYPD."

Chapter Three

_____

Leon Spinks University was an impressive campus constructed in Neogothic-style red brick and granite with a looming clock tower that stood in the center of the grounds. An attractive and slightly curious concierge directed us to the Archives library were we found Dr. Graham Whitlock engrossed in his examination of a collection of antique volumes detailing the practices of an ancient secret society know as The Order of the Black Booty Bitches. Whitlock was a slight man with a bald head and graying beard who spoke with an accent that lead me to believe that he was either British or incredibly pretentious.

As Solomon and I explained the incredibly strange reasons for our visit, the man paid us little attention as he went about his work, seeming endlessly distracted by the volumes laid out on the table in front of him. The scholar grunted acknowledgement and nodded a few times to convey the questionable idea that he was actually listening to us—all the while scrutinizing the brittle, yellowed pages of his books through the lens of a large magnifying glass, fascinated by whatever antiquated secrets they revealed.

Finally, the odd, little man stared up at us with cold, blue eyes that seemed nearly as spooky as the strange comings and goings at Hull House. "What you're suggesting defies all reason, gentlemen."

Solomon nodded in agreement. "You're preaching to the choir, Doc. It all sounds like a bunch of insane bullshit, but we're not the Brothers Grimm and we didn't come here to bend your ear with fairytales. Despite appearances, Mr. Matheson isn't as crazy as he looks."

Dr. Whitlock looked me over. "I'll have to take your word on that, Detective."

I turned to Solomon. "Show him the photographs."

Solomon fished the collection of Polaroids he'd taken in the laboratory from his coat pocket and passed them to Dr. Whitlock.

Somewhat warily, the scholar examined the first of the photos and then gazed up at me with a grimace. "Is this you in a costume gripping an enormous penis?"

I snatched the picture from the stack. "That looks really weird taken out of context."

Dr. Whitlock returned his gaze to the stack of photographs, examining the Polaroids through the lens of his magnifying glass.

I leafed through Solomon's notebook, examining my frantically scribbled notations. "What can you tell us about Shiverdecker's Theory of Malignant Reversal, Doctor?"

Once again distracted, Dr. Whitlock half-mumbled his further responses to my questions as he examined Solomon's photographs. "Albrecht Shiverdecker was a scientist and astronomer who claimed that he'd discovered evidence of some kind of evil parallel dimension. He was committed to a mental hospital sometime in the mid 1800s. The man was catatonic for nearly a year after his confinement, but eventually he began to paint as a form of therapy. His paintings were quite horrific—hellish landscapes populated by grotesque monsters and demons. He insisted that his works were prophetic visions of some horrible place that he likened to the Hades of Greek mythology. He called this world the Scorpius Plane. He maintained that one day, a human simpleton would be tasked with navigating his way through a gauntlet of horrors and monsters to retrieve the hidden secrets of the Lovejoy codex in this wicked world, and he hoped that his paintings might offer clues to this brave simpleton during his daunting quest to save mankind from some kind of demonic apocalypse. Only through the success of this simple-minded individual would the process of malignant reversal be able to be set in motion."

"And the Lovejoy Codex ... was this also one of Shiverdecker's inventions?"

"It was another recurring theme in his work ... part of his all-consuming obsession with this evil world. He described the codex as an ancient relic that detailed the history of the Seven Legions of Darkness. Shiverdecker claimed that incantations hidden within the codex could be invoked against the evil forces that he believed would one day rise up against the human race. He said that he could see these hidden incantations because he'd been exposed to some kind of toxic mist that spewed forth from this gateway that he'd discovered. A toxic mist that gave him visions of this hellish world beyond our dimension."

"The Orias Nebula," I said.

"I believe we have a book of Shiverdecker's paintings and correspondence somewhere here in the archives."

"We'll want to have a look at that. What are the prophecies of Shemrach Theydarian?"

"Fire and brimstone texts from the late 17th century that predict the end of the world ... demons, pestilence, rivers of gore, rampant insanity—the stuff of snake handling tent evangelists talking in tongues. The exact same sort of nightmarish fantasies that you've been describing to me."

Dr. Whitlock closed his eyes and began to quote the Theydarian texts from memory. "From his grave the man-demon rises, hailing the twilight of humankind. Assembling armies of devils against us, and breeding madness in the mind. The legions of darkness awaken, sending monsters forth from Hell, to rule the world with terror. Destroying all who dare rebel."

"Sounds like the lyrics to a Black Sabbath song," Solomon quipped nervously.

Dr. Whitlock had no comment—either about Solomon's wisecrack or, thus far, about the photographs the detective had taken in the laboratory at the mansion. Breaking the eerie silence that had crept into the library, I prompted the strange, little man to continue. "And what about this Opus Demonium? Is that some kind of spell book?"

Dr. Whitlock gazed up at us with his creepy, blue eyes. "What? Oh ... no, it's not a book of spells ... you might call it *Everything You Always Wanted to Know About Demons But Were Afraid to Ask*. It's an elaborate study of demonology compiled by Shemrach Theydarain ... a kind of demon slayers' handbook is the best way to describe it, I suppose. It's farfetched, horrific stuff. In his apocalyptic visions the man apparently saw these creatures he describes in the book as being a type of lycanthrope."

"Werewolves?" I said.

"Of a more demonic variety, able to turn from human into many variations of demonic form. He wrote the book as a sort of safeguard for mankind—a way to detect and slay the varieties of demons during their assault on our world. I'd say the person who assembled this laboratory is quite interested in the Opus Demonium as well."

"What gives you that impression?" I said.

"Here in these notes you photographed. Someone has written *Opus Demonium, Theydarian Society for the Study of the Black Arts, Goblin's Dong, Connecticut.*" Dr. Whitlock placed the photograph showing the notation atop the library's central table and held his magnifying glass over the picture, enlarging the image so that the writing was clearly visible.

Solomon sighed. "It appears we have a cobra in the buttermilk."

"A what?" I said

"You know, that old expression."

"No. I'm not familiar with that one."

"Fart on a plum! It's just like when you say *'Bing bong! Grandpa licked the flypaper!'* or *'Foolish is the Dutchman who ice skates on a lake of frozen diarrhea.'* It's all the same idea."

"What does any of that even mean?" I said.

Solomon pulled the Smith and Wesson .38 special from its shoulder holster beneath his jacket and checked the rounds in the cylinder. "It means we'd better get our asses to Goblin's Dong, posthaste."

"You should've just said that in the first place."

Solomon snapped the cylinder back into place, satisfied. "Well, nobody wants to be a chicken in the dung heap, my friend."

I turned to Dr. Whitlock. "I don't suppose that we could persuade you to join us for a little road trip, Doctor?"

The man looked incredulous. "You can't be serious?"

I'd hoped that our visit would not result in an unavoidable kidnapping, but Whitlock's unshakable skepticism was quickly narrowing our options. "We need your help, Doctor."

The scholar crossed his arms, observing us with a wry grin. "You gentlemen actually believe all of this, don't you? Ghosts and demons and magic books."

Now it was my turn to play the skeptic. "For a man who spends his days studying the secrets of arcane mysticism, you certainly seem to lack any kind of professional curiosity about any of this. Aren't you in the least bit interested?"

Dr. Whitlock considered the question for a moment. Finally he tucked his magnifying glass and Solomon's Polaroid photographs into a battered, black, leather bag that lay on the table next to a pile of his scattered notes. "For the sake of urgency, we'll take the book on Shiverdecker's work along with us."

Solomon and I breathed a sigh of relief as the doctor donned a soft tweed hat and woolen scarf that he'd pulled from his bag.

"I'll warn you now. Professor Hiller will never let the Opus Demonium out of his sight," Dr. Whitlock said. "I'm afraid he isn't the most accommodating man that you could hope to work with, so I wouldn't expect a very warm reception. The unpleasant bastard is likely to slam the door in our faces."

"We're not just a couple of nuts, Doc," Solomon said.

Dr. Whitlock raised an eyebrow. "That remains to be seen, gentlemen."

Chapter Four

_____

During the drive to Goblin's Dong, we examined the book chronicling Albrecht Shiverdecker's paintings and correspondence and discussed what significance they might have to our own peculiar case. Thanks in no small part to my own exposure to the poisonous revelations of the Orias Nebula, I found a chilling familiarity in Shiverdecker's work that could only have been achieved by someone who had also experienced the horrors of the malignant cloud firsthand.

Dr. Whitlock—with a slightly removed, yet genuine fascination for the events that were unfolding around him—was quick to point out the similarities between the monstrous creatures roaming Shiverdecker's hellish landscapes and the horrible specimens visible in Solomon's Polaroid snapshots of the Hull House laboratory. "If this is a hoax," Dr. Whitlock observed, "it's certainly a very elaborate one. It's really quite extraordinary."

"I'm glad we managed to pique your interest, Doctor," I said

Dual photographs of Albrecht Shiverdecker taken in a brief one-year span before and after his confinement in the asylum revealed a shocking transformation in the man's appearance. The first revealed a well-dressed, bespectacled gentleman of slight build with short-cropped, dark hair and an intense look of sharp intelligence in his eyes—a night and day difference from the second portrait, which showed a disheveled, vacant-eyed lunatic with a wild head of white hair gazing into the distance with a look of utter confusion. Had I seen the second photograph out of context, I would have easily mistaken it for a police mug shot of a rum-soaked, middle-aged hobo.

The obvious similarities to my own ordeal with the horrible nebula were certainly not lost on the ever-observant detective at my side, and Solomon was not reluctant to make mention of the connection. "Looks like you're not the only unsolicited dentist to pry a few of the devil's teeth loose, Stanley."

Gazing with insuppressible, mounting terror at the grainy, black and white eyes of my crazed and unfortunate predecessor, I could only pray that fate might offer me a more merciful outcome in my battle with the Legions of Darkness than that of the all-consuming madness that had devoured my once-brilliant forerunner. As I stared at the second Shiverdecker photograph, one thought kept repeating over and over in my mind: *Jesus H. Christ! Do I look that insane?*

"That's why Stanley looks so insane," Solomon explained. "He was also exposed to some type of toxic mist when he was investigating the Hull family mansion in Dorchester. It shot red lightening into his brain matter ... gave him some kind of weird telepathy. It sounds just like how Shiverdecker describes his ordeal."

From the strange conclusions to be drawn from our discussion, there was one that stood out as an absolute certainty. It hit me like a brick with a note tied to it that read: "*Hey Stanley, one of the most logical conclusions that you could arrive at would be that Albrecht Shiverdecker located the Gateways of the Seven Legions of Darkness for Leland Hull.*

P.S. Don't forget to renew your subscription to D Cup Debutantes and pick up some wheat germ.

Love ya!

Stanley's Mind"

"Shiverdecker found the Gateways of the Legions of Darkness for Leland Hull," I said.

"It would certainly stand to reason," Solomon agreed. "Do you think that was on purpose?"

Dr. Whitlock suddenly chimed in from the back seat. "Sometime in the early 1800s, Leland Hull supposedly came into possession of a grimoire ... an ancient book of spells. The book's name was roughly translated as meaning: To Summon Those That Come From Darkness. It was said to contain incantations that summoned evil spirits from other worlds.

"There were coordinates listed in the book ... coordinates that supposedly revealed the location of the Gateways of the Seven Legions of Darkness. Leland Hull was rumored to have consulted with Albrecht Shiverdecker about the validity of these coordinates. This was shortly before Shiverdecker's commitment to the asylum.

"There might be something to the story, although no one that I know of has ever actually seen this grimoire of Hull's."

"I have," I said.

Dr. Whitlock was stunned. "What?"

"I destroyed it, three years ago—to prevent anyone from ever being able to exploit its evil power again. I also sabotaged one of the gateways by harnessing the malignant forces of the Orias Nebula."

Dr. Whitlock's eyes widened. "The idiot," he muttered.

"Idiot?" I said.

The scholar pointed at me, looking somewhat incredulous. "You're the idiot."

"Well ... thanks for the vote of confidence. I think under the circumstances I didn't do too badly. You think it's easy to blow up a porthole to an evil dimension?"

"The passage from the prophecies of Shemrach Theydarian that I mentioned ... there's more to it," Dr. Whitlock said.

"The poem you recited about the man-demon assembling armies of devils?" I said.

Dr. Whitlock recited the quotation once more, "From his grave the man-demon rises, hailing the twilight of humankind ... assembling armies of devils against us, and breeding madness in the mind. The legions of darkness awaken, sending monsters forth from Hell, to rule the world with terror, destroying all who dare rebel ... but the idiot plots against them, to disrupt their rein of terror, armed with his moronic gift for success through bumbling error. In the ruined house of horrors, his motley band unites, to retrieve the Lovejoy Codex, turning darkness into light."

"Perhaps something got lost in the translation. Maybe this Shemrach Theydarian used a word that meant brilliant, unconventional warrior or something like that, and the person that translated the poem misinterpreted it," I suggested.

"No, I'm fairly certain that the translation is correct," Dr. Whitlock said.

"Maybe you *are* the idiot," Solomon said.

"Well then, in this case I'll just take that as a backhanded compliment," I said.

It was nearing dusk when we arrived at our destination; a place as distinctly unwelcoming as it was overpoweringly malodorous. The cloying stink of low tide hovered in the air like the aroma of a fish oil cologne. Dark storm clouds loomed on the horizon, rumbling and pregnant with rain.

An isolated New England fishing village established in 1702, Goblin's Dong was a damp and dreary place inhabited by dour, long-faced curmudgeons who seemed less than thrilled by a surprise visit from three out-of-state interlopers.

As the three of us exited my rented Mercedes Benz, the scowling, frog-eyed locals ogled us as if we'd stepped forth from a time machine, appearing suspicious of our modern day attire and sophisticated "big city" ways.

We approached a pair of mistrustful townsfolk who busied themselves with paintbrushes, touching up a large wooden statue of what appeared to be a monstrous fish creature rising from the ocean tide with the much smaller body of a man clutched in its hideous jaws. The apprehensive twosome eyeballed us like we were a trio of greedy, gypsy vagabonds who had descended upon their pungent hamlet to pilfer their simple trading coins fashioned from lead.

We inquired about the location of the Thaydarian Society for the Study of the Black Arts, and—after appeasing the surly duo with our purchase of a t-shirt emblazoned with the slogan: *I caught crabs in Goblin's Dong*—we were directed to a local tavern called The Whale's Bladder Inn. There I was to ask for the proprietor, a man named Angus McFishfucker.

The Whale's Bladder Inn was, not surprisingly, a gloomy establishment seemingly untouched by 20th century sensibilities, as evinced by the dim light thrown off by the antique oil lamps that lit the smoke-filled interior of the tavern. On one of the dingy walls hung a fearsome oil painting of the same horrible sea monster depicted in the wooden statue we'd just seen outside.

Our entrance was met with a collection of perturbed stares and cautious, mumbled remarks from the collection of hatchet-faced locals who sat hunched over the drinkery's worn, wooden tables.

Feeling like fish out of water in a town populated by people who actually looked like fish out of water, we approached the hulking barkeep with some trepidation. The man stood with his back to us, polishing a pint glass and attempting to ignore us with the obvious hope that we might simply vacate his establishment without troubling him for a drink. In an attempt not to unduly upset the imposing brute, I tapped a knuckle lightly on the bar to get his attention and begged his pardon for the unwelcome intrusion. The elephantine barman turned about face, glaring at us with the same look of spooked apprehension that was so characteristic of his fellow townsfolk.

"Help ye gentlemen with something?" he grumbled. His voice was gravely and baritone-pitched—thick with an accent that sounded like a mixture of Gaelic and Yiddish as spoken by a stroke victim with a mouthful of oatmeal. Any in-depth discussion with the man would have required an interpreter from whatever undersea kingdom he'd originally hailed from.

Raising my voice slightly, as if I were speaking to someone who was partially deaf, I explained our predicament to this gargantuan, mongoloid lovechild of Jack Elam and Peter Lorre. "We were told that Mr. Angus McFishfucker, the owner of this fine, dimly-lit establishment, could direct us to Professor Hiller at the Theydarian Society for the Study of the Black Arts."

"Professor Hiller?" one of the patrons squawked, as if the very mention of the man's name was tantamount to blasphemy.

The lumbering barkeep frowned and then reached over the bar, seizing me by the shirt collar with his ham hock-sized fist and jerked me forward until I was but inches from his scowling face. His toxic breath wheezed into my nostrils—a foul mixture of seafood and hard spirits that nearly rendered me unconscious. "And why would the likes of ye be wanting a visit with that mad, old bastard, eh?"

Solomon and Dr. Whitlock attempted to calm the man, pleading for him to release his stranglehold on my crumpled esophagus. The troglodyte reluctantly unhanded me and I dropped to the tavern floor gasping for breath. My stunned associates helped me to my feet as the other patrons observed us without offering any assistance whatsoever.

"Ye lot best make yourselves scarce around these parts or ye soon learn the meaning of Goblin's Dong hospitality," one of the customers warned.

The gargantuan bartender pointed a beefy index finger in our direction. "Ye head south down a Witch's Teat Road, then left up Devil's Anus Trail to Gorgon's Crotch Hill ... there ye find the place ye seek. Now go! Get out of my tavern, ye foreign bastards!"

We immediately took our leave, fleeing the unabashed hostility of the tavern's customers before we could be physically removed from the establishment.

Rushing to the Mercedes, we found the car drenched in a bloody splatter of rotting fish intestines retrieved from some nearby fish market. *"Go Home!"* was written across the windshield in slimy reddish-pink blood.

"Quite the welcoming committee," Dr. Whitlock mused.

"I guess all of that inbreeding must put you in a really foul mood," I said.

"What's with the sea monster god? First the wooden statue, then that painting in the tavern," Solomon said.

"Carthalluulffthh," Dr. Whitlock said.

Solomon smirked. "Come again, Doc?"

"It's known as Carthalluulffthh. Part of the local folklore," Dr. Whitlock explained, removing the handkerchief from his coat pocket and using it to open the car's back left side door. "The legend goes that the founding fathers of this village made some kind of horrible pact with this ancient god of the sea to provide them with a source of industry ... fishing and whaling, etcetera, and in exchange, the god Carthalluulffthh was offered human, female virgins with whom it could mate to produce its abominable offspring."

"Getting a gander at these fish-faced fuckers, I don't exactly find that hard to believe," Solomon said.

"Should no virgins be available, a blood sacrifice would be offered to Carthalluulffthh. It's rumored that some of the more superstitious locals around these parts still worship this deity out of some deep-rooted fear ... afraid of some kind of reprisal if it isn't appeased during the annual festival held in its honor," Dr. Whitlock said, somewhat matter-of-factly, as he climbed into the backseat of the Mercedes.

Solomon and I climbed into the front seats and Solomon cracked the passenger side window as he lit a cigarette. "I can't say that I've seen any signs of our rivals from Hull House just yet," he said, blowing cigarette smoke from the car's window.

"Well, the night is young, my friend. Perhaps they're lying in wait," I said, turning the key in the ignition and then flooring the gas pedal as we sped away toward Witch's Teat Road.

With petal pressed firmly to metal, we made the short trip to the top of Gorgon's Crotch Hill in under ten minutes time and pulled the car into a wooded area just out of sight of the road. As we exited the Mercedes, Solomon stomped out his cigarette and then drew his .38 special and cocked back the hammer.

Treading as lightly as possible along the grass that lined the roadside, we quickly made our way to the two-story stone building that housed the artifacts and library of the Theydarian Society. At first glance, the former cooperage appeared undisturbed, but a few telltale droplets of blood splattered about the gravel that surrounded the building spoke volumes about what awaited us inside.

We approached the sturdy, oak door of the building with Solomon leading the charge.

Our predecessors apparently felt very little need to cover their tracks and had left the front door slightly ajar, revealing a faint glimpse of what appeared to be a human liver lying on the floor near the entryway. Flies swarmed about the bloody organ and the high-pitched hum of their buzzing wings turned the skin of my arms to gooseflesh.

Solomon kicked the door aside. It squealed in its hinges as he leapt inside the building in a slightly squatted firing stance, aiming his pistol about the dimly lit expanse of the building's ground floor. "Sweet chocolate Jesus!" he grumbled.

Dr. Whitlock and I stepped inside, stopping abruptly in our tracks as our eyes meet the butchery that Leland Hull's bloodthirsty henchman had performed in the already foreboding interior of the morbid museum.

What remained of Professor Hiller looked like the unfortunate recipient of an all-over-the-body briss performed by a psychotic rabbi with a rusty linoleum knife. The flesh had been stripped from the scholar's corpse, leaving what resembled a large meatloaf sculpted into the shape of a human body. The brutalized carcass had been garnished with slices of pineapple and partially eaten, as evinced by the bloody paper plates and plastic utensils that surrounded it atop a large rectangular display case. Discarded party hats, party horns and a clown-shaped birthday candle rammed into the body's mutilated groin lead us to the obvious conclusion that the sadistic butchers had thrown one hell of a party before our arrival.

The professor's decapitated head sat in the center of a large, black walnut desk, impaled atop a metal notepaper spike. In his mouth was stuffed a rolled sheet of parchment paper tied with a red ribbon.

We approached the mutilated crania and extracted the viscera soaked parchment paper from its mouth, knowing full well that the note had been left specifically for our perusal. Solomon pulled the ribbon from the scroll and unrolled it. Written in what appeared to be Professor Hiller's blood was the following message:

Dear idiot,

We now have the Opus Demonium, so don't do anything idiotic—although, since you are an idiot, that may prove difficult. Any actions taken against us on your part would be sheer idiocy.

Solomon passed me the note. "It's for you."

Dr. Whitlock removed his hat and absentmindedly wiped the beads of nervous sweat from his brow with the sleeve of his jacket as he stepped back from the desk, looking pale and on the verge of fainting. "This is pure sadism! What kind of monsters could do such a thing?"

Solomon and I rushed to his aid, quickly taking hold of each of the man's quivering arms before he collapsed onto the blood-streaked floor.

"Easy, Doc," Solomon said. "Maybe you could use a little fresh air."

Suddenly, from high above, a thunderclap rumbled and roared in the darkening, evening sky like some terrible omen warning us to vacate the area immediately.

We scrambled back to the front door of the building with the doctor in tow. A hasty escape from Goblin's Dong seemed to be the wisest option available to us under these rather gruesome circumstances.

As we were about to exit the building, Dr. Whitlock suddenly halted, wrestling his arms from our grip. "Wait!" he shouted. We observed him anxiously as he regained his composure, donning his hat once again. "Whoever murdered Professor Hiller was obviously anticipating our arrival. This could be some kind of trap, gentlemen," he said.

As if cued by the doctor's grim warning, another thunderclap ripped through the sky like cannon fire.

"There's a window on the second floor. It might offer us a useful vantage point," Dr. Whitlock said, rushing off toward a stairwell located at the far end of the building. "Latch that door shut!" he shouted as he rushed up the stairs. We followed his orders without question, sliding the front door's heavy iron bolt into its latch and then rushed up the stairwell to join him.

As we reached the top of the staircase, Solomon took aim and nearly fired upon a wax figure clad in the ceremonial robes and strange sea monster mask of the high priest of the Carthalluulffthh cult that was posed next to the figure of a screaming young woman tied to a crucifix. A diorama painted behind the two figures depicted the monstrous image of Carthalluulffthh rising from the sea to accept its sacrificial offering. Beyond the figures stood Dr. Whitlock, gazing silently out of the large bay window at the front of the building.

The second story window overlooked the hillside on which the former cooperage sat, revealing a panoramic view of the seaside town nestled in the valley below. Hovering above the village was a gargantuan Orias Nebula, stretching nearly four miles across in each direction. The horrible cloud was the color of molten lava—a swirling mass of blood red nightmares and pitch-black evil that sent bolts of crimson lightning shooting downward into the streets below from its amorphous mass. Screams of terror and madness echoed in the distance, carried up the hillside on a malodorous wind that smelled of blood and rotting shellfish.

Suddenly, I felt a familiar, stabbing pain in my head and gasped in horror as images of the madness taking place in the village flashed in my mind's eye. Black globules of gelatinous, oily muck rained down from the sky, quickly collecting across the cobblestone streets like steaming pools of rotting salmon eggs. Psychosis quickly overtook the frightened population as they painted fake eyebrows on their foreheads with Dijon mustard and exposed their private parts to campaign posters urging local residents to re-elect Senator Bert Davis to the Connecticut State Senate.

As the insanity consumed them, random villagers brutally mutilated their own faces with shards of broken glass and then performed expertly choreographed song and dance routines from *Seven Brides For Seven Brothers*, while others drank fabric softener out of martini glasses and wrote bad checks for subscriptions to Nudist Lifestyle Magazine. I saw blood and carnage—crazed villagers running amok, gathering weapons of every sort and frantically donning the ceremonial tunics and hoods of the Carthalluulffthh cult. In a blasphemous chapel, a terrified congregation kneeled before the image of their terrible sea monster deity, screaming warnings of the nightmare gods that had awakened—*The ancient evil ones of the Legions of Darkness: Athvenog, Selurach, Yazalaryat, Urisyazram, Slogarath, Hemyulac.* *"The strangers!"* they shouted—*"It is the strangers who have brought the evil to Goblin's Dong! Their blood must be spilled in sacrifice! Carthalluulffthh must be appeased! Only the god of the sea can protect us!"*

My brain felt as it were on the verge of a volcanic eruption when darkness abruptly swallowed me like a leather sex gimp mask with no eyeholes. I felt my legs give out beneath me as I collapsed to the floor and faded into oblivion.

Somewhere in the foggy purgatory of my subconscious emerged a vision of my beloved Charlotte, swimming hazily before me like an apparition of a buxom mermaid with flowing strands of cotton candy for hair. Instinctively, I reached for her ample breasts, imitating the whistle of an old time, steam-powered train engine: *Woo Woo!*

Charlotte gently batted my hands away from her bountiful bosoms and issued a stern warning. "There's no time for that now, Stanley. You must escape from Goblin's Dick."

"Dong," I corrected. "Goblin's Dong."

"Dick, dong, ding-a-ling, schlong! The Legions of Darkness now have the Opus Demonium ... they will be overly confident that they can defeat you, and yet they fear you. They're well aware that you destroyed the Krelsethian witch coven and blew up the seventh porthole. They know that to underestimate you would be dangerous. They will want to make an example of you ... and example so horrifying that no one else would dare take a stand against them."

"You mean like they did with Professor Hiller?"

"Precisely."

"I don't like the sound of that."

"I don't imagine you would ... unless being emasculated and eviscerated alive and then having your intestines and genitals fed to a sea monster before your dying eyes sounds particularly appealing."

I thought for a brief moment. "No ... I'd have to say that would be pretty low on my list of appealing scenarios." Charlotte's mountainous cleavage beckoned, her bountiful bosoms seemingly longing for the groping touch of my sausage-like fingers. "I'd better cop a feel while I'm still physically able," I said, reaching out for a quick squeeze of her bodacious boobies.

Suddenly Charlotte's image blurred and faded away, replaced by the irate specter of Dr. Bernard Harvey looming before me. Dr. Harvey slapped my groping hands away roughly. "Christ, Matheson! Are you mentally retarded?"

"Dr. Harvey? What are you doing here in my imaginary brain thing?"

"I thought my little appeal might be best served by my appearing you to as your girlfriend, Stanley, but I've obviously underestimated your ability to pay attention to anything other than a pair of big tits waving in your face."

"Wait, what's all this about a pair big tits waving in my face?"

"Listen, you idiot, while the demonic manifestations of the Legions of Darkness walk the earth in their human form, they are vulnerable. The bodies they inhabit are susceptible to injury and even death if their weaknesses are discovered and exploited correctly."

"Wait a minute. Are you saying that while the demonic manifestations of the Legions of Darkness walk the earth in their human form, they are vulnerable? That the bodies they inhabit are susceptible to injury and even death if their weaknesses are discovered and exploited correctly?"

"Yes, that is nearly word for word what I am saying, Stanley. Now, can your tiny brain comprehend the meaning of the words you just repeated back to me as if they were your own?"

"You mean like finding an Achilles heel somewhere on their bodies? Like say ... the elbow?"

"Or perhaps, the heel?"

"Or the nose."

"Or perhaps the heel?"

"If you're going for the obvious, sure, then the heel would be fine, I guess."

"I am your eyes and ears at Hull House, Stanley. Unfortunately, I cannot compensate for your walnut-sized brain, but I am doing my best to assure that you will not meet your terrible end at the hands of the Legions of Darkness."

"I appreciate that, Doctor."

"I'm doing this for the greater good, Stanley, not for your benefit. As much as I dread the fact, it behooves me to prevent your untimely demise. The only upside is that the longer you walk the earth, there isn't any chance of us running into each other here in the afterlife."

"I still detest you too, Doctor, if that makes you feel any better."

"It doesn't, but I'll take that as a compliment. Now listen to me, Stanley, the six humanoid manifestations of the Legions of Darkness were given specific instructions by Leland Hull for their visit to

Goblin's Dong. First, they were to retrieve the Opus Demonium from Professor Hiller before you could get your hands on it. Then they were to make an example of you. One of the demonic humanoids was to appear to the people of Goblin's Dong in the guise of the god, Carthalluulffthh, to rally them against you, working them into a psychotic religious frenzy. The one who will make his appearance in the form of Carthalluulffthh was formerly the teenager, Ronald Dickey. He incessantly whined about a sever allergic reaction to shell fish when informed that Goblin's Dong was a seaside town who's main industry was crab fishing. He claimed that he would go into anaphylactic shock if he were to ever accidently eat any kind of shell fish. "

"Anaphylactic? Is that like when you have a really tiny head?"

"No, Stanley. Eating shellfish will not give him a really tiny head. It's an allergic reaction that can cause breathing difficulty and circulatory failure and can be fatal without emergency medical attention."

"So we should give him emergency medical attention?"

"No, you idiot. You should give him shellfish!"

"But why would someone with prophylactic shock want to appear as a sea monster god when the sea is full of sea food—specifically shell fish?"

"Because he's a showoff, Stanley, and he simply couldn't resist the opportunity to play Carthalluulffthh. Even in demonic form, he's still a showboating little shit."

"What about the others from the Legions of Darkness? Are we supposed to slip them some crab cakes too?"

"The others will have already moved on, moved on in search of Jamie Lynn Faraday, spreading madness and death wherever they go. They know she's escaped from Hull House, but they've not yet discovered her location. Like you, she is to be made an example of. If they find her, her death will be horrifying."

"They'd better not harm a hair on that kid's head. These assholes are fucking with the wrong idiot."

"I couldn't have said it better. You are definitely the wrong idiot for this job."

"Don't get your ghostly Fruit of the Loom, control top briefs in a bunch, Doc. If they want an example to be made, they're going to get one. I'm going to be administering an enema full of my own brand of raw, undistilled justice to these corpse-eating turd jugglers!"

"I'm not sure what that even means, Matheson. Just don't get too cocky. Remember, foolish is the Dutchman who ice skates on a lake of frozen diarrhea."

"Point taken, Doc. I never trusted the Dutch anyway. Anyone who carves their shoes out of wood has got to be little weird."

Dr. Harvey smiled, drew back his fist and then punched me in the face.

I awoke with a jolt, lying on the floor with thick, foamy saliva running down my chin and blood pouring from my nostrils. Dr. Whitlock and Detective Solomon kneeled over me with terror in their eyes, each man holding one of my arms to the floor. One of them had shoved a large wooden penis between my teeth to prevent me from biting down on my tongue—obviously some kind of fertility symbol used in black magic that had been hastily grabbed from a display shelf during my seizure.

They reluctantly loosened their grip on my forearms after I came to.

"I didn't shit my pants did I?" I mumbled, momentarily unable to pry my teeth loose from the wooden penis clenched tightly between my upper and lower jaw.

Solomon patted me on the shoulder and grinned with relief. "I don't think so ... but you did practically everything else. We thought we were going to have to call a goddamn exorcist."

I jerked the fertility symbol loose from my jaws and grabbed both men by the lapels of their jackets. "Doctor, you were right. This was a trap laid by those donut fuckers from the Legions of Darkness.

They mean for the psychotic villagers to sacrifice us to Carthalluulffthh!"

"You had a vision ... from that nebula," Solomon said

"Yes. Most of the villagers have been infected with the Death From Medusa's Uterus Plague carried here by the Orias Nebula. They believe that we are responsible for bringing the evil to their town and that the only way to end their terror is by sacrificing us to their weird god. And you better believe that Carthalluulffthh will be putting in a guest appearance tonight."

"But Carthalluulffthh is only a legend! Just local superstition," Dr. Whitlock said. His tone sounded desperate—as if a plea for rationality might actually restore it to our bizarre situation.

"Carthalluulffthh will be one of the shape-shifting, demonic humanoids that we saw in the caverns at Hull House that has taken the form of the hideous sea god. This is going to get real ugly, boys. I'm afraid the Legions of Darkness mean to make an example out of me. I mean like a disemboweled example with my own penis crammed into my mouth, and I don't mean that in the weird way you try during puberty that turns out to be physically impossible. I mean they're going to cut it off first! But I have a little ace up my sleeve!"

Solomon's eyes glimmered with faint hope. "Ace?"

"Tonight the part of Carthalluulffthh will be played by a humanoid with a deadly allergy to shellfish. Apparently that annoying idiot Ronald Dickey just couldn't help showing off, despite his Achilles elbow."

"You mean *heel*," Dr. Whitlock corrected.

"I'm just trying to think out of the box here, gentlemen. Maybe Achilles had a vulnerable elbow that no one ever discovered because they were too obsessed with his goddamn heel, " I said.

Solomon smirked. "A sea monster with a shell fish allergy?"

"It sounds like one of Aesop's Fables," Dr. Whitlock said.

"Or an idiotic plot twist created out of sheer desperation," Solomon said.

"Well it's better than anything in *Juicy, Black Love Jumbo*," I said.

Dr. Whitlock looked baffled. "What on earth is that?"

"Nothing. Forget about it ... just some perverse, third rate erotica—probably written by a Dutchman. You can never trust those dike-fingering, tulip snorters."

Solomon and Dr. Whitlock helped me to my feet. I winced, now feeling the dreadful, squishy mess I'd excreted into my trousers. "I *did* crap my pants!"

"Maybe a little bit, buddy" Solomon said with a guilty grin and patted me on the shoulder again.

Whitlock's eyes went wide as he gazed out of the window in shock. "The nebula ... it's gone."

Angry shouts for vengeance drifted up the hillside, coming from the rapidly approaching mob.

"I guess that would be our cue to run for our lives," Solomon said.

"Sounds like as good a plan as any," I said, bolting for the stairwell.

Solomon and Dr. Whitlock followed closely behind me as we charged out of the building and onto the road in a desperate rush toward the car. Suddenly Dr. Whitlock cried out in agony and froze in his tracks, clutching a bloody whaling harpoon that had speared him through the upper right thigh. "God almighty, " he groaned, tottering weakly away from us and stumbling into the trees lining the roadside. Then came a pained shriek as the diminutive scholar lost his footing and tumbled down the hillside just beyond the cooperage. Solomon and I stared helplessly in stunned silence as Whitlock disappeared from view.

Before we could even react to the assault on our colleague, we were trapped—swallowed up in a pair of fishing nets that had been heaved at us with expert precision. The .38 special gripped in Solomon's right hand fired off a random, wild shot as he struggled to take aim beneath the cloying grip of the damp, tangled mesh that had been cast on top of him. Another shot rang out before I caught a fleeting glimpse of Solomon's right hand being kicked at by one of our assailants. The gun flew out of the detective's hand and skidded into the brush lining the roadside.

The strategically weighted nets seemed to grow tighter around our limbs as we attempted to wrestle ourselves free, leaving us as helpless as a pair of houseflies trapped in the web of a hungry spider. We were kicked and beaten unmercifully before the hooded, torch-wielding mob finally hoisted us roughly onto the bed of a horse-drawn, wooden cart and then knocked us unconscious with a pair of fish-shaped clubs.

Solomon and I awoke with a start some time later as we were doused with buckets of freezing seawater. The villagers had tied the two of us to a pair of driftwood crucifixes, the bases of which had been nailed to a wooden pallet affixed with wagon wheels on either side like a makeshift rickshaw that could be pulled through the streets by hand. The enraged townsfolk stood before us like a hooded mob of Ku Klux Klansman, screaming curses and waving knives, cleavers and torches in front of our terrified faces.

A powerfully built gorilla of a man stepped forward, growling his disgusted remarks in a voice that was instantly recognizable as that of the hospitality-impaired barkeep from the Whale's Bladder Inn. "Ye little friend won't get far. Not with that harpoon in his leg he won't!" The lumbering lummox loudly cleared the phlegm from his throat and then spat at us. "Uh! Shit!" he grumbled, realizing that the hood he wore over his head had blocked the stream of saliva from hitting its intended mark. He lifted his hood slightly and wiped the phlegm from his chin, flinging it to the ground and then wiping his fingers on his pant leg. "Ye bastards! Ye tricked me with ye powers of black magic!"

Solomon spat blood and then cried out, "No! We know nothing of black magic! This is all a misunderstanding. We're representatives of the Salty Seaman Fishstick Company. We were only here looking for a location for our new factory!"

Another villager stepped forward, pointing an accusatory finger. "Lies! I own the Salty Seaman Fishstick Company, and I've never seen these ye bastards before!"

Solomon looked briefly confused, "Oh ... well then, we're actually from the Minty-Fresh Spearmint Gum Company ... and we're looking for a place to build our new gum factory!"

Yet another villager stepped forward, eagerly. "I like gum! It's chewy and minty in my mouth!" he said, before being shushed by his fellow townsfolk.

"We don't want ye gum around here, ye warlocks!" the barkeep grumbled and then attempted to spit at us again, dousing the inside of his hood with phlegm for the second time. "Goddamn it! They tricked me again!"

"They just attempted to rape me with a large stick of peppermint candy!" a woman shrieked. The mob roared in anger and then began to pelt us with handfuls of fish entrails.

"Let the Feast of Carthalluulffthh begin!" another townsperson screamed.

The makeshift rickshaw cart that held us was pulled forward by a pair of hooded runners and then paraded down the main street of the village. The verbal abuse and throwing of rotting fish entrails continued, accompanied by rhythmic chants of "Carthalluulffthh! Carthalluulffthh!"

"Please don't throw a shitload of shellfish at us!" I shrieked. "Please! Anything but that! Don't throw any shell fish at us to appease your god of the sea who probably loves him some tasty shellfish!"

Solomon moaned in horror. "Yes! For the love of Carthalluulffthh, please don't pelt us with shellfish!" The detective turned to me and winked, giving me a strained thumbs-up with his right hand.

"Hey! Let's throw crabs at them!" an enthusiastic villager screamed. His suggestion was met with shouts of approval and several of the abusive villagers rushed off to gather crabs from the fish market.

We soon began to regret our ingenious plan when several villagers began pelting us with large Dungeness Crabs, whose hard shells shattered upon impact with our skulls, leaving large mounds of crabmeat piled upon our shoulders and caked about our jackets, ties and shirtfronts. My face exploded with white-hot pain as a crab shell cracked the bridge of my nose and spilled gouts of blood down my chin. "Fucking fuck!" I screamed. "Okay! I think your goddamn sea monster god will be adequately appeased! You can stop throwing fucking crabs now you assholes! You can go back to throwing soft fish intestines at us, your crab quota has been met!"

"Oh God! Please don't throw marshmallows at us!" Solomon pleaded, attempting to change the villager's focus.

"Perhaps we could calm them down by singing a few bawdy sea shanties," I suggested. "Do you know *Johnny Come Down the Hilo* or *Jinny Wren Bride*?"

Solomon considered the suggestion. "No, I don't know those."

"Crap. Neither do I," I said. "I'm not even sure if those are actual sea shanties."

"Well they do sound delightfully bawdy, nonetheless," Solomon said.

"Yeah," I said, weakly. All hope had drained from my voice as I attempted to resign myself to our terrible fate.

"I always thought that I might be killed in the line of duty," Solomon said. "I just never saw something like this in the cards."

"I guess our one consolation prize is knowing that these assholes will watch their sea god choke to death on a couple of half-assed do-gooders who did their small part to try to save the human race from a fate worse than death."

Our humiliating procession finally came to an end as we were left to rest at the edge of a stony precipice overlooking the foamy, grayish-green turmoil of the Atlantic Ocean. Waves exploded against the jagged rocks below us as the icy ocean winds ripped through our hair. The rhythmic chants of "Carthalluulffthh! Carthalluulffthh!" continued behind us as a small man clad in the robes and mask of the high priest of the Carthalluulffthh cult rounded the cart and stood before us with a large ceremonial dagger in his hand. The man spoke in a strange language that I did not recognize, his arms outstretched to the ominous darkness of the sky above.

"Casathaflashacasaflthhhh!" he roared. "Twatlick gurgleslorp!" The high priest fumbled with his bulky mask for a moment, then he continued his strange tirade. "Slathalack maltholus caracathos!"

The Lilliputian cleric approached us, grunting in pain as he limped forward. "Don't worry. I'm not going to castrate you," he whispered. The pained limp and British accent told us that, against all odds, Dr. Whitlock had managed to infiltrate the cult by donning the high priest costume on display at the Theydarian Society. "I'm afraid I had to kill the real high priest," he whispered. "I haven't done anything like that since I was in black operations back in the 1950s."

A collective gasp of terror and awe from the manic mob that surrounded us directed our attention seaward once more. From the foamy brine of the tempestuous Atlantic arose the scaly, tentacle armed horror now so familiar from the village's strange religious iconography. The amphibian monstrosity loomed above the crashing waves, floating like a phantom against the turbulence of the churning clouds of an indigo sky. Its slimy wings flapped madly, like a manta ray taken flight. Finally the creature descended, landing upon the jagged edge of the precipice that jutted out before us over the crashing surf below. The abominable monster cackled with wicked glee, emitting a series of bubbling croaks that sounded as if the creature was suffering from chronic bronchitis.

Staring into its awful, cackling maw, I was struck with a sudden inspiration. I tilted my head toward my shoulder and opened my mouth as wide as possible. I chomped madly at the awful crab meat caked upon my jacket—forcing in as large a mouthful as I could. I then turned to Solomon, who was eyeing me with bemusement.

"Hungry?" he asked.

I grunted frantically and gestured toward the terrible sea monster with my head, spitting slimy bits of crabmeat down my chin as I tried to make my intentions clear. Suddenly the detective's eyes widened with realization and he cried out to Dr. Whitlock.

"Punch the fucker in his fishy, octopus balls, Doc!" Solomon screamed.

In the heat of the moment, Dr. Whitlock became confused by Solomon's command and bolted forward in my direction, punching me full-force in the testicles. The hideous blow caused me to spit my mouthful of crabmeat into the face of the cackling sea monster that stood before us, splattering the shellfish mush into its eyes and down its throat. The creature began to choke, its confused eyes staring at us with helpless terror. It wrapped its tentacles around its throat as its eyes bulged and its neck began to swell like some sickly, mutant toad. The monster fell to the rocky ground, as its wings flapped about frantically, sending clouds of sandy gravel into the air. The creature twisted and turned as it went into seizures, gagging and gasping for air.

The confused townsfolk gazed upon their dying sea monster god in helpless horror as Dr. Whitlock quickly cut the ropes that bound us to the driftwood crosses with the ceremonial dagger. Solomon and I stumbled to the ground, now free of our restraints. The hulking barman from The Whale's Bladder Inn charged at Dr. Whitlock, shrieking and waving a previously bloodied meat cleaver. With the agility of a trained assassin, the doctor heaved his dagger at the oncoming assailants throat, lodging the blade in the man's jugular vein. A shower of blood sprayed from the man's neck and drenched the three of us with a spray of crimson gore. The powerfully built assailant fell dead as yet another crazed villager rose to the occasion, charging at us with a bloodied axe. Without hesitation, Dr. Whitlock seized the meat cleaver from the deceased barkeep's hand and brought the blade down with intense fury on the oncoming attacker's skull, imbedding the cleaver in the man's forehead and killing him instantly before he could even draw back the axe in his hands. Dr. Whitlock pulled the axe from the dead man's clutches and passed it to Solomon and then drew a sawed-off, double-barreled shotgun from beneath his ceremonial vestments.

The crazed villagers gasped in shock and then backed away, now seeming more than a little apprehensive about mounting a full-on attack against us.

"The possession of the fire weapons is forbidden by Carthalluulffthh," a stunned villager protested.

Dr. Whitlock removed the bulky ceremonial mask and scanned the mob with squinted, gun fighter eyes.

"Anyone else feeling particularly bloodthirsty this evening?" he inquired, in his manner-of-fact way.

"I am," another monstrously built villager growled, stepping forward from the mob and shoving a few of his less impressive colleagues aside as he ripped the ceremonial hood from his head. The deranged goliath then tore his vest and shirt from his muscular body, as if they were made of nothing more than Kleenex, and flexed his arms until the veins protruded from his thick neck.

"I wouldn't shoot my mouth off, if I were you, lad," Dr. Whitlock warned.

The muscular man balked, "Oh yeah? And why's that, old man?" The Herculean challenger took a step toward him, defiantly.

Dr. Whitlock leveled his shotgun at the man's face and pulled the trigger, blasting the man's scowling features to kingdom come. The crowd fell silent, staring at the blood-spewing mess of the challenger's face as he fell backward, dead as a doornail.

"Even without a follow-up wisecrack about me being the one pointing the shotgun at his mouth, I would have thought the reason would be completely obvious," Dr. Whitlock said, shaking his head with puzzled disbelief. "Now, if no one else feels the burning desire to shuffle off from this mortal coil this evening, I might suggest that you all disperse, posthaste, ladies and gentlemen." The smallish, shotgun-toting, killing machine voiced this last proposal to the crowd with all the calmness of a university professor dismissing his class for the day, and—after brief consideration of the warning—the townsfolk fled in terror, scattering into the streets of Goblin's Dong.

With the threat of the murderous mob now quelled by the surprisingly murderous crowd control techniques of Dr. Whitlock, we were finally able to return our attentions to the vile, shapeshifting imposter that convulsed upon the ground not five feet away from us. The creature had shriveled from the imposing form of the ghastly sea monster god to the shivering, naked figure of a humanoid male with sickly-pale, grayish flesh, jagged, rat-like teeth and eyes as black as onyx.

The humanoid monstrosity moaned, emitting a blood-curdling alien wail as it glowed red with intense heat and then disintegrated into a smoldering pile of ashes before our eyes. As the smoking soot was quickly swept away by the lashing winds of the Atlantic Ocean, the churning indigo clouds of the night sky came suddenly alight with a strange series of colorful bursts of red and green luminescence and then abruptly went dark once again. Thunderclaps sounded far off in the distance.

"I'm hesitant to burst out singing *Ding, Ding the Witch is Dead*, just yet, Stanley, but that was some nice work," Solomon said, patting me on the shoulder as I gripped my swollen testicles.

I attempted a pained grin. "It's just a band aid on a severed limb, Mort. This one got a little too big for his demonic britches. I don't think the others will make the same mistake. This was human error. The human aspect of Ronald Dickey caused this one to get careless ... the same way Ronald Dickey got those other teenagers to make the careless mistake of throwing their little Halloween party at the ruins of the Hull Mansion. We got lucky this time. If you can call any of this *lucky*," I wheezed.

"And we have very little time to make our escape," Dr. Whitlock warned. "It will only be a matter of minutes before these people launch a counter attack," Dr. Whitlock warned. "I give us ten minutes at most to get clear of this village before we're torn to shreds."

Shrieks of fury and the sounds of shattering glass in the distance verified our mounting paranoia as we limply jogged back into the streets of the village, taking cover in whatever shadows we could duck into as we ran for our lives.

The village chapel was now engulfed in flames and many of the townspeople ran through the streets, screaming and confused, their mutilated faces bloody and their eyes wide with insane terror. We paused for only a moment to catch our breath as Dr. Whitlock reloaded another shell into the shotgun. The man's hands were steady. He was strangely calm under the circumstances.

"So you were with black ops? That's license to kill, covert shit, Doc," Solomon said.

"Ancient history." Dr. Whitlock answered.

"Well it explains how you could take a whaling harpoon in the leg and then come back swinging," Solomon said. "Where'd you procure the shotgun?"

"Professor Hiller was a dear friend, my boy ... a complete and utter bastard, but a dear friend nonetheless. I knew he'd have a firearm hidden somewhere. He was incredibly paranoid. He wholeheartedly believed in the prophecies of Shemrach Theydarian and often proclaimed that they would come to pass in the very near future. I assumed that since there were no signs of a struggle at the cooperage that they must have caught the man completely off guard. Luckily, in this case, I assumed correctly, Mr. Solomon."

"I'm just glad you're on our side ... such as it is," I muttered.

We pinned ourselves flat against the exterior wall of a barbershop to avoid the attention of a nude man wearing a spaghetti colander on his head as he sprinted down the street toward us. The naked man streaked past without taking any notice of us, screaming that he was "Emperor Snickerdoodle Pumpkinfart of Astronaut Junction."

At that moment, the strangest twist in an evening chock full of strange twists occurred when a horrible caterwauling came bellowing out of the crashing surf in the distance. We turned seaward yet again, as what could only have been the *real* Carthalluulffthh arose from the breaking waves, ascending into the stormy clouds of the ominous night sky. Its horrible, slimy wings flapped rhythmically against the freezing ocean mists that cascaded across its smooth, shimmering flesh.

The sea monster shrieked once more, its throaty scream carried into the village streets on the ice-cold ocean winds. The monster soared into the hamlet like some gargantuan bat and plucked Emperor Snickerdoodle Pumpkinfart from the street with the stealth of a hawk. With its screaming prey clutched in its tentacles, the monster descended to the rooftop of a feed store and then began to devour the screaming villager, backlit by the hellish red and orange flames of the burning chapel behind it.

"The chanting must have summoned the real beast from the sea," I said.

Dr. Whitlock stared at me, looking slightly dumbfounded. "You don't seem to be the least bit surprised by any of this."

"The only thing that surprises me is that we're still alive, Doctor," I said.

Dr. Whitlock hugged the shotgun. "The car isn't far. Your keys fell out while they were beating the shit out of you in the fishnets. I parked it as close as I could without the risk of being seen," he said and then stumbled around a corner and down a dark alley. Solomon and I limped along behind him, trying desperately not to collapse from sheer exhaustion as the three of us attempted a slow, wobbling jog.

Another crazed villager wearing a lobster bib and who had peeled away most of the flesh of his own face met his untimely end at the hands of Dr. Whitlock when he charged at us wielding a meat tenderizing mallet. A shotgun blast to the chest sent the man flying backward into a collection of trash cans, dispatching a throng of rats to scurry off into the shadows of the dank alleyway.

A nearly deafening explosion sounded in the village streets as we, rather miraculously, reached our car. Dr. Whitlock passed me the keys as he helped Solomon into the front seat of the Mercedes and then dove into the backseat. As I opened the driver's side door, my heart leapt into my throat as I spotted a regrouped coalition of insane villagers charging madly toward us from the alleyway we had so recently exited. I threw myself into the car and shoved the key into the ignition. The engine roared and I floored the gas pedal, pealing away from the oncoming horde with only seconds to spare.

The screaming mob and the burning village shrank quickly into the distance behind us as we sped away into the night, with the haunting shrieks of Carthalluulffthh echoing through the darkness.

Chapter Five

_____

After our incredible escape from Goblin's Dong, we drove nonstop to Newark, New Jersey to deliver our Medusa's Uterus plague sample to Diseases 'N' Stuff. Once we'd found the discount epidemiology center, I carefully tucked the specimen into one of the paper drop box envelopes provided by the center, along with a note detailing its destructive symptoms as described by Dr. Harvey: *Containment required. Specimen is a parasitic organism that secretes a corrosive enzyme into the tissues of the brain. Desire immediate cure for prevention of worldwide epidemic.*

I also included a few of Detective Solomon's Polaroid photographs of the lab at Hull House—photographs that captured the strange medical notations and biological formulas scrawled on the chalkboards and notebooks in the bizarre laboratory. Perhaps there was some vital clue in those snapshots that might help the epidemiologist combat the spread of this biological terror.

I sealed the parcel and addressed the envelope to the attention of Dr. Cynthia Quinlan, adding Charlotte's phone number at the Poontang Palace as my emergency contact. As instructed, I was careful to also add the warning: "DO NOT ATTEMPT TO JUGGLE in bold letters across the package. Then I crammed the envelope into the after hours drop box slot and crossed my fingers.

Our wounds required immediate medical attention, and Solomon—the seasoned New York City Police detective—called in a few favors from some friends in low places to make this happen. We didn't want to risk alerting the authorities to our involvement in the disastrous events in Goblin's Dong, and so, thanks to this precaution, we ended up in the embalming room of a New Jersey funeral parlor being treated by an irritable Russian physician with trembling hands, bloodshot eyes and vodka on his breath. The doctor chain-smoked as he worked, mumbling curses in Russian one minute and then chuckling to himself at some private joke the next.

Whatever skills the fermented Frankenstein lacked as a conversationalist, he more than made up for as a battlefield surgeon. Despite the tremors in the pickled paramedics hands, our wounds were cleaned, stitched and dressed in what must have been record time. The rapidity of the man's work, though perhaps not exactly reassuring, was beneficial nonetheless. It was only a matter of time before the other demonic humanoids could get their claws on Jamie Lynn Faraday. We needed to get back to the Danvers State Hospital as soon as we possibly could.

After incinerating our filthy clothes in a makeshift bonfire that smelled like a septic tank explosion, Solomon and I changed into the clothes we'd brought with us and then procured a cheap black suit for Dr. Whitlock from the funeral home's storage room.

We then fumigated the car's pungent interior as we waited for Solomon's underworld contact to supply us with a few firearms.

"Demon slayers," Dr. Whitlock muttered, as if he was trying the title on for size.

Solomon lit a cigarette. "One down and only five more to go."

"Just exactly how do you plan to extract this Miss Faraday from a maximum security state mental hospital, gentlemen? Something tells me that informing her doctors that her life is in danger from five shape-shifting humanoids from another dimension might not cut the mustard in this situation," Dr. Whitlock said. "Unless, of course, you're planning on some kind of inside job after you're both committed for observation."

"Well that's where the next step becomes a little murky," I said.

"How murky?" Dr. Whitlock said.

"Like a deep brown murky," I said. "We're going to have to get very creative."

Solomon's shady underworld firearms connection came through for us with flying colors, arming us with enough weapons to stage the climax of a Sam Peckinpah movie. What good this portable arsenal would do us could not be predicted, but the guns and explosives did provide us with a comforting, if perhaps, false sense of bravado for the time being.

We sped to the Danvers State Hospital using a route that was well off the beaten path, keeping clear of the major highways after hearing early news reports on the car's radio of the carnage now taking place in Connecticut. The vague, but sinister news hinted at a quickly spreading hysteria over shocking outbreaks of homicidal violence in the area. Despite the cautious nature of the reports, the message was clear: the madness of the Death From Medusa's Uterus Plague had quickly gained a foothold in the region in the span of only a few hours. In very little time at all, the plague could escalate to epidemic proportions.

As we drove, Dr. Whitlock sat quietly in the backseat paging through a large antique book that he'd taken from the Thaydarian Society.

Solomon eyed him in the rearview mirror. "What do you remember about this Opus Demonium, Doctor? Can you remember anything that we might be able to use to our advantage?"

Whitlock gazed up from the book and rubbed his bloodshot eyes. "I remember that approximately four months ago, Professor Hiller became extremely paranoid that sinister forces were conspiring to steal the book. He said he'd been having flashes or visions in his dreams of the very demons that the book was created to safeguard the human race against. Quite frankly, I thought the man might be going a bit senile. It was as if he'd suffered some sort of mental break with reality. He was always high strung and paranoid, even during our days at Cambridge back in England—but this was something altogether different. He was not a man who was frightened or intimidated easily, but the tone in his voice when he spoke about this subject seemed extremely fearful ... terrified actually. He would never admit that, of course. Whether this was prophecy or sheer coincidence, the man at least had the foresight to create a counterfeit copy of the book."

"A counterfeit?" I said.

"A very convincing counterfeit copy, as evinced by the fact that our murderous predecessors were content to procure the decoy compendium left on display by Professor Hiller, rather than tear the museum apart looking for the authentic volume that he'd secreted away."

"A you telling us that you found the Opus Demonium?" Solomon turned to face the doctor, who seemed oblivious to the fact that he hadn't announced this rather fortuitous victory.

"That is what I'm telling you."

"You didn't mention any of this before," Solomon said, sounding a bit miffed.

"Mr. Solomon, forgive me, but I'm still trying to wrap my mind around all of this. Until today, I'd always considered the Opus Demonium the work of a delusional madman, and that Professor Hiller's rather strange obsession with it was simply a result of his rather extreme eccentricity. Telling me that *this* book wasn't actually a work of fiction would have been the equivalent of informing me that Bram Stoker's *Dracula* was a realistic account of actual vampirism. "

I chuckled. "Vampires! Now *there's* a ridiculous idea."

"I simply didn't wish to unduly excite you both before actually reviewing the text," Dr. Whitlock explained in a calm tone of voice that was almost, but not quite, patronizing.

Solomon smirked. "And now that you've had a chance to preview this volume—before Stanley and I wet our pants with undue excitement—what is your professional opinion?"

"My professional opinion is that erring on the side of caution under such fantastic circumstances might actually serve us well, which is why I also procured all of the demon slaying paraphernalia that Professor Hiller had assembled in the recent months in accordance with the instructions given in the Opus Demonium."

I was as thrilled by the news as I was shocked. All I'd brought to the table was a battered, steel-plated bowler hat, a copy of the collected works of Leland Hull and a strange resolve that I was somehow supposed to save humankind from the evils of the Seven Legions of Darkness. This was certainly a step in the right direction. "So we now possess both the Opus Demonium *and* a collection of demon slaying weapons?"

"Precisely ... for whatever good they'll actually serve," Dr. Whitlock said.

Solomon chimed in. "What are we talking about here? Wooden stakes and garlic and silver bullets? What the hell does 'demon slaying paraphernalia' even mean?"

"Well, something like this, for example." Dr. Whitlock paged through the text of the Opus Demonium and then, finding the appropriate diagram, displayed a Leonardo da Vinci-like sketch rendered with incredible detail. But, detail notwithstanding, what the device actually was or what possible purpose it might serve remained mysterious.

Solomon voiced his perplexity in no uncertain terms. "What *in the hell* is *that*?"

Dr. Whitlock re-examined the drawing. "According to the text, this is a blueprint for a demonic extermination ray gun fashioned from the bones of children who died in childbirth, as well as those of dead kittens, puppies and baby arctic seals. It would emit a blast from two cylinders containing a pair of human, infant fetuses soaked in a concoction of holy water, garlic, mandrake root, ginger and mercury. The apparatus would be constructed using the aforementioned bones as well as a combination of silver and brass. It would also be adorned with a symbol from every known religion ever practiced by mankind: Christian, Hebrew, Hindu, Muslim, Taoist, and so on. The exterminating, poisonous blast would work on the concept of it being fueled by the inherent goodness of earthly innocence and all of the powers of human faith that there is an actual hierarchy of good and evil operating in the universe."

"Well ... that's certainly creative," I muttered.

Solomon considered the notion for a moment. "Are you actually saying that Professor Hiller built this goddamned thing?"

Dr. Whitlock lifted a canvas bag from the floor of the car and placed it onto the backseat, then unzipped the satchel. "He managed to assemble a version of it using medical school specimens and former carnival sideshow attractions he'd procured," the doctor said as he removed the gruesome apparatus from the pack.

I glanced back at the monstrosity held in Whitlock's hands—mumbled, "Oh ... a dead baby gun ... there's something you don't see every day ... thankfully," and then turned back to face to the road.

"That one has two heads!" Solomon gasped, observing one of the fetuses floating inside one of the two glass cylinders attached to the weapon.

"As I said, the man obviously made due with what was available," Dr. Whitlock reiterated.

"Well I've got two daughters and a baby grandson back at home! I'm not touching that goddamned thing!" Solomon warned.

I could feel Dr. Whitlock eyeing me in the rearview mirror. "I think Stanley would be the most obvious recipient," he said, matter-of-factly.

I was puzzled by the dubious honor. "Why *me*? Hiller was *your* buddy. I wouldn't even bring that thing to a Malice Frankenstein concert!"

"You will wield this horrible weapon, Stanley, because—like it or not—that would seem to be your destiny," Dr. Whitlock said. "For whatever reason, you seem to possess a kind of idiot savant's talent for smiting down the incredibly powerful forces of evil that have risen up to enslave humankind."

"That's probably just all of those painkillers that the weird Russian doctor fed you talking," I said.

Dr. Whitlock giggled inadvertently. "Well they certainly took the sting out of all of this shit! I can't feel a thing," he said, staring at his hand as he opened and closed his fingers repeatedly with intense fascination. "It's like I swallowed a rainbow! I certainly wouldn't mind getting my hands on more of those pilly, rainbow, psychedelic, pill things!"

"He's completely stoned," Solomon said. "But he makes a valid point."

"Like William S. Burroughs. I guess the dead baby gun is my cross to bear," I muttered.

"It's like in the Greek myths, when Zeus provided his son, Prometheus with all of those weapons, like the golden dildo and the unicorn and the sword of Damocles," Solomon muttered, sounding, understandably exhausted.

"Well, your grasp of Greek mythology might be slightly cloudy, but I get your point," I said.

"This might all be your fate, Stanley ... like Herpes and his flying shoes, delivering all of those flowers to people for the hermaphrodites," Solomon slurred.

"You took a bunch of those painkillers too, didn't you?"

"'Bout a handful," Solomon muttered, examining his twiddling fingers with intense fascination.

I glanced up at Dr. Whitlock's face in the rearview mirror. "I hesitate to ask what else you procured from Professor Whitlock's collection," I said.

Dr. Whitlock giggled, looking exhausted and now, very high on painkillers. "It doesn't get any prettier, Stanley," he said, carefully tucking the strange weapon back into the canvas bag.

Solomon unsuccessfully fought back a yawn. "That goddamned thing belongs in a carnival sideshow tent," he muttered, crossing his arms and closing his eyes for a nap.

Carnival sideshow tent; the words immediately spun my mind back to my tempestuous association with the gifted and tragic clairvoyant, David Collins—the man who'd played such a vital role in the original Hull House investigation. Given the fact that Collins was nearly killed during the ordeal, Charlotte forbade me from soliciting his help in re-opening the case.

Not that the man would've even considered such a dubious invitation. The last time we collaborated, he ended up with saber shoved through his lower intestine. I could never possibly expect the man to stand at my side again, not after literally having dragged him into and then out of that godforsaken haunted mansion like I did. I hadn't heard a word from Collins in over two years, yet I couldn't deny the sinking feeling that, wherever he was, he must sense the terrible things that were happening. The question was: would he ignore the pull of the Legions of Darkness trying to drag him back to New England? Would he feel at all obliged to help me confront these apocalyptic evils? If not, I suppose I could scarcely blame the man for sitting out yet another opportunity to die in the line of duty.

Beside me in the passenger seat, Solomon began to snore. The detective was down for the count. Gazing into the rearview mirror once more, I saw that Dr. Whitlock was also now fast asleep. Thankfully I'd brought along my own painkillers to dull the aches in my problematic leg and was not under the influence of the rainbow of fruit flavors that now coursed through the bloodstreams of my dozing colleagues.

I drove on into ominous blackness of the night in silence, not wishing to hear the impending horrors that were unfolding on the car's radio news broadcasts. In the eerie quiet, my mind wandered. Suddenly I felt something creep across my brain like a spider—as if some other entity had slipped in through an unguarded mental backdoor. It wanted me to think of Jamie Lynn Faraday. It wanted to know where she was.

A familiar voice sounded in my brain—a voice I'd heard before in a terrible nightmare, three years ago during my stay at the Hull mansion.

"Those that come from darkness see you as you see we!" the voice whispered.

As a defense mechanism, I flooded my brain with a strange stream of thoughts and visuals to conceal the information that the intruding entity was prospecting for.

Jamie Lynn Faraday? Is she that elderly black woman who's always talking to herself at the International House of Pancakes?

My brain began to ache with a sharp, stabbing pain—as if an ice pick was being slowly plunged into my tender and highly imaginative grey matter.

(Those that come from darkness see you as you see we!)

Oh THAT Jamie Lynn Faraday, the main character in the underrated Charles Dickens novel "The Glass Dildo." Or was he the gay, heroin-addicted star of Andy Warhol's film, "Garbage Man?"

(Those that come from darkness see you as you see we!)

Finally, I felt the cloying, telepathic tentacles of the alien intruder wrap tightly around a hidden thought: *Danvers State Mental Hospital.* Before I could block the image, the face of Jamie Lynn Faraday flashed in my mind's eye. Seconds later, the creeping, phantom sensation was gone. My brain relaxed, expanding like a sponge soaking up water.

"Son of a bitch!" I hissed and then floored the gas pedal.

Hang on, Jamie Lynn! I'm not going to throw you to these goddamn wolves! I'm coming! And I've got a few surprises for these fuckers!

Chapter Six

_____

The imposing, red brick facade of the Danvers State Hospital's central administration building loomed behind a thick mist of November fog, looking ominous, but, as yet, undisturbed by any interfering demonic forces.

This rather overly optimistic impression was drawn from my first glance at the building as I pulled into the parking lot, and changed quite drastically with a subsequent examination, obtained when I stepped out of the car to stretch my legs. As I gazed at the asylum, somewhat perplexed, I began to wonder if my eyes were playing tricks on me.

I blinked, then rubbed my eyes—cleaned the lenses of my glasses and blinked again. My vision was fine. It was what my vision was seeing that was the problem. What my vision saw was the Danvers State Mental Hospital, rising out of the November mist now looking like some candy-coated cottage pulled straight out of a children's' storybook. The formerly red brick facade had been replaced by an enormous gingerbread structure trimmed with colorful frosting and elaborate candied adornments that lined its windowsills and doorways. Plump, mechanical, German children clad in lederhosen and dirndls beckoned visitors toward the entrance with a happy song.

"Welcome, welcome, everyone! To our chocolate land of fun! Candy-coated, sticky treats! Fun for all that can't be beat!" the chubby, automated Aryans crooned, as they danced about in robotic repetition.

I could hardly believe my good fortune! Swept up in the enchantment of the place, I abandoned all logic and rushed toward the vision of sugary wonders with giddy anticipation—leaving my still-dozing colleagues lying fast asleep in the car.

In hindsight it seems more than a little odd that a grown man wasn't the least bit suspicious of an insane asylum being magically transformed into a colorful candy factory, but I wasn't exactly thinking clearly at the time. I was compromised by the thoughts of Tangy Chews and Googlie Bars dancing in my head.

I scrambled toward the entrance like a gimpy Charlie Bucket, waving a silver entry ticket that had inexplicably materialized in my hand. "Oh boy! A silver ticket that admits one lucky winner! How on earth did this suddenly appear in my hand?" I said, experiencing slight reservations about having left my two colleagues and all of our demon slaying weapons back in the car.

As I drew closer to the building, my eyes beheld a golden sign above the front doors that read: *Trouserfudge Confections, Chocolates and Sweeties.*

A ginger-haired gentleman wearing a purple top hat and green frock coat made his way down the front steps with open arms and a broad grin. "Welcome, young man! Welcome to Trouserfudge Confections! I'm the proprietor, Mortimer Trouserfudge."

I was awestruck. "Wow! *The* Mortimer Trouserfudge? The creator of Wiggly Doodle Pies and Orangey Prang Slingers?"

"The very same, my boy! I hope you brought your appetite!"

"I sure did! I have a sweet tooth the size of a saber-toothed tiger's fang!"

"And now, so do we!" Mr. Trouserfudge announced—pulling a set of bucktoothed, dentition from the pocket of his frock coat. "Sweet Teeth! Edible sugar dentures for the frail and elderly."

I clapped, giddily, "You think of everything, Mr. Trouserfudge! But then, what else could I expect from the creator of Creamy Curd Sugar Tinglers and Luscious Lemon Lickies?"

"And let's not forget Winkle Slurps, Snorkel Glops and Custard Wigglers, my boy!"

"How could I forget those, Mr. Trouserfudge?"

"And just what brings you out to our factory today, young man?"

"I've got a sliver ticket! I've got a silver ticket!" I exclaimed in my best singsong voice, waving the aforementioned ticket frantically back and forth in the face of the eccentric candy maker.

"My goodness! You're the winner of the free tour of my magical candy factory! Eligible for a free, year's supply of Caramel Cream Nougat Snorters and Pumpkin Spice Wang Twisters!"

"Likewise!" I said, passing the ticket to the grinning candy baron.

Trouserfudge read the name printed on the ticket and gave me a wide, warm grin. "Welcome, Stanley! Welcome to Trouserfudge Confections!" he said, wrapping his arms around my neck and waste in an inappropriately intimate embrace. He pulled me close and breathed heavily into the flesh of my neck for an uncomfortably lengthy period of time. Trouserfudge began to sob softly and then whispered, "I've done such horrible things. So many lives."

At that point, I gently shoved the man away from me and attempted to lighten the mood. "Where are your little purple-skinned slaves? Like in the television commercials!"

"The stunted grunties? Oh they're about! Everywhere and nowhere at all, as usual."

"Off making Winkle Slurps and Juicy Wanks, I'd wager," I said.

"Yeah, those little eggplant fuckers are around here some place," he muttered under his breath.

I was shocked at the venom in his voice. "Excuse me?"

"Nothing ... I'm rambling. I haven't been sleeping well since the police came sniffing around here looking for those two, missing, teenage detectives," Trouserfudge grumbled.

"Hmmmm, maybe now isn't the best time for a tour," I said, stepping away from the man.

"Oh, don't be a silly Billy, Stanley! We need to fill you full of Fickle Pew Pew Twerps, Sticky Licks and Spooge Creamies!"

"Well, maybe I can just take a rain check for the time being," I suggested.

"Since when is Stanley Matheson such a gloopy poopie, plop plop pants?"

"Well I've been having quite a few stomach issues as of late, Mr. Trouserfudge," I said, backing further away.

Suddenly, I found myself surrounded by purple-skinned little people clad in fishnet tank tops and adult diapers. The short-statured servants pawed at me in gentle awe, as if I were a holy relic rumored to possess healing powers of heavenly grace.

"Please don't leave us, Mr. Stanley. Your skin is so pale and smooth ... like mayonnaise," one of the violet-hued stunted grunties pleaded, stroking the flesh of my left hand, gently. "You shall recline, nude, on a bed of raw oysters as we hand feed you Bugle Squirts and Lemon Fizzle Sizzlers."

"That's okay, my skin gets itchy when I'm nude around people of shorter stature," I said, pulling my hand free.

"No ... please ... we must give you pleasure through your oral hole," another said.

Mortimer Trouserfudge cackled with glee. "Come, Mr. Matheson, we have such delights in store for you! Snoogleberry Plops! Pink Panty Diddlers! Twinkle Stix and Chicory Colon Cleanse Chews ... our least popular confection!"

"Ew!"

"Did I mention that those are our least popular confection?"

"I don't find that too hard to believe."

The stunted grunties danced around me in a circle with their hands joined, singing discordantly. "Custard Wigglers! Tata Jigglers! Winkle Bites and Anal Sizzlers!"

I waved my hands about like an orchestra conductor, joining in the fun and frolic, but stopped when I noticed the glowing specter of Dr. Harvey hovering above me with arms crossed and a scowl on his face.

"Having fun?" Dr. Harvey grumbled.

"Not particularly. This is actually pretty disturbing," I said.

"Hardly surprising, considering the source," he said.

"Source?"

"You're dreaming you moron! Wake up!"

As they danced in circles around me, the stunted grunties offered me handfuls of bloody human body parts and entrails dripping with gore. I shrieked in horror as one of them placed the decapitated head of David Collins in my hands.

"He's going to die just like you, Stanley. No one can help you, now," the purple-skinned midget said with horrid glee.

I snapped awake, abruptly—driving on the wrong side of the road and heading straight toward an oncoming semi truck. The driver blasted his horn, frantically as I jerked the steering wheel to the right, veering quickly into the proper lane. The truck roared past, missing the car by mere inches. Moments later we passed a sign reading, "Danvers State Hospital next right," and I wondered with exhausted dismay just how long I had been sleep driving.

Four minutes later, I steered the car into the asylum's parking lot.

It certainly didn't take a rocket scientist to figure out that the Orias Nebula's poisonous rain had preceded our arrival at the mental hospital—although actually having a rocket scientist along with us might have come in handy, as we might have been armed with heavier artillery than our mini arsenal of guns and bizarre collection of demon slaying weapons. Normally, having enough firearms to arm a Columbian drug cartel might have put one at ease, but under the circumstances, I wasn't feeling all that cocky, and neither were my two accomplices.

The murky morning sky rumbled above us like the sour stomach of some Greek God with a bad case of gas, and dreadful pools of the steaming, toxic, black ooze of the Death From Medusa's Uterus Plague were scattered about the parking lot in front of the central administration building of the state hospital. An ambulance, with its mars lights still lazily rotating and aglow, had been ambushed and now sat, parked askew, in the middle of the parking lot with its back doors swaying creakily in the breeze. The bodies of two unfortunate paramedics lay dead and brutalized only a few feet from the vehicle. From the severity of their wounds, it was obvious that the pair had been unmercifully mauled in some savage frenzy.

A small army of patients roamed freely about the grounds clad in nothing more than their pajamas and bare feet, looking confused and heavily medicated. The telltale bloodstains splattered around their mouths and down the fronts of their pajamas led us to the immediate assumption that—despite their dementia—the lunatic collective were not as harmless as they might appear.

Solomon surveyed the carnage as he loaded a .44 Magnum. "I guess the cavalry rode in a little late to save the day."

I eyed a deranged patient gnawing absent-mindedly on a bloody tongue that extended a full two inches past his chin. "But on the bright side, it looks like we're just in time for breakfast."

"You really think Faraday could still be alive?" Solomon said, stuffing a cigarette between his lips.

"She's managed to slip through their clutches before."

"So have we, Stanley—but I'd imagine we're really pushing our luck at this point. We go in there—and those creatures get their hands on us—well, I guess I don't even want to imagine the rest."

I extracted Professor Hiller's monstrous, infant bone weapon from the canvas bag that Dr. Whitlock had been hauling it around in and felt its weight in my hands. It looked like something crafted by a demented child murderer and felt revoltingly slimy to the touch. It was a test of will just to be able to hold the abomination in my hands, let alone carry the horrid thing around with me for self-defense. I shouldered the weapon and passed the bag containing the remainder of the strange demon-slaying ammunition to Dr. Whitlock. "Don't forget your party favors, Doc."

Dr. Whitlock sighed. "You realize that even if we find Miss Faraday ... she might be afflicted with this murderous insanity?"

"Let's just address *that* troll under the bridge when we cross it, Doc," I said.

Once fully armed, we began to ascend the steps leading up to the state hospital's central administration building. The front doors of the main entrance had been ripped from their hinges and lay askew on the stone steps with their glass windows shattered. Just as we were about to enter the asylum, the three of us froze in our tracks as the vast ensemble of disturbed patients roaming the grounds behind us began to suddenly chant in unison.

"Walpurgisnacht," they whispered over and over again, keeping a strange rhythm in their chanting.

We paused at the top of the stairwell and turned to face the warbling throng below.

"Walpurgisnacht," they mumbled, grinning stupidly, and yet menacingly up at the three of us.

Solomon turned to Dr. Whitlock. "That chant ring a bell with you, Doc?"

Dr. Whitlock's brow wrinkled. The man looked uncharacteristically perturbed. "It's the name of a legendary witches' Sabbath that dates back to the Seventeenth century—" his voice trailed off into silence as he gazed down at the assemblage of mentally ill vagabonds gazing up at us with their glassy, dangerous eyes. "When beings spat forth from the blackest depths of Hell roamed freely through the world of humankind."

I looked to the demolished front doors of the central administration building, fighting my overwhelming urge to rush way screaming like a twelve year-old girl. A horrible, low-pitched cackle sounded from somewhere deep in the halls of the asylum, making the three of us start in unison.

The throng of chanting mental patients began to advance slowly toward us, marching in formation toward the foot of the administration building's stairwell.

"They seem to be under some kind of mass hypnosis," Dr. Whitlock said.

I descended a few steps toward the advancing legion and held my arms aloft. "Pimpslap churgen fart!" I bellowed, gazing skyward as I adlibbed my obscure incantation.

As is if on cue, a clap of thunder roared overhead, causing the demented collective to back away in fear. The timing was pure luck and nothing more, yet the illusion of my power to summon some kind of otherworldly forces kept the patients at bay.

"I am Hashish Pumpernickel, Grand Zandith of the Order of Yarlock the Great Deceiver," I announced with as much bravado as I could summon. "We have come here from the fourth dimension. We have come for Walpurgisnacht."

"Walpurgisnacht," the mad assemblage echoed in unison.

"We have a big party planned with loads of games and prizes and yummy food and human sacrifices to the dark gods of the outer realms of the octogenarian sex planet of Herpes Simplex Twelve. You're all invited ... it should be really fun ... like a big carnival. You'll each get four complimentary drink tickets and all-day passes for the swell rides we're going to have.

"But before we can all start having loads of fun, we need to summon the carnival from Herpes Simplex Twelve and we'll need your help. You'll all need to close your eyes real tight and chant the magical incantation: *The clown be makin' sex juice in his pants of baggy size ... The clown be makin' sex juice in his pants of baggy size!*"

Slowly the group began to close their eyes and mimic the chant in greater and greater numbers until the entire horde was happily repeating the nonsensical phrase over and over again. As they did so, we crept slowly up the remaining steps and into the hospital.

The asylum's interior was a smoldering wreck. Patients' files lay scattered about the bloodied floor along with shattered bottles of medications and broken syringes that crunched under our feet as we explored the nearest ward. The florescent lights overhead flickered on and off at random, and at times we were forced to forge ahead in almost total darkness, guided only by the weak, jaundiced flame of Solomon's cigarette lighter.

Eventually we came upon more gruesome evidence of our demonic adversaries' handiwork. In a ransacked electroshock therapy room we found one of the asylum's doctors strapped to a gurney. The top of his skull had been removed and some kind of horrific brain surgery had been performed on the unfortunate physician. As the glow of Solomon's lighter fell upon the man's face, the mutilated doctor gasped and spat a thick stream of blood down his chin. "She's escaped! I've already told you! We found her cell empty in the middle of the night!" he shrieked.

"Who's escaped?" I said, rushing to the gurney.

"Miss Faraday! She's gone! Please don't torture me anymore!" the doctor pleaded.

"Who did this to you, Doctor?"

"Those monsters! The things that came from darkness!"

I began to unbuckle the restraints fastened around the maimed psychiatrist, but before I could set the man free, he began to convulse violently. He screamed in agony as his partially exposed brain began to squirm and pulsate like a mound of bloody worms. My two companions and I backed away from him in horror as ghastly, blood-soaked tentacles extended from the twisting brain matter and undulated in the air, as if searching for a grip on the intruders in the room. The doctor's eyes glowed red like burning coals and his flesh faded to pale shade of grey. His facial features expanded and transformed into something monstrous and serpentine. He smiled at us with bloodstained teeth.

"Walpurgisnacht," he croaked and chuckled with sickening glee.

The doctor's horrible metamorphosis sent us charging back into the corridor whence we came. As we gathered our wits, the florescent lights above us flickered in the gloom and then came alight, casting a weak bluish glow about the hallway.

"Let's get the hell out of here before something else jumps out at us," Solomon said.

"Too late," Dr. Whitlock muttered, staring into the distance to our left. Solomon and I turned our gazes in the same direction.

A black widow spider the size of a Volkswagen bus crept down the hallway toward us. Straddling the monstrous arachnid was a voluptuous feminine figure who radiated such overpowering sexual magnetism that just laying eyes upon her was akin to being blasted in the face with a pair of hydrogen bombs shaped like enormous tits that had been loaded with Powdered Poontang, boner-inducing instant drink mix.

The succubus was humanoid, incredibly buxom and completely nude. Her bright red flesh and black, insect eyes shimmered under the weak luminescence of the florescent lights as she rode toward us. With her jet-black hair, ebony horns protruding from her forehead, bat wings and pointed tail, she was the very exemplification of the "she-devil."

"It's one of them. She's one of the Legions of Darkness," I said. "I can feel her in my mind."

The curvaceous creature was stunningly erotic to behold, and I felt a twinge of horror as I found myself becoming hopelessly aroused by the sight of the demon as she dismounted the gargantuan black window and slinked toward us.

"My God," Dr. Whitlock murmured. "What are you waiting for? Kill it, Matheson! Before it gets the upper hand!"

Despite the doctor's understandable pleas for action, my gut told me to stand down and see what developed other than the rock-hard erection in my pants. "Easy, Doc. Just trust me here. I might be able to get something useful out of this beastly bitch."

The demon paused a few yards away from us and then hissed—
extending a forked tongue that waved wildly about in the air before
her beautiful face.

"I can taste your terror," she cooed and then licked the tip of her
pointed tail, seductively as she looked me over. "So you are the idiot
spoken of in the prophecies of Shemrach Theydarian."

"In the flesh," I said.

"Temporarily," she taunted. "I think I will save your hide for a
throw rug." The she-devil examined me, swinging her tail in circles
like a cattle rancher's lasso. "We have the Opus Demonium, yet you
still hunt us." She sounded almost impressed by the idea. "Foolhardy
... yet strangely fascinating. You are the human who destroyed the

Krelsethian Coven. The slayer of the Athvenog demon in Goblin's Dong."

"I am them that is he," I said in a monotone voice, attempting to sound completely unfazed by the creature's hypnotic sexuality. As an afterthought, I lifted my right hand in a Vulcan salute that I had seen on the Star Trek television show.

"You're quite bizarre—even by human standards," she said.

"Yes, I've heard that before," I said without a trance of irony. I drank in the vision of the wicked creature. "You are the succubus queen, Sexulina Clitorasus, coven leader of the Selurach ... you're a war criminal, guilty of mass genocide, cannibalism and necrophilia. You were banished for eternity to the great, hellish labyrinth of the Scorpius Plane." Only after my mouth had voiced these facts, did my brain realize that it somehow culled this information from the mind probing I'd sensed during the lengthy car ride to the asylum.

The she-devil chuckled. "Impressive. You're just full of surprises. You're like an especially annoying tick sucking on the ass of the Legions of Darkness, Mr. Matheson."

"Likewise," I said—distracted by a strategy slowly forming in my head.

The she-devil grinned, seductively. "Tell me, weird one—who is David Collins?"

"David Collins?"

"Don't be coy, Mr. Matheson. You were thinking of this man shortly before I probed your mind looking for the location of Miss Faraday. Who is he, and how is he relevant to your mission?"

"He was my flatulence instructor," I lied.

"Flatulence?'

"It is a form of mysticism practiced by certain warrior monks in my world."

"An image I culled from your mindscan matches the description of the man who helped Miss Faraday escape from this asylum for the insane. He is obviously an ally, and a potential danger to the Legions of Darkness."

"Collins is what you might call a mystic ... a necromancer," I explained, as I began to execute an admittedly strange and risky plan. "He was a level 12 chocolate beaverlick ... a very powerful dark priest of the Blackalicious Thunder Booty." I wondered just how long I could improvise this sort of gibberish while I attempted to probe this creature's mind without being detected.

"He sounds like quite a nasty piece of work," the she-devil whispered as she slapped the tip of her tail across her open palm. It snapped like a bullwhip. "Nasty!"

Once again, I felt the telepathic tentacles of the succubus slithering across my grey matter like a curious cobra. This time, I responded in kind—welcoming her into the comfort and luxury of the compartmentalized mental masturbatory research facility that I liked to call *the Stanley Matheson Sexual Fulfillment Center*. Who would have thought that all of that masturbating would have eventually played such a vital role in my attempts to save mankind? Touché! *Come on in sweet thang! Take a sip of my smoldering and intoxicating sexuality! Pimp Daddy Matheson gonna put a smack on that round, red booty of yours, you nasty little bitch!*

With the succubus now temporarily preoccupied, I mentally catapulted myself into the demon's twisted psyche, hoping that this kinky, psychic game of cat and mouse would divert her attention for a few fleeting moments while I performed my reconnaissance. And so—as my libido attempted to distract the succubus with large-breasted blowjob fairies and bisexual female vampires clad only in black, spider web panties—the more analytical portion of my mind went prospecting for information on the Scorpius Plane.

The demon's mindscape was an eerie, alien wasteland of treacherous, rocky terrain shrouded in thick billows of fog. A nauseating stench of decomposing flesh wafted through the air, carried on ice-cold winds that chilled the marrow of my bones—which was odd, given the fact that I had left my bones back in my physical body.

Agonized moans echoed from somewhere off in the distance and grew louder and clearer in my ears as I trudged through the wasteland. Finally, I came upon a swampy field riddled with elevated, rusting iron cages. The cages had been forged in humanoid shapes and imprisoned a small army of naked and emaciated captives within their torturous frames. Monstrous ravens pecked away bits of the prisoners' wrinkled, grey flesh as they hopped from cage to cage, indulging themselves on the meat of their helpless prey. The moaning captives craned their heads in my direction, searching instinctively and frantically with blinded, empty eye sockets for some savior in the mist—as if they had caught my scent in the foul air. As horrible as the sight of these wretched captives was, more horrible still was the sense of déjà vu I felt upon laying eyes on them. I'd seen this nightmarish vision before in a painting by Albrecht Shiverdecker.

Terrified, I charged off into the putrid, swirling fog, covering my ears to block out the tormented cries of the prisoners banished to this purgatory of horrors. Moments later, I spied the spires of a tenebrous cathedral-like structure rising out of the mist a short distance away from where I stood—another familiar image from the Shiverdecker paintings. It beckoned me with an odd, hypnotic power and seemed to be the obvious stronghold for the Lovejoy codex in this hellish realm.

Dodging horrible, steaming pools of blood and bile that squirmed with thick layers of maggots, I navigated my way toward the sinister ebony temple. As I drew closer, I was given pause by the strangely shaped skulls impaled upon wooden spikes that littered the grounds surrounding the tabernacle of terror. The fear instilled in me by the dreadful skulls was miniscule compared to the sheer, pants-dampening horror I felt upon coming face to face with the monster that guarded the entrance to the stronghold.

The thing was muscular and humanoid in body shape, but its head was that of a behemoth housefly with grotesque, red, compound eyes and a spiky labellum and pseudotracheae that extended down from the chin of its bulbous cranium and dripped milky, acidic bile. The beast clung to a jagged club fashioned from a humanoid skull and spinal column that it raised above its head upon laying eyes in me. The creature croaked out some guttural warning from its fleshy snout and then swung the weapon though the air, shattering another skull impaled on a spike that jutted from the ground a few feet away. It gurgled at me, spewing foul sputum and then gestured obscenely to its now erect penis. The ghastly, elephantine member swelled between the monster's thick legs and dripped green puss from its swollen head. Seconds later, I received the freak's message with crisp telepathic clarity: "*I'm going fuck you in ass with infected cock!*"

I was about to retort with, "*Over my dead body*," but then thought better of it, since that would hardly seem a deterrent to this demented abomination. Instead, I feigned excited amazement and pointed off into the mist. "Holy cow shit! Isn't that Polish singing sensation, Bobby Vinton out there in the fog signing autographs?"

To my utter surprise, the rather desperate ruse proved quite effective. The monster let out a delighted, high-pitched squeal—sounding like a star-struck teenage girl—then dropped its revolting club and buzzed off into the fetid mist, carried aloft by veiny wings that protruded from its back.

Following the ferocious flying freak's fluttering farewell, I fumbled frantically for the fearsome facade of the fortress of fright.

As I climbed the jagged steps to the front doors of the towering structure, the hideous fly monster descended from the fog and landed with a damp thud directly before me. Staring into the creature's horrible face in close-up, I let out a shriek of terror that could have shattered glass. As the monster gurgled and jittered furiously, another telepathic blast stabbed at my brain like an ice pick.

"No Bobby Vinton! Lies you tell! Wanted autograph on favorite Bobby Vinton album, Take Good Care of My Baby!"

The beast seized me by the throat and lifted me off the ground like an exceptionally handsome, pencil-necked ragdoll.

"There must be some confusion. Isn't this the clown college?" I croaked.

There came more furious gurgling from the monster, then another telepathic stab.

"None shall pass threshold! Guardian of codex will sodomize your corpse!"

"Oh, well then I'll just nip in and use the rest room and be on my way," I squealed.

The situation wasn't exactly unfolding in my favor, and I was quickly becoming envious of the other half of my subconscious that was holding court back at the Sexual Fulfillment Center.

Desperately, I stretched my neck to the left and pointed off into the mist, yet again. "Oh my god! There's Coop Jerrison, the star of the hit television sitcom, *Bingo and the Chooch*!"

"No more lies! I rip balls off!"

Time was of the essence here, and as much as I was enjoying my visit to this little shit-soaked anus of the universe, my patience was running thin. Drawing upon the questionable telekinetic gifts that I had once displayed at the Hull mansion, I concentrated on drawing one of the wooden spikes from the ground and into my grasp. Suddenly, their was a whoosh of air past my hand and a wet ripping sound—after which, the monster slowly released its grip on my throat and dropped me back to the ground. As the creature backed away, I saw that the desired spike had soared passed my hand and into the monster's muscular gut. The thing clutched at the bloodied stake as it stumbled backward.

I straightened my shirt collar with great bravado. "Listen to me, you puss-spewing fart bag! I don't know if you get the papers out here in this gonorrhea-caked fuckhole, but there's a new sheriff in town, and he's here to kick some ass all up in this joint!"

As it shuffled backward, the monster waved its arms about defensively, gurgling and spewing its foul acidic saliva. Gazing into the reflections of its hideous, compound eyes, I caught sight of at least a hundred identical flashes of a gigantic, mustachioed man wielding a massive flyswatter. He scowled down at the creature and then administered an abrupt and fatal swat that sent the monster's putrid entrails showering over me in a sickening rain of gore.

Gagging with disgust, I looked to the horizon. Towering over me was a gargantuan Caucasian man with handsomely chiseled features. The giant sported a plaid, flannel shirt, feathered, sandy blond hair and the aforementioned thick and impressive moustache. He grinned and then addressed me in a manly, baritone voice. "You looked like you needed some help. I thought I would lend a hand, little friend."

"You're the Felcher's Paper Towel Giant! The one from the commercials!"

"No, I'm a trademark-free spoof of that copyrighted character, once created in your imagination while you were high on marihuana. I'm not surprised that you don't remember me—you were really baked when you came up with this whole idea. You named me the Slurpo Paper Towel Man. I think you wrote the concept down on a cocktail napkin at a bar."

"Your moustache ... it's so manly. You must be very popular at your local discothèques."

"My moustache is the stuff of legend, my little friend. It is fashioned of hair from a loin's mane and meticulously groomed with a comb crafted from the rib cage of a mighty lumberjack."

"Wow, that's pretty excessive."

"Not as excessive as my raffling off tickets for moustache rides to the ladies for five dollars a pop."

"Wow, you're a lot weirder than I remember when I scribbled this character down on the cocktail napkin."

"Well I'd say that's the pot calling the kettle black in this instance, but you were pretty fucked up. Anyhow, these raffle tickets aren't gonna sell themselves. Anything else I can help you with, little buddy?"

"You could bust these doors down for me, my exceptionally macho friend."

"Sure thing, Ace," the giant said and then thumped his middle finger against the heavy wooden doors of the temple. They burst open with a squealing crash, clearing my path to the gloomy interior of the foreboding fortress.

I waved at the giant. "Thanks a million, Slurpo!"

"Actually, the name's Brick Champion. Slurpo was only the name of the phony paper towel brand."

"Well, then, thanks, Brick! You've certainly lent a *big hand* in my efforts to save mankind."

"Don't thank Brick Champion, thank that weed you smoked." The giant then donned a motorcycle helmet decorated with an American flag design and gave me a supportive thumbs-up. Then he suddenly dissolved into the ether, leaving behind only a cloud of tinkling fairy dust.

With the ingress thus cleared, I crept inside. The dreary, cavernous interior smelled of death and decay and of things best left hidden away in dark places ... like underpants made of actual human genitalia and buttock flesh.

Once I was inside the horrible hall, the front doors slammed shut behind me with an echoing thud. Eerie red lights illuminated the venue, giving it a cheery ambience that brought to mind a New Orleans whorehouse operated by Satan worshipers. The place was a cobweb-shrouded museum of bizarre relics that appeared to have been procured over the course of several centuries. Most of the curios were beyond my comprehension—collections of texts written in strange and ancient tongues, antiquated statuary sculpted into mind-boggling representations of beings and places from other worlds that staggered my imagination.

I began to explore the mausoleum of mysteries, ducking spider webs that were as thick and sticky as cotton candy, but a lot less tasty. The Lovejoy codex was buried here somewhere amongst these trophies—but where? It would take me a hundred years to examine every rotting relic secreted away in this dreadful keep.

Suddenly, the metallic clack of a spotlight being switched on directed my attention to a familiar figure seated on a stool atop a wooden stage to my right. Beside the stage, a boxy stairwell led the way into a colorful circus tent lined with canvas banners that touted the freakish horrors to be witnessed within.

Seated upon the stool and bathed in the harsh white glow of the spotlight was my deranged (and quite deceased) uncle, Harrison Hull. The questionably talented ventriloquist/comedian and multiple murderer was dressed in a gaily-colored seersucker suit, bowtie and straw boater hat. Propped up on his knee was his identically clad ventriloquist dummy, Charlie Chuckles.

Ever the consummate showman, Harrison took to the role of otherworldly carnival pitchman with undeniable relish— gesticulating wildly toward the gruesome sideshow banners with the tip of his bamboo cane as he unashamedly ballyhooed the stomach- churning horrors to be found within the canvas enclosure. "Hur-ee, hur-ee, hur-ee! Step right up, folks! Witness, with your very own eyes, the most jaw dropping—the most awe-inspiring—the most maniacal menagerie of monstrosities to ever maim and mutilate mankind!"

Dumbstruck, I approached the stage.

Charlie Chuckles, batted his bushy eyebrows. "Get a gander at the slack-jawed yokel! Somebody get this kid a lobster bib! Close your mouth, Sonny Boy! You look like a Venus flytrap in a cheap suit!"

Harrison chastised his rude companion. "Now, now, Charlie ... it's not nice to talk about the rubes that way."

Charlie leaned forward. "Are you here to join the sideshow,

weasel-face?"

"What? No!"

"You sure? You could make a pretty penny with that weird-lookin' kisser of yours."

As I gazed, slack-jawed at my murderous uncle and his dummy sidekick, a second Harrison Hull doppelganger passed by—this one sporting a bowler hat and sleeve holders and pushing a concession cart offering fried sewer rat and frozen clown dicks covered in what looked like (but probably wasn't) chocolate syrup.

The clone tipped his hat. "Frozen clown dick?"

I was taken aback by the question. "No ... no thanks. I'm trying to cut down."

"I've got turdcicles, syphilis chews ... hot cup-o-puke."

"No ... I'm not really hungry ... thanks."

Harrison #2 tipped his derby and then continued on his merry way as his double, seated upon the stage, resumed his spiel. "A more gruesome gaggle of grotesque gargoyles has never before been gathered for your gawking gaze! Can your timid ticker take the tension of the terrors trapped in this tent of torments?"

Charlie Chuckles batted his eyebrows once more. "A weasel man before me stands, with chicken guts and shaking hands. A yellow streak runs up his back. He might just have a heart attack."

Harrison laughed and resumed his colorfully foreboding ballyhoo, waving his cane about, wildly. "Gaze in horror at Beef Pinkman, the human meat jerky baron and alligator rapist of Kremlar 12! You will gasp with terror at the sight of Pimlak, the unsolicited colonoscopy monster, and Prang Slinkfelder, the rabid, two-headed grizzly bear with a moray eel for a penis! Chuckle with glee at the delightful antics of Toots Feldstein, the farting golem, and Horkmeer, the walleyed bowel squeezer and murder enthusiast! Fight back the bile rising in your throat as you behold Hershey Phlemslurp, the transsexual, Flemish testicle collector and modern art enthusiast!"

"Excuse me," I interjected. "Could you direct me to the Lovejoy codex?"

Harrison ignored the question. "Can your heart stand the sight of Perry Pumpernickel, Jr., the indestructible, multi-limbed, many-headed, sharp-toothed thing of indescribable horror?"

"Now ... about this Lovejoy codex you mentioned."

Harrison rapped me across the top of my skull with his cane. "Take a hike, kid. You're camping my style."

"What style?" This quip got me another crack on the head.

"I guess some folks just can't take a hint, ladies and gentlemen! I guess some folks don't know when to flee in terror from Anal Butthole, the monster with an asshole for a face, or to scurry off in horror before laying eyes on Therman Slutfuck, the flesh-eating pederast and booger collector."

Was Harrison actually trying to give me some kind of signal? "So ... are you hinting that I should actually run away from this horrific carnival freakshow of terror, instead of just standing here interrupting you with questions about the Lovejoy codex and the hidden messages in your dazzling sales pitch?"

Before Harrison could reply, a growling, malformed monstrosity tore its way through the circus tent with razor sharp claws and burst onto the stage. The vicious brute snarled at Harrison, spewing slimy saliva through a mouthful of twisted, pointy teeth, and then abruptly tore my uncle's head from his body with the strength of a sliver back gorilla high on PCP.

I bolted away as the abomination roared with animalistic fury. The monster and its terrible ilk would surely soon give chase. I had no defense against their attack and searched the relics for any kind of weapon I might use to ward off their impending attack. Instead of a bludgeon, I found something even better—a battered, brass oil lamp that resembled something straight out of the *Arabian Nights*. Had I happened upon a genie trapped inside of a magic lamp? There was only one way to find out. I rubbed the lamp with all of the frenzied urgency of a back alley handjob. Eventually, my efforts brought forth a luminescent cloud of green vapor—in the center of which hovered a scowling humanoid face.

I stepped toward the entity. "I wish to find the Lovejoy codex!" I commanded. "I wish to undo the horrors visited upon my planet by the Seven Legions of Darkness ... then I wish to be back at the Poontang Palace with my face buried in Charlotte's cleavage."

The scowling green spirit scoffed. "Why the hell are you asking me for all that shit?"

"Aren't you a genie of the lamp?"

"A genie? Fuck no! I'm Halitosis Von Toiletbreath, the horrible, bad breath monster!"

"Oh ... well, never mind. You can go back in the lamp."

"Oh no, it's too late for that, genius. You're summoned me. Now you must pay the penalty. It's the old magic lamp ploy. It works like a charm!"

"No ... no, that's okay. You go back in the lamp now."

"I don't think so, shit-for-brains!"

The malodorous cloud suddenly engulfed me in its fouls stench, hovering about my head and shoulders.

I charged blindly forward, waving my hands about in a futile attempt to ward off the pungent entity. From somewhere close behind me, a creature let loose a vicious growl.

I struggled to keep my wits about me. I had to use my head. Seconds later, I did just that when I used my head to bash open a pair of double doors that were blocking my path.

I stumbled for a few feet and fell flat on my face, as the bad breath cloud suddenly evaporated with a tortured squeal. I arose to find myself standing in a gloomy corridor that led directly to an enormous ebony gateway dripping with what appeared to be blood sweat and tears, but in hindsight, was most likely blood, semen and mucus. To the left of the gateway was a ticket booth manned by a smiling, animatronic ticket salesman.

As I approached the booth, the puppet mouthed a pre-recorded greeting. "Hello, and welcome to the Labyrinth of Terror, brought to you by Applebaum's disposable dildos; the durable, double-sided dildos that taste sort of like peppermint. Please insert your admission fee now."

Hastily, I extracted the two-dollar admission fee from my wallet and inserted the money into the bill slot. Seconds later, a red receipt popped out of the ticket dispenser.

"Please take your admission voucher now."

I took the stub as instructed.

"Thank you for your patronage, and enjoy your visit to the Labyrinth of Death," the salesman said.

"Death?" I said.

"Did I say *death*? I meant terror," the automated salesman muttered with a plastic grin.

The massive doors leading into the maze squealed and began to open. As they slowly parted, a cauldron of warm vomit was dumped over me from a hatch in the ceiling. Then a bucket of bloody chum showered down on top of me from a 2nd hatch door. It was quite the welcome wagon, indeed. But the best was yet to come. Entering the labyrinth, I waded into an ankle-deep pathway filled with raw, steaming sewage, batting madly at the swarms of flies that buzzed through the air in great black clouds.

Walking further into the maze, I noticed that that the gore-splattered walls were lined with shards of broken glass and jagged shanks of rusted metal.

Behind me, the hellish menagerie from the sideshow tent tore their way through the doors of the admission hall. I shrieked with terror and charged through the river of piss and shit as the monster squad closed in on me with frightening speed.

As I approached a corner that led into a narrow corridor marked "Evisceration Alley," I thought it might be wise to vacate this malodorous land of wonders before I ended up being worn as an undeniably stylish skin vest with matching facemask accessory. Short of taking flight within the next few seconds, I had very few options for survival—so you can imagine my surprise when, seconds later, I suddenly took flight and soared like a mighty hawk into the sky above the horrible maze. The bird's eye view was breathtaking, or maybe that was just the overpowering odor of burning flesh that wafted through the air.

Just as I was about to burst into a rousing rendition of, *Up, Up and Away,* the moment was spoiled by the irate voice of Dr. Harvey coming from behind me. "Christ, Matheson, I can't leave you alone for two seconds!"

The ghostly curmudgeon had "spirited" me away from the turmoil of the horrible maze below, before I was given the chance to evacuate my imaginary persona from this world of horrors and return to my physical form back in the other world of horrors at the asylum.

As was fairly typical of the doctor, he began to lecture me about my foolhardy approach to the matters at hand. Ignoring the scolding criticisms of the bitchy banshee, I tried to take in every detail that the view from above might offer me from such a strategic position. From this soaring vantage point, I spied what could only be the Lovejoy codex situated at the opposite end of the maze from where I had entered. Nightmarish beasts of inconceivable ghastliness ambled and writhed throughout maze, divided by pools of steaming blood and bile that were littered with the bloated, maggot-covered corpses of my unfortunate predecessors. This was a hell that I couldn't have imagined in my worst nightmares. It looked like a safari park designed by H.P. Lovecraft.

Leland Hull's prophetic words echoed in my brain: *Well, Mr. Serdgurglar from the Heldethrach Herald, if you are referring to Shiverdecker's theory of malignant reversal, the odds of a human saboteur surviving the horrors of the Scorpius plane and locating the Lovejoy Codex are a million to one.*

A million to one—I had a hunch that I was staring down at that unfortunate other million floating lifelessly in the pools of sickening gore below me at that very moment. Perhaps the single glaring mistake of my forerunners had been the misguided idea that they might somehow successfully navigate this maze of unconquerable horror and torment to reach the Lovejoy codex and save the day.

Maybe the simplest solution to this insurmountable problem was to bypass this quagmire of abhorrence altogether. If I could not navigate my way through this death-laden shithole, I would fly over it—fly over it just like I was doing right now.

I would just need to shut Dr. Harvey up long enough for him to comply with my instructions. "The Lovejoy codex! It's positioned at the far end of the labyrinth! Get me closer so I can see if Shiverdecker's incantations are visible!"

Amazingly enough, Dr. Harvey actually shut his mouth for two seconds and complied with my request. We soared over the terrors of the labyrinth like Hawkman and the deformed cousin of Casper the Friendly Ghost, but as we neared the codex, I began to detect the rank odor of garlic, cigar-smoke, onions, whiskey and bleu cheese engulfing me in a foul embrace. It was not unlike the foul stench of Halitosis Von Toiletbreath, the bad breath monster that I had tangled with only moments before entering the maze—in fact, it seemed to be oddly identical to the smell of the horrid odor entity.

"You know I was just being sarcastic back at the Hull Mansion when I referred to you as a talking fart cloud, Doc ... but the afterlife seems to have really taken a toll on your oral hygiene habits."

The apparition clutching me in its pungent grasp cackled with glee. "Well, if it isn't Aladdin, the magic lamp molester."

"Halitosis! I thought I smelled trouble. Are you sure you don't grant wishes? Because I sure wish you'd fuck off."

"Bask in the glory of my appalling odor as you take in the view, dipshit. You wanted to find the Lovejoy codex. Drink it in, Einstein. It'll be the last thing you ever see! Foolish is the Dutchman who ice skates on a lake of frozen diarrhea!"

"So, you're the cobra in the buttermilk, eh Halitosis?"

"Bing bong! Grandpa licked the flypaper!"

"I still don't get that expression."

"That doesn't exactly surprise me, whiz kid. You'd have to be playin' with half a deck to come pokin' your nose around this neck of the woods in the first place."

"Well, I'd *have* to be an idiot to poke my nose anywhere near your vicinity."

As we traded verbal barbs, I kept my eyes firmly on the prize as we drifted closer and closer to the Lovejoy codex. Below us I beheld a granodiorite stele, an enormous, jagged section of smooth, ebony stone—intricately carved with stunning three-dimensional detail. Resting upon a pulpit situated at the top of the stele was the prize I sought; a tattered section of vellum adorned with hundreds upon hundreds of printed passages and painted depictions of the crimes of the Legions of Darkness. As I gazed down at the codex, a series of hieroglyphics emerged from the vellum, glowing red like molten lava. The symbols shimmered and swayed as if I were viewing them through waves of intense heat. The ancient hieroglyphics curled and twisted into words that were nothing from the English language, but were recognizable nonetheless thanks to my telepathic connection to the horrible creatures of the Legions of Darkness. These were decrees of sentencing that possessed the power to hold the monsters in bondage. This I knew more through intuition, rather than from a true understanding of the words themselves.

At that moment the image of Sexulina Clitorasus materialized in the reddish black sky above the labyrinth. The succubus laughed with delight.

"You don't think that I can feel you fumbling about in my mind like a blind, retarded child? You truly *are* an idiot."

"Idiot like a fox!" I said, hoping my defiance was justified.

"Your torments have only just begun, Mr. Matheson. I wasn't kidding about the skin throw rug idea. I actually intend to do that. It would create a nice warming effect in my breakfast nook. But first, I think it's time to run you though the maze like the despicable little rodent that you are!"

"Grelfracht unktalus omlotgar Selurach!" I commanded.

The succubus let loose a blood-curdling shriek upon hearing the strange words.

Suddenly everything around me went black and I felt the forceful, sucking sensation of being cast out of the demon witch's mind and back into my own physical body.

Seconds later I was back, standing before the enraged she-devil in the corridor of the state hospital. Solomon and Dr. Whitlock stood at my side with their guns drawn looking concerned and slightly perplexed.

The infuriated succubus spread her bat wings and roared like a hungry tiger.

I held my ground and raised the horrible baby bone weapon. "Sadas elkras pradasus, Selurach!" As I vocalized this command, a blast of luminescent liquid suddenly shot from the barrel of the horrible water cannon and sliced through the demon's flesh like a white-hot laser beam. The glowing solvent bisected the succubus at the midriff of her torso, spraying blood in all directions throughout the hallway. There was a moment of stunned silence from everyone—then the demon's two slashed body sections dropped to the floor with a sickening, wet, slapping sound.

"Sweet monkey shit, Matheson!" Solomon mumbled.

The enormous black widow spider reeled up like a spooked horse, and bicycle-pedaled its front legs about in the air as it fired a thick stream of webbing at me from its abdomen. A silken blob spattered against my upper body, pinning my right arm and the bone weapon to the corridor wall. Solomon and Dr. Whitlock took careful aim and then blasted the spider in the face with several rounds from their handguns. The arachnid's head exploded in every direction, splattering the hallway with even more blood and copious helpings of insect gore.

"Looks like it's safe to assume that your reconnaissance was successful, Stanley," Dr. Whitlock said.

"I take it you got a gander at that Lovejoy codex, Dirty Harry," Solomon said.

"Shiverdecker was right ... all of it ... his visions weren't the delusions of a madman. He saw the Scorpius plane ... and believe me it's no wonder he ended up in a nuthouse after that dubious pleasure.

The exact same thing *literally* just happened to me."

"So what's next on the agenda?" Solomon said.

"Two down, four to go," I said. "I'm afraid there are more delightful adventures in store for us, boys—provided we can get the hell out of here in three, solid, human-shaped pieces."

In lieu of shooting our way through a collection of unarmed mental patients, I was able to keep the throng occupied with a phony Walpurgisnacht talent show audition that sent the inmates into an excited frenzy of odd, impromptu performances as we made our escape.

Chapter Seven

_____

Desperately in need of rest, we checked into the Jolly Bedbug Inn for some much needed shuteye. After a few hours of restless sleep, I revisited Dr. Whitlock's book on Albrecht Shiverdecker and my own copy of the Collective Works of L.B. Hull—piecing together the strange components of Shiverdecker's theory of malignant reversal.

Reports of violent outbreaks and mass hysteria taking place across the Eastern region of the United States dominated the local news on both television and radio. Speculations concerning the origins of the Orias Nebula ranged from a catastrophe brought about by pollution, to chemical weapons falling into the wrong hands, to a sign from God that the Rapture of the Book of Revelations was at hand.

The Connecticut office of the Center for Disease Control issued an official statement that citizens should "bow down in servitude to the Legions of Darkness and prepare for the terrible coming of Yarlock the Great Deceiver: Eater of Souls."

Even Dr. Pepper got in on the action when a spokesman for the soda pop company announced their brand as "the official soft drink of the impending apocalypse."

Inevitably my thoughts soon returned to the fates of David Collins and Jamie Lynn Faraday. Collins had swept in and rescued the young woman from certain death mere hours before the demons had arrived at the asylum, which told me that my intuitions about him were true: his powers of clairvoyance were just as sharp as ever.

David Collins was very near—I felt it in my gut. This sensation was chiefly due to the fact that that man had just snuck up behind me and stuck the blade of a large hunting knife to my gut and wrapped his left arm around my throat in a chokehold.

"Boo, mother fucker," Collins whispered.

"Long time no see, David."

"Not long enough, Matheson ... not by a long shot."

"You haven't been exposed to that shit pouring out of the Orias Nebula have you? You seem a little tense."

"Fuck you, asshole! I wouldn't even have to be the least bit crazy to gut you like a prize hog after all the shit you pulled at Hull House, pal!"

"I concur."

Collins released his grip on my neck and slid his knife into a sheath on his belt as I turned to face him. He was dressed in a dark navy pea coat, dark knit sweater cap and a white orderly's uniform that was covered with flecks of dried blood.

He offered me a liquor bottle wrapped in a crumpled paper sack. "Commode Merlot, raisin-brewed toilet wine?"

So as not to insult the man, I accepted the bottle and took a sip. The liquid burned as it slithered down my throat. "Wow! You can really taste the toilet in that vintage."

I passed the bottle back to Collins, who took a long drink. "Christ, Matheson, you look like you just clawed your way out of a coffin! Are those bags under your eyes or did you stick your face in a hornets' nest?"

"You're not looking so spry yourself, Peter Pan."

Collins took another long swallow from the bottle and then screwed the lid back on. "As you might have guessed, I've had a lot on my mind lately—all those visions and night terrors tend to take a toll on one's boyish good looks."

"Faraday ... how is she?"

"The kid's tough. She's holding up ... reasonably well under the circumstances."

"Those monsters would have eaten her alive and then eaten her dead after she ceased to be alive anymore if you hadn't rode in like the cavalry and gotten her out of that nuthouse. I know—I've seen their handiwork. She could've ended up as a bucket of Sloppy Joe mix. Then who would be here to smoke all of those cigarettes?"

"She's pretty flipped out, but she thinks it might be wise to stick close to us for the time being."

"*Us?*"

Collins unscrewed the top of his liquor bottle and took another swallow. "Well golly gee, Stanley, I wouldn't dream of letting you have all the fun without me. Now can I *please* join your ragtag gang of dysfunctional, yet loveable misfits?" He belched and winced as he offered me another drink from the bottle.

I took it, reluctantly. "You'd better be careful—that thinly-veiled sarcasm just might hurt my feelings." I took a quick swig of the grape-flavored battery acid and managed to keep it down without gagging. "You're timing is impeccable. We were just about to have matching t-shirts made."

"Good, maybe when this is over I can wrap mine around your neck and strangle you with it."

"You'll have to get in line. Charlotte would kill me in cold blood if she found out I'd sucked you back into this crazy bullshit."

"Well you certainly suck, Matheson, but I guess your better half will just have to accept the fact that this time I was crazy enough to hitch my wagon to your little doomsday Donner Party of my own free will."

Our witty banter was suddenly interrupted by the click of Jamie Lynn Faraday's Zippo lighter slamming shut. "Christ, you two bitch at each other worse than an old married couple."

"Stockholm syndrome," Collins muttered, screwing the cap back on his liquor bottle.

Jamie Lynn picked up the hideous baby bone holy water rifle that I'd placed atop the nightstand next to my bed. "Jesus Christ, I guess you really aren't screwing around here."

I winced, staring down the tip of the barrel. "I'd be careful with that. It just sliced one of our enemies into a split personality across the center of her torso."

Faraday cringed and then gingerly returned the baby bone squirt gun to its place on my nightstand.

Collins smiled at the obviously exhausted teenager. "I think Mr. Matheson and I better have a little powwow about what we know and don't know about all of this shit before we get down to our belated hug session, Kiddo," Collins said, plopping warily down on my queen-sized bed and patting the mattress to welcome his guarded charge to lay down for a much needed rest. "You might consider taking a little nap while we rekindle our rather tenuous working relationship."

The teenager snuffed out her cigarette in one of the many ashtrays provided by the seedy motel and laid down next to Collins, wrapping the blankets tightly around her body as she curled into a fetal position and fell fast asleep not five minutes later.

As the teenager dozed, my battle-scarred colleague and I examined my notes while I attempted to explain what we now knew about the strange Prophecies of Shemrach Thaydarian and Shiverdecker's oddball theories about how to reverse the evil doings of the Legions of Darkness. We were soon joined by Solomon and Dr. Whitlock, as well as another man who identified himself as "Duncan Langston: the man with the plan." Unfortunately Mr. Langston had no real "plan" to speak of and turned out to be just a local degenerate who'd spotted Jamie Lynn being snuck into a sleazy motel full of admittedly ragged looking middle aged men. Dr. Whitlock had mistaken the pervert for the motel's handy man, which was understandable given Langston's grubby coveralls and the battered toolbox he carried at his side.

"I thought he was a maintenance man," Dr. Whitlock protested.

"I am," Duncan said, opening his toolbox. "I maintain this box of big hard cocks!"

After sharing this information, the man removed a gargantuan black dildo from his toolbox.

Collins displayed the knife on his belt for the benefit of Mr. Duncan Langston. "Take a hike, fuckstick ... before I give you a few more holes to poke your dildos into."

Mr. Langston looked disappointed. "Don't be that way, David," he pleaded, addressing Collins by his first name, learned from our recent introductions.

Solomon pulled his .44 Magnum and pressed the barrel to Langston's forehead. "You been stickin' those things in your ears, shitbird?"

"Once in a while," Langston said, quickly packing up his toolbox and backing toward the door. "I'm telling Jerry about you guys!" he warned.

"Who the hell is *Jerry*?" I said.

"My friend down at the syrup plant! He used to be a security guard in Vermont! He has a gun too, and he's not afraid to shoot rats down at the junkyard with it!"

"Well you tell Jerry to keep his mind on monitoring the proper levels of boysenberry flavoring in his syrup and keep his nose out of our business, smart guy," Solomon growled.

"They make lots of flavors besides boysenberry, smartass! You're a bunch of weirdoes! Weirdoes and freaks!" Langston screamed as he slammed the door behind him.

Jamie Lynn stirred on the bed and opened her eyes. "What the hell was that?"

"Nothing ... probably just a local pitchman for Applebaum's disposable dildos, the durable, double-sided, dildos that taste sort of like peppermint. Just go back to sleep," I said.

"Works for me," she mumbled and then closed her eyes, pulling the bedclothes tightly around her. Seconds later, she began to snore.

Thanks to Dr. Whitlock's encyclopedic knowledge of the prophecies of Shemrach Theydarian and their relation to

Shiverdecker's theory of malignant reversal—as well as our possession of the Opus Demonium—we now had the knowledge to orchestrate a plan of attack against the Legions of Darkness. But the clock was ticking; Surely, the remaining demons would hunt us down and crucify us upside-down with our own sexual organs stuffed into our mouths for a big demonic laugh—and so, rather than fleeing in terror, we would bring the fight to their doorstep.

We would return to Hull House and destroy the remaining portholes, along with the Heldethrach army and the demonic manifestation of the spirit of Leland Hull—this, we reasoned, would be achieved by our resourceful "pioneer spirit" and with the help of the demon hunting gear constructed by Professor Hiller from the strange blueprints from the Opus Demonium.

Granted, our bravado was extremely optimistic given the dire circumstances, but we chalked all of this up to our "desperate times call for desperate measure" attack strategy. This would be a Walpurgisnacht celebration like the Legions of Darkness had never seen!

I phoned Charlotte at the Poontang Palace to let her know that I was still alive and to make certain that she was safe. She informed me that she'd spoken with Dr. Quinlan at Diseases N' Stuff and that the doctor was indeed making some progress in combating the symptoms of the Medusa's Uterus virus. Dr. Quinlan told Charlotte that her big breakthrough came by a happy accident—apparently the note reminding her not to attempt to juggle the virus sample came loose from the Petri dish at some point and the epidemiologist had absentmindedly mixed the deadly sample in with a collection of colorful balls she kept handy in her laboratory for the purposes of juggling practice.

Dr. Quinlan had recently taken up juggling in the hope of one day being able to leave the field of medical research to pursue a career as circus performer. The hobby was also a welcome distraction from the unending pressures of her regular nine to five work. According to her own admission, the aspiring amateur juggler clumsily dropped the Medusa's Uterus sample into a cure for a deadly strain of syphilis she was developing to infect an ex-boyfriend with and the mistake resulted in an instant "Eureka" moment. According to Dr. Quinlan, common penicillin might prove the key to reducing the terrible side effects of the disease being spewed out by the Orias Nebula, and her subsequent tests on multiple lab rats showed great promise— reducing the homicidal rages of the test subjects to relatively harmless, off-key and poorly choreographed song and dance performances from the musical, *Guys and Dolls*.

The news was promising, but held no guarantees for a successful containment of the epidemic and certainly didn't bode well for a Broadway revival of *Guys and Dolls*.

Charlotte's other revelations were also encouraging, if not a great deal stranger. Apparently my mother, Margot, had recently begun to suffer strange spells, during which she levitated about the house, talking in tongues, urinating on the shag carpet and shouting warnings about the coming of "the age of the thousand agonies of man."

In desperation, the two women conducted an impromptu séance' with Charlotte acting as their conduit to the spiritual world. During the séance they were visited by the spirit of 1st American President, George Washington, who angrily demanded that they craft him a pair of comfortable dentures using leftover Halloween candy corn and then sew him a pair of "scandalously sexy" undergarments employing the finest of Asian silks. "Embroider a snarling, golden dragon on the groin of the underwear, or you shall suffer my wrath from beyond the grave!" the deceased president instructed them. Moments later, the ghostly commander in chief began to moan in the throes of some otherworldly agony and vanished in a puff of smoke, never to be heard from again. The phantom founding father's spirit was soon replaced by an apparition who identified himself as Albrecht Shiverdecker—who proceeded to repeat the same demands as his predecessor, but then admitted that he was only joking and offered a half-hearted apology.

Shiverdecker explained that the tormented souls who haunted her ancestral home were now crying out for Margot's help to end the horrors of that dreadful place once and for all. Her grandfather's spirit—who welcomed these evils into our world in his vain lust for power—had returned, and only she and I could end his rein of terror. Like me, she had an obligation to undo the evils perpetrated by those of her bloodline.

Shiverdecker—who had known Leland Hull personally during his lifetime—vehemently warned Margot to never underestimate the man's devious nature. "He was the human embodiment of Yarlock, the Great Deceiver. The two have *always* been one in the same. With Leland Hull's reincarnation, we now fall prey to the wrath of this master of lies, this Satan made flesh."

The visitation from the realms of the great beyond must have made quite the impression, as both Margot and Charlotte were now absolutely determined to meet us in Dorchester for our planned assault on Hull House. No amount of pleading on my part could convince them to do otherwise. Margot had already taken her wardrobe trunk and disguise kit out of mothballs. She'd also pulled a few strings to commandeer one of the hotdog-shaped "wiener" mobiles retained by the Oscar Meyer hot dog company for their nation-wide promotional campaigns and publicity photos. In order to keep a low profile, Margot intended to drive the vehicle to Dorchester disguised as a flamboyant, homosexual rodeo clown character she'd created named, "Loopy Lavender." "Loopy" favored purple rawhide chaps, fringed orange gloves and a ten-gallon hat covered with pink sequins.

Apparently our ideas of a "low profile" differed dramatically.

Margot's logic was that—given the copious reports of widespread insanity taking place across the country—when in Rome, one must do as the Romans do. When I mentioned the fact that the aforementioned reports made no mention of widespread incidents of flamboyant, homosexual clowns driving vehicles shaped like enormous hot dogs, Charlotte accused me of being a racist.

When I suggested that, in this case, my mother's past stint as a performer on a humorous television variety show might have tainted her better judgment, my concerns fell on deaf ears. Neither Charlotte nor my mother would be deterred. When I insisted that Margot's husband, Dick accompany them on their journey, I was told that he was currently in Italy producing a ribald, all-midget cast re-envisioning of "Caligula." In a final attempt to insure their safety, I suggested that they at least bring Isabella Hull's mystical oracle along for consultation purposes during their journey. My great grandmother's crystal ball could only help in guiding them on their way back to Hull House, and in the event of an assault could be bashed over an attacker's head, if worse came to worse.

We said our goodbyes with only a dim glimmer of hope that we would ever see each other again. The fates of my one true love and the mother that I somehow always loved, but had never really known, were now placed in the hands of some drunken fate that I was helpless to predict—somewhere far away, they rode off into the sunset in a vehicle shaped like a gargantuan frankfurter, dressed as gaily-attired, homosexual rodeo clowns.

Chapter Eight

Now that Shemrach Thaydarian's predicted "motley band" of oddballs had been drawn into my poisonous orbit, it behooved us to actually set the wheels of our strange battle plan in motion. Our first order of business was to convince the spiritual medium in tow, David Collins, to dust off the cobwebs of his venerable talents and conduct a séance in the hope that we might contact our "eyes and ears" at Hull House: the spirit of Dr. Bernard Harvey.

After a few more belts of his terrible, toilet-brewed hooch, the rusty necromancer instructed us to gather around the rickety Formica table provided by the motel and join hands. By the light of a malodorous citronella candle foraged from a bathroom cabinet, we assembled in a cramped circle with hands joined and held our breath as Collins went to work, chanting his incantations in a monotone voice. A few moments of silence in the room seemed to stretch into eternity as we awaited word from the great beyond—but just when it seemed that our efforts to pluck the ghostly fruit from the trees of the afterlife had yielded a basket of dried up, worm-eaten figs that would not be suitable as ingredients for a cookie called "Shitty, Dried-Up Fig Newtons With Worms in Them by Nabisco"—the pungent citronella candle flickered and suddenly went out. Its light was replaced by a dim, green radiance emitted by the specter of Dr. Harvey. The apparition hovered above the center of the table like an ill-tempered hologram. The doctor waved his ghostly arms about in the air, muttering "Woooo," at his stunned audience.

Dr. Whitlock gasped. "Bernie! My god! It really *is* you!"

"Yes, unfortunately. You can imagine my embarrassment—being conjured up at a séance! Talk about insult to injury."

"But it's remarkable!"

"Remarkably annoying! I imagine Matheson suggested this."

Jamie Lynn addressed the apparition. "You ... you're the spirit that pulled me from the wreckage of Ronald's van."

"Yes, I'm a regular Casper the Friendly Ghost these days, young lady."

Dr. Whitlock was utterly astounded by Dr. Harvey's materialization. "You must tell me, Bernie, what is it like? What does one experience in the great beyond?"

"Well, currently, I teach a course in *Existential Skepticism in the Afterlife* and continue my research in the hope of one day disproving my own existence. Despite overwhelming evidence to the contrary, I'm still extremely suspicious of all of this supernatural gobbledygook. Ghosts, and witches and demons —hogwash!"

"Well I hope you can put your feelings aside for the time being, Doctor. Without you, I'm afraid we don't stand a *ghost* of a chance," I said, suppressing a snicker.

"Oh shut up, Matheson!" Dr. Harvey growled.

"Don't goad him, Stanley," Dr. Whitlock scolded.

"I was just trying to raise the pasty poltergeist's spirits, Doctor. He just seems so haunted."

"Your brain belongs on display inside of a jar, Matheson. But, unfortunately, I think Gerber baby food might object to such questionable ingredients. Perhaps, one day, Dr. Frankenstein can just transplant it back into the skull of the retarded chimpanzee he pilfered it from," Dr. Harvey said.

I chuckled. "He's just grumpy because ectoplasm gives him the trots."

Dr. Whitlock was quickly losing patience with our verbal

sparring. "Gentlemen, please—this is no time for juvenile name calling, so please stop acting like a couple of faggoty, little dickholes!"

"But I haven't made my joke about Ecto Bismol yet," I said.

Solomon interjected. "Boys, we're already all skating on a lake of frozen diarrhea here. Let's try to move this along before it's too late to purchase our tickets for the impending apocalypse."

"We're planning to mount a counter attack on the Legions of Darkness, Bernie. What can you report about the situation at Hull House?" Dr. Whitlock said.

Dr. Harvey looked grim. "I wish I had more encouraging news, but unless you like the idea of imminent death by brutal disembowelment, what I have to tell you might be just a wee bit disheartening."

"That bad, eh Doc?" Solomon said.

"Yes, I'm afraid it is. There's been a rather disturbing tread in acts of necrophilia being perpetrated by the Heldethrach man-demons as of late ... so just a heads up on *that* news."

Jamie Lynn looked as if she was about to be sick. "You mean they're having sex with the dead bodies of their victims?"

"Well, yes, young lady. And I'm afraid that's just for starters. Believe me, you don't want to know the rest. There are some things that you just can't un-see. I'm a goddamned ghost, and their depravity frightens me."

"Yeah, those Heldethrach really throw one hell of a party," Solomon said.

Dr. Harvey observed David Collins presiding over the séance in a deep trance. "Oh, I see you've managed to Shanghai David Collins, once again. Kudos, Matheson—you're more cunning than a trapdoor spider."

Jamie Lynn spoke up in my defense. "He's here of his own free will, Doctor. Mr. Collins rescued me from a mental hospital before the demons were able to track me down and have sex with my mutilated corpse."

"Well then, I stand corrected. Let's hope the association ends on a more pleasant note than their last collaboration," Dr. Harvey said.

"Hope springs eternal," Collins muttered in a distant, monotone voice.

"No need to throw more kerosene on that fire, Jacob Marley. I may be the enemy of David Collins, but I'm also the enemy of several of his other enemies, which makes me his temporary friend ... until he can eliminate all of his other enemies that he needs my help eliminating before he can finally kill me. By that time, maybe I can either change his mind and actually become his true, misunderstood friend, or accidently be responsible for his premature death—but we'll cross that rickety bridge when we come to it."

"Spoken like a true idiot, Stanley," Dr. Harvey said.

"You're such an asshole, Matheson," Collins muttered in his monotone trance state voice.

"Well, we'll agree to disagree on that for now," I said.

"No one is disagreeing," Collins mumbled.

Changing the subject I addressed the more pressing business at hand. "Doctor, you were taken into one of those portholes. You can travel back and forth between the alternate dimensions I take it?"

"Yes, I suppose that would stand to reason, if that's the proper word for this situation."

"Then we need to travel through the Selurach porthole and into the world of the Scorpius Plane."

"*We?*"

"*We* ... I and me and you."

"But you wouldn't survive for more than ten seconds on the Scorpius Plane, Stanley!"

"That's why you're going to help me fly over it. You pulled Miss Faraday out of the wrecked van at Hull House."

"Yes."

"So I need you to help me soar over the labyrinth and all of the other delightful tourist attractions in that shit pit to retrieve the Lovejoy Codex, as mentioned in the prophecies of Shemrach Theydarin. I've seen the codex, Doctor—in the Selurach witch's mind ... I used an incantation from the codex against her and it activated Professor Hiller's demon slaying weapon."

"Interesting," Dr. Harvey said.

"Do you know which porthole leads to the Scorpius Plane, Doctor?" I said.

"I do. The Scorpius Plane was where my spirit was cast from my body during those vile rituals I told you about."

"Maybe you could accidentally drop Stanley into the labyrinth after you acquire the codex," Collins mumbled.

"You sure are opinionated for somebody in a deep trance, Collins," I said.

"I wish I could offer a retort to your insinuation that I'm not actually in a deep trance, but I can't because I am in a deep trance," Collins muttered.

"Well you must have accidently floated back into the shallow end, Captain Nemo," I said.

Harvey interrupted. "You must make haste, Matheson. The great Walpurgisnacht sabbat is to take place in the gateway of the Seven Legions of Darkness upon the rise of the full moon, two nights from now.

"Your corpse and the corpses of your companions are wanted and desired for the festivities at Hull House. There is, in fact, a bounty on all of your heads. The first demon to deliver you to the master of ceremonies wins a free Frosty Slurp ice cream cake from Baskin Robbins Ice Cream and a twenty five dollar gift certificate for Rockin' Rudy's Records and Tapes. I can tell you from first hand knowledge, the only thing that these monsters like more than necrophilia is free ice cream."

"This doesn't leave us much time," Dr. Whitlock said.

"On the other hand, it doesn't leave the demons much time to track us down before Walpurgisnacht," Solomon said.

"Aside from our corpses, who else is on the guest list for the big Walpurgisnact bash?" I said.

"The members of numerous occult societies will be in attendance ... members of the Order of Yarlock the Great Deciever, the Order of the Golden Dragon, the Coven of the Crimson Talon and local members of the Boxcar Willie Fan Club are all expected to gather for the sabbat," Dr. Harvey said.

"Which gives us a better shot at blending in with the crowd," I said.

"They'll also be live music provided by a pop band called the Peppermint Gang, if that's of any use to you," Dr. Harvey said.

A series of gunshots suddenly popped in the distance, startling all but Dr. Harvey and David Collins. A pair of helicopters chopped through the sky above the motel and faded into the distant, rumbling chaos to the south of our location. Then came the bowel-shivering boom of a great explosion a few miles away.

"Things are going to hell out there fast," Solomon said. There was an understandable apprehension in his voice. "Maybe we'd better get a move on."

Dr. Harvey's image began to fade quickly, like a cool mist evaporating in the heat of the afternoon sun. His disembodied voice echoed, as if from far away. "Then I say Auf Wiedersehen and David Collins collapses from psychic exhaustion ... Auf Wiedersehen."

Suddenly, David Collins collapsed upon the table. Dr. Whitlock rushed to his aid, quickly assisted by the others. They placed him upon the lumpy motel bed as I remained at the table, dumbfounded by an overwhelming sense of déjà vu. Everything seemed suddenly so familiar, as if I was watching a rerun of some old movie on television.

Dr. Harvey says Auf Wiedersehen and then David Collins collapses from exhaustion. "Then someone knocks on the door," I mumbled.

Solomon turned from the bed. "What's that?"

There came a light tapping at the door and then a nervous voice spoke in a loud/soft stage whisper. "Wizard! Hey, man, it's Rainbow Ron."

Solomon pulled his .45 as everyone stared at one another wondering what to do.

"Another dildo enthusiast?" Dr. Whitlock whispered.

I searched my memory for a quick moment. "It's a drug deal. The guy has the wrong room ... then the coven arrives to kill us!"

"What are you going on about, Stanley?' Dr. Whitlock said.

Another quick knock at the door, then a frantic plea; "Wizard! Hey man, it's the candy man! Open the goddamn door before someone calls the cops."

"This is part of the dream ... the night terrors," I said. "I've seen this before."

"Seen what?" Jamie Lynn said.

"Chance favors the prepared mind, Jamie Lynn." I looked at Solomon. "Well, detective, it's time for a little impromptu narcotics bust. We need to get this weirdo's stash and send him on his merry way."

Jamie Lynn was baffled. "You wanna get high?"

Solomon signaled for quiet and walked to the door with his weapon drawn. With lightening quick speed, he jerked the door open and seized the shaggy-haired dope pusher by the collar of his Foghat t-shirt and then tugged him into the room, placing the barrel of his .45 firmly against the shocked dealer's nose.

The man was terrified. "What the shit?"

"Whatcha' got in the bag, Jimi Hendrix?'

The pusher was nervously defiant. "Who wants to know, man?"

Solomon looked to me and shrugged. "Detective Brian Cocksure, narcotics division of the local police department, dirtbag!"

"Are you kidding, man?"

"Do I look like I'm kidding, Pink Floyd? What's in the goddamn bag?" Solomon cocked his pistol.

"Acid, man! Purple sunset! 40 sheets!"

The detective looked to me once more with a raised eyebrow. "Well, Detective Mumford? What's the plan?"

"Confiscate it ... you can cut the deadhead loose," I said in a gruff voice.

Solomon released the grubby dope dealer, who scrambled out the door without further comment. I followed and watched the shaken narcotics salesman as he jogged across the motel parking lot and quickly past a beefy, long-haired biker dismounting his Harley Davidson motorcycle. This greasy gentleman was obviously "Wizard," the intended recipient of our seized drug booty. "Hey where the fuck you goin', Ronnie?" the biker inquired as his associate breezed past him without bothering to answer.

I pointed at David Collins. "Get him up ... and fast!"

Jamie Lynn obeyed, rushing into the bathroom and filling a drinking glass with water. She returned to Collins's side and then tossed the water in his face. Collins rose up on the bed, gasping.

"You passed out," Jamie Lynn explained.

Solomon squeezed my arm. "I take it you have something very special in mind for our friends at Hull House."

"I have an idea, yeah ... that is if I'm actually correct about our next surprise guests."

Dr. Whitlock placed our cache of weapons on a chair and unzipped the bag. "What was that about a coven coming to kill us, Stanley?" he said, drawing a sawed-off double barrel shotgun from the bag.

"The Coven of the Black Sacrament," I said—instinctively donning my bowler hat brain helmet.

"Those are the freaks they blamed for all those cult murders around the country a few years ago," Solomon said.

"Yes. They are infamous Satanists and practitioners of the black arts," Dr. Whitlock said. "Their leader, Sinclair Montebello, is rumored to have partaken of the flesh of a human infant during a black mass in Paris during the late 1960s ... but that has never been actually proven."

Jamie Lynn grimaced. "That's sick!"

We all froze in silence as the tinkling chimes of an ice cream truck broadcasting a cheery rendition of *The Entertainer* by Scott Joplin grew louder and louder in the distance.

"That would be them," I said.

"Driving an ice cream truck? What kind of perverts are these bastards?" Jamie Lynn said.

"Very dangerous ones, Jamie Lynn, and I can assure you that they are not coming here to sell us some ice cream," I said.

We watched the road leading to the motel parking lot as a small motorcade came into view. The sight was eerie, even by the standards of the madness we had witnessed thus far. A large black, Cadillac hearse led the procession. Atop the car's hood was impaled the decapitated head of a police officer. The badge of his uniform cap shimmered in the silvery moonlight.

The motorcade rolled slowly forward at the speed of a bulky parade float, as if to give us the time to fully comprehend the horror of its arrival.

"These pricks certainly know how to make an entrance," Solomon said.

In the parking lot, the biker observed the approaching vehicles. "Oh, fuck that noise, Jack," he grumbled as he quickly remounted his Harley and started the engine. Seconds later he was gone, speeding off into the night like a bat out of hell.

Beneath the jolly tinkle of the ice cream truck's crackling speaker, a repetitive, monotone chant could be heard being recited by the occupants of the vehicles.

We armed ourselves—quickly and heavily, with Jamie Lynn selecting a small crossbow for protection. Dr. Whitlock was in full black ops mode once again, strategizing the defensive and offensive options for our impending showdown. "We should fan out around the parking lot. We're sitting ducks if we get corned in this room."

Solomon concurred.

"This is gonna get real ugly, folks," I said. "Thankfully, if my premonitions are correct, these assholes have spent a lot more time eating babies and engaging in sex orgies than they have practicing their marksmanship."

We followed Dr. Whitlock's lead and spread out across the parking lot, ducking behind cars for cover.

The parade route came to a stop at the far end of the motel's parking lot. The hearse had led a procession of two vintage limousines and the aforementioned ice cream truck following aft. Three shivering captives, clad only in filthy rags stumbled behind the second limousine, manacled at the wrist to lengths of chain hooked to the car's rear bumper. The frightened prisoners were battered and bloody and barley able to stand. The sight of them was heart wrenching. This was pure sadism.

A small gang of pasty-faced Satan worshipers clad in black robes stepped from the vehicles, armed with ornate silver daggers and German Luger pistols. A goateed man wearing Egyptian style eye makeup and bizarre red war paint stepped forward. From his lofty manner, I surmised that the man could only be the infamous Sinclair Montebello. He spoke with an overly confident arrogance, in a voice that was slightly affected and theatrical. "I will say this once and once only! Come out voluntarily and we shall spare you all from a fate worse than death ... which is better than you deserve."

Seconds later, a haggard-looking prostitute clad in a mini skirt and skin-tight t-shirt that read *Happiness is a tight pussy,* exited the motel with her hands raised in the air. "You wanna date?" she said. "We could run a train, or I can do you three at a time."

Montebello grimaced. "Take a hike, Phyllis Diller. We're not here for your saggy ass!" The devil worshipping dickhead fired a shot at the prostitute, sending her sprinting away in terror.

One of the battered female captives suddenly spoke up. "Don't listen to him! He's lying! They're monsters! Cannibals!"

Montebello turned to the defiant prisoner, took aim with his Luger and shot the unfortunate woman between the eyes. The other two captives screamed in horror.

"Shut *up*!" he hissed, quieting them down instantly. He turned back to the motel. "Well?"

"Apparently they're going to play hard to get," a female coven member said.

"We can smell the fear wafting off of you like the stench of a nest of sewer rats," Montebello said. He sniffed at the air and then waved his hand before his nose with sarcastic distaste.

Suddenly Collins spoke up. "Hey, Sniffles ... have a whiff of this!" He peered around the car that shielded him and lobbed his knife at Montebello, hitting the Satanist in the center of his nose. The blade sliced the man's proboscis in two, spraying blood in all directions as if it were shooting from the nozzle of a fire hose. The stunned occultist raised his shivering hands and then dropped to the ground, stone cold dead.

The other coven members fired at Collins, missing him as he ducked behind the car.

I felt a quick, stabbing pain in my head and then experienced a flash of familiar horrors. One of the demons was among them ... which would explain how the coven could have located us with such ease.

Dr. Whitlock pulled the pin from, and then launched a hand grenade at the coven. The projectile hit the blacktop and skittered beneath the second limousine. The ensuing explosion sent our assailants scattering in all directions. Some fell, mortally wounded, to the debris-scattered ground. Others ran in terror as we all opened fire.

I saw one of the assassins take an arrow to the throat from Jamie Lynn's crossbow and then another lose his right leg, courtesy of Dr. Whitlock's shotgun. Solomon fired steadily, in rapid succession, knocking coven members off like they were mechanical ducks in a shooting gallery.

I rushed back to the motel room and seized Hiller's baby bone demon extermination device. Then I grabbed the Opus Demonium and scurried back into the parking lot, ducking fire. A bullet ricocheted off my brain helmet, vibrating my skull from side to side like the clapper of a church bell.

Whitlock and Collins took down two minions clinging to the ice cream truck. The bloody firefight was over in only a few minutes, thanks to our aggressive, Saint Valentine's Day Massacre-style defense.

"Get us loose from here! Oh God! Please!" one of the manacled captives pleaded.

Collins started off toward the frantic woman.

"Wait!" I warned. "One of these persons isn't a people ... it's a demon from the Legions of Darkness. I can feel it in my mind." I stepped from behind the Mercedes with the bone weapon at the ready. I read a passage from the Opus Demonium: "Demonus incognito forbitas sacrileum e conjorum necronomicus!"

I paused—scanning the prostrate bodies of our adversaries sprawled about the parking lot, surrounded by quickly expanding pools of blood.

Suddenly, one of the pools of blood began to move in reverse—as if it were being sucked back into the body whence it came by a powerful vacuum.

"It's not dead!" Jamie Lynn warned.

"Not yet, it isn't, " I said.

I approached the body cautiously. The female coven member's facial features began to morph, softy. The change was sudden and startling. I gasped as I stared down at the face of my beloved Charlotte. "Stanley," she whispered.

"No!" I growled, taking a step back.

"They found me, Stanley ... and oh what terrible things they did to me."

"You aren't her! You goddamn demonic freak!" I backed away,

stumbling clumsily over the body of another dead coven member and falling on my ass.

Collins stepped forward. "Don't listen to it, Stanley. It's just trying to distract you."

The demon Charlotte rose from the ground. "Where were you, Stanley? You left me to die. Do you know what they did to me, lover?"

Dr. Whitlock rushed to my side and seized the baby bone weapon. "It's stolen the image from your mind ... don't fall under its spell."

"Kill that fucking thing!" I pleaded.

"Read the passage," Dr. Whitlock instructed.

I tore my eyes away from the demonic replica and quickly read from another section of the Opus Demonium. "Demonus abortum necronomicus!"

Another translucent blast shot from the barrel of the bone weapon in Dr. Whitlock's hands and hit the monster in the face. The creature shrieked in agony as blobs of bloody, steaming flesh dripped from its face and splattered across the black top.

The demon glared at us with its single remaining eye. It pointed at Dr. Whitlock and me as its melting lips attempted a wicked grin. "All things sadistic and profane shall slither forth from their putrid, torturous hells and spill, flopping, onto the earth, like a squirming litter of venomous snakes! We will devour your flesh and shit you into your shallow, premature graves, you pathetic, terrified maggots!"

The utterly condescending arrogance of the demon's proclamation brought my blood to a steady boil. "Listen, fuckface, we've already got more than enough maniacal assholes on this planet trying to shit us all into early graves without *your* help! We're doing just fine with our atomic bombs and genocide and pollution without assistance from a bunch of yokel dickheads creeping in from their shithole alternate dimensions, trying to hone in on our territory! We've got more than enough rope to hang ourselves with, and we certainly don't require an army of sadistic alien interlopers to march in and don the executioner's hood to insure our imminent annihilation! If you don't think that the human race can inevitability self-destruct due to its own misguided arrogance, hatred and greed, then you have drastically underestimated your opponent, you cocky, alien, corpse fuckers!"

The stunned demon took a cautious step backward as I rose to my feet, filled with rage and defiance. "Go ahead! Go ahead and *try* to stick your syphilitic, puss-dripping, alien cocks up the polluted asshole of our over-crowded, slowly dying world, you degenerate scumbags! It's only a matter of time before this little green and blue ball is reduced to a pathetic, dusty, dead star drifting through the universe without rhyme or reason, or *purpose*!"

The maimed demon cringed. "You're a pessimist! That's what you are, Mr. Gloomy Gus! Every cloud has a silver lining!"

"And here's yours, shit for brains ... Demonus abortum necronomicus finalante!"

Another radiant blast shot from the barrel of Hiller's weapon and splattered across the demon's face. The creature's head exploded in a shower of gore that filled the air with a cloying stench that nearly choked us all. Its convulsing body dropped to the blacktop and quickly melted into a stinking puddle of revolting, rainbow-hued custard.

My shocked associates eyed me with apprehensive glances as I surveyed the bodies of our enemies. "We'll have to commandeer some of these robes ... one for each of us. I'll grab the LSD. And one of you make sure there's actually ice cream in that ice cream truck and not just frozen human body parts or some crazy shit."

"What for?" Jamie Lynn asked.

"Because, my dear, as Dr. Harvey says, if there's one thing that the Heldethrach demons at Hull House like more than necrophilia, it's free ice cream, baby!" I said.

"*That's* why these freaks were driving around in that truck. They were bringing the ice cream for Walpurginacht," Jamie Lynn said.

Solomon grinned. "And you want to dose all of that ice cream with LSD."

"We'll create our own Orias nebula for those freaks, Timothy Leary-style," I said.

Solomon whistled. "Forty sheets of acid ... that aught to shoot a rocket to Venus straight up their ass."

Chapter Nine

After our carnival of carnage had concluded, we freed the coven's
two surviving prisoners, bandaging their wounds and dressing them
in what clothes we could part with. What we could not provide they
took from the bodies of the dead coven members. We bid the two
traumatized women adieu, giving them each a pistol and ammunition
with which they could better defend themselves against another
assault. They drove off into the night in the coven's remaining
limousine.

We opted to add the coven's hearse and ice cream truck to our
own convoy, hoping that the hearse would provide us with the
desired dramatic effect for our arrival at Hull House. We hit the road
with enough LSD and ice cream in tow to throw a children's party
for the Grateful Dead.

The fact that not one local police officer had responded to our
little bloodbath offered us a clear indication of just how dire things
were getting in this neck of the woods. I could only imagine that
people must be drinking a shitload of Dr. Pepper lately.

Our plan, such as it was, would require our group to march
directly into the lion's den posing as invited members of the Coven
of the Black Sacrament. Hopefully with a little Egyptian-style eye
makeup and a bit of red face paint we could pass as baby-munching

Satanists without raising a red flag. We would be playing it by ear, with an eye out for trouble. We had to keep our chin up and not get too cheeky. Hopefully the Heldethrach man-demons wouldn't get too nosy and we wouldn't feel the need to give them any lip once we were face to face.

As before, we steered clear of all main roads and highways, instead navigating our way to Hull House through a series of winding, desolate, country roads traveled only by solitary, free-spirited hoboes and solitary, free-spirited serial killers seeking isolated body dump sites.

The weather had taken a turn for the worse and our convoy presently wound its way slowly through the rain slick country roads in a torrential downpour, accented by occasional bursts of thunder and lightening.

We'd already jeopardized our mission by so casually stopping to rest at the motel, yet by this point in our bizarre quest we were all running solely on fumes. Our exhaustion and fatigue would only impair our judgment, and we could scarcely afford to get sloppy this late in the game. Another impromptu battle with the demons might just do us in for good. At this rate, we'd be rolling into Hull House in electric wheelchairs—the scent of Ben Gay pain-relieving ointment prematurely trumpeting our arrival with a pungent fanfare of menthol-scented fumes.

There was only one place that I could think of where we might find sanctuary, but I was quite certain that my return would not be met with open arms. I had not seen my adoptive parents, Richard and Adrienne Matheson, since I left home at eighteen years old. Our relationship had always been somewhat strained. They never let me forget the fact that I was not their *real* son. Growing up, I'd always felt a bit like Pinocchio—if he'd been crafted from dog turds.

The Mathesons were vain, greedy, spiteful assholes, and only the possibility of my group and me being slaughtered in our sleep could inspire this desperate attempt at a family reunion. This was truly a case of "any port in a storm."

The spooky, bluish-yellow flashes of lightening played tricks on my tired eyes, and—more than once, I thought I'd spotted sinister shapes stalking us through the trees that lined the roadside. Even these lonely country roads now bore a distinct air of menace, as if permeated by the evils rained down by the Orias nebula. I tried to put the thought out of my mind, yet I knew that now all bets were off. Anything could be fair game for the evils of the Legions of Darkness and the side effects of their genocidal interloping.

Leaning forward to better see through the heavy curtains of rain being whipped away by the windshield wipers of the hearse, I chuckled nervously at the thought of a possible confrontation with a grove of murderous apple trees in this creepy forest.

Dr. Whitlock spoke up—he'd been lying in the back of the hearse with a flashlight, attempting to memorize passages from the Opus Demonium and cross-referencing them with passages from the Collected Works of L.B. Hull and the letters of Albrecht Shiverdecker—"Something on your mind, Stanley?'

"It's just such a lovely night for a drive."

"It's even nicer back here. You know I was actually hoping to avoid having to been driven around in the back of a hearse for a few years yet."

"Any progress with the Opus Demonium?"

"I'm putting the pieces together ... slowly ... but I'm beginning to get a more complete picture of what sort of evils we're dealing with here. Whether all of these spells and incantations can actually save any of us, only time will tell."

"I'll apologize in advance for what we're about to submit ourselves to. I haven't seen the Mathesons since I told them to drop dead and left home as a teenager. My hope is that we just find their place empty ... and perhaps covered with telltale blood splatters and claw marks."

"Were they actually that horrible, Stanley?"

"If it wasn't for my biological mother's generosity over the years, those two freaks would have probably been feeding me through a slot in the cellar door."

"Perhaps they've softened over the years."

"Like moldy bread."

"I wanted to discuss something about that terrible business back at the motel. You said you'd experienced some sort of premonition about what was about to happen. You knew the coven was coming after us."

"Yes ... the premonitions. David Collins can tell you all about that. He's experienced them as well—I'm sure that's how he found us. There's something about the poisonous aura of Hull House ... the place has invisible tentacles that can reach you anywhere."

"You know, Stanley, I think that's no coincidence. I think the wheels of this battle were set in motion centuries ago."

"Well wheels can often roll over you and crush you to death, as we unfortunately saw with that skunk a few miles back."

"You were drawn back to Hull House like moths to a flame."

"When you say 'you,' don't you mean, 'we?' You're the one riding around in the back of a hearse during an electrical storm like Frankenstein's monster ... on your way to Hull House, I might add."

"Yes, I didn't mean to remove myself from the Hull House equation. I too am trapped in its tractor beam of evil."

"They probably actually have one of those there, by the way."

"From what you've told me, I don't doubt it."

"I just hope we're not on some death march here, Doctor."

"Well ... at least we'll go down swinging punches, my boy."

"Drawn like moths to a flame ... I'd hate to be the guy that has to empty that light fixture when this is all over."

"I wouldn't sell us too short just yet, Stanley. I believe this plan might actually have a chance at working—if we can survive long enough to attempt it. Buried in between your great grandfather's ads for the rectal pear of love and that awful, rubber fisting mitten are passages predicting just such a Walpurgisnacht celebration. A celebration of the dawning of the age of the thousand agonies of man."

"So he wasn't insane? I mean—apart from the obvious things like all of the murders and him breeding demonic mutants in his underground lair."

"He predicts the spread of the plague, the mass insanity. His ego is astounding ... and it may prove to be his undoing. It might have sounded completely mad in 1863, but after what I've witnessed, it all sounds downright prophetic. He's practically handed us a copy of his entire game plan for this play at world domination. He intends to create a hell on earth, freeing the evils of the Legions of Darkness to rule a planet held in a stranglehold of malevolent chaos."

"Well, destiny or no destiny, I still wish we didn't have to visit my parents. I'd rather spend the night in the abandoned rectal suppository factory a few miles away, but that would be too much of a pain in the ass ... and I'm not making a pun. Getting over the barbed wire would be pretty horrible. I've tried it. I still have the scars on my ass."

"You tried to break into an abandoned rectal suppository factory?"

"Yeah."

"What on earth for?"

"Well, I'm still asking myself the same question. I was just a kid. Back then it was the abandoned denture cream factory, a few years later it became the abandoned rectal suppository factory. Everyone thought the place was haunted by all of the workers who had died during the tragic denture cream accident." I rubbed my eyes, feeling dizzy from exhaustion. "You'll have to excuse me, Doc. I'm rambling nonsense."

Dr. Whitlock patted my shoulder. "Not to worry. I'm used to that by now, Stanley."

"The last I heard, the Mathesons had converted their Victorian country estate into a boarding house. They were hard up after blowing through all of the cash my real mother had paid them as hush money over the years. I imagine they didn't take it very well when Margot cut them off after she'd told me about my true family heritage." I chuckled at the thought of my parents' misfortune. "They must have flipped! I sure as hell can't wrap my head around the thought of those two sociopaths running a boarding house. You might go to sleep in your room, and then wake up in a bathtub full of ice with a kidney missing."

"They sound utterly charming."

"Oh yeah, their a couple of real characters, alright. Just keep an eye on your watch and hide your wallet."

We arrived at Chez Matheson at 8:30 am—although with the dreadful winter storm, it could have just as well have been 8:30 pm. The stormy night had segued seamlessly into the stormy day. We parked a good distance from the house, so that our hearse and ice cream truck would not be visible when we knocked on the front door. Solomon, Collins and Dr. Whitlock stayed behind in the vehicles while I felt things out with the Mathesons, taking Jamie Lynn along to pose as my teenage daughter, Emily.

Bringing a daughter to meet the parents that I so despised was not much of a cover story, but I could scarcely think of another legitimate reason to revisit the Mathesons, aside from coming back to murder them in cold blood. The pain from my old leg wound was nearly unbearable thanks to the recent stress on my body, and I chose to employ the use of my cane when I finally presented myself to my adoptive parents. I figured the sight of it might wring a few ounces of needed sympathy from their ice-cold hearts if my cover story failed to work its questionable magic.

As we approached the house, Jamie Lynn observed me tucking a snubnose revolver into my jacket. "Are you worried that they might have thrown away your soccer trophies?"

"Just keep an eye on your valuables."

We knocked on the door and then stepped back, waiting for the sparks to fly. There was a commotion inside the house, accompanied by muffled protests and slamming doors.

After waiting nearly two minutes for an answer, I approached the door again and was greeted by the barrel of a shotgun pointed at my face. Adrienne Matheson glared at me from the dimly lit foyer. "We ain't got no vacancies. You'll have to try a place in town." The foul tempered concierge withdrew the shotgun and slammed the door in

144

my face.

Jamie Lynn let loose a stunned chuckle. "Jesus, they really roll out the red carpet at this place."

I pounded on the door. "Mother! Adrienne Matheson! It's Stanley!"

A shocked voice from inside the house: "Stanley?"

"I used to be adopted by you and Richard. Remember?"

"Stanley Hull?"

"Ah, yes ... technically, although I still go by Stanley Matheson. God knows why. Just a filthy habit I guess."

"What the hell do you want?"

"I came to visit?"

"What? Why?"

"Oh, well ... that's a good question. I was just in the neighborhood and I thought I'd show you this teenage daughter I had a few years ago."

"What are you babbling about, Stanley?"

"I just thought we could try to make amends ... patch things up."

"Are you drunk or something?"

"No, but that's not a bad idea under the circumstances."

Adrienne peered out of a window at us. "That girl don't look a thing like you!"

"Thank God!" Jamie Lynn whispered and elbowed me in the ribs, snickering.

"You probably brought that little jailbait here for elicit sexual purposes! I don't know what you heard but this ain't some goddamned whorehouse—no matter what the neighbors claim they saw!"

"No, she's not a teenage prostitute. This is Emily. Emily Matheson, my precocious teenage daughter."

Jamie Lynn frowned. "Precocious? I'm not six years old, *Dad*."

"I mean she's precious—my precious little girl. I'm so proud of her that I just had to show her off to my adoptive parents." I patted Jamie Lynn on the head and she brushed my hand away, annoyed.

Adrienne was losing patience. "What the hell did you come here for, Stanley? That bitch mother of yours cut off all our money! I ain't got nothin' to say to you!"

"Oh, well that's the other reason I came to visit. I heard that you were a bit strapped for cash and I was going to write you a check to show how appreciative I am for all that you and Richard did for me."

There was a moment of silence and then Adrienne opened the front door, eyeing me with suspicion. "Just who do you think you're bullshitting with that line, Sonny? I didn't just fall off a goddamned turnip truck."

"No, if you had, you might have broken your neck and wouldn't that have been a tragedy?"

"So, the prodigal wart on my ass returns, bearing monetary compensation and a full grown daughter who doesn't look a goddamned thing like him. That's what I'm supposed to swallow here, Stanley?"

I smiled pleasantly. "Well you could try the barrel of that shotgun, if that works better for you."

Adrienne scowled. "Still a goddamned wiseass, I see." She lowered the shotgun barrel and waved us inside. "I don't know what you're playing at, but I'm not going to turn down your money."

"I thought not," I said.

We entered the stuffy, dimly lit house and winced at the stench that greeted our nostrils. The unmistakable scent of decaying meat lingered in the air, despite the obvious camouflage of air freshening spray used in a futile effort to mask the foul odor.

Adrienne Matheson waved her hand through the air. "Meat freezer broke down a couple of days ago. We lost 60 pounds of venison. Whole place reeks to high heaven. Perfect timing for such distinguished guests," she explained, and then curtsied sarcastically, as if she were in the presence of royalty. Then she turned away and walked off down the hallway. "We can talk in the kitchen. I had to make chili out of cans. It's all we got around here that's decent at the moment."

Adrienne turned and entered the kitchen as Jamie Lynn and I lingered behind in the front parlor, whispering to each other.

Jamie Lynn grimaced. "Christ, it smells like a slaughter house in here."

"Just try to ignore it. Tell that old witch whatever she needs to hear. We need a hideout and sleep and food. This is the safest place I can think of in this area." I took the teenager by the arm and gently tugged her down the hallway and into the kitchen.

Adrienne was spraying Lysol disinfectant around the dark room. A pot of chili bubbled on the stove. The aroma masked the odor of rotting meat.

Jamie Lynn and I took a seat at the kitchen's wooden table. "So ... where's Richard?"

"He's down in the cellar," Adrienne muttered.

"Burying the other boarders before the police investigation?" I said, attempting to lighten the mood.

Our disgruntled hostess snorted with irritation and then returned to tending her pot of chili heating on the stove—keeping her back to us, as if making direct eye contact with me might make her nauseous. "I'm afraid we don't have a fatted calf to slaughter in honor of your magnificent return."

"I think the chili will do just fine," I said, attempting to sound grateful.

Adrienne chuckled sarcastically. "I don't even know when I last laid eyes on you. You sure haven't aged well, sonny boy. Too much hard living?"

"Let's just say I've wrestled with a lot of demons."

"Well you look like you belong in a rest home, Methuselah. Walking with a cane at your age ... what are you going to do, sign over your social security check to me?"

Jamie Lynn raised her eyebrows in disbelief and mouthed, "Fuck!"

I nodded, offering assurance that my adoptive mother could be such an unbelievable gorgon's cunt.

I chuckled. "Well, I'm not collecting social security just yet, *Mother*, but—as you know—Margot is still quite wealthy ... I can make this little visit very worth your while."

"Oh, yes ... that rich bitch has done quite well for herself."

"We need to stay the night, Adrienne. We're tired. We need rest and food."

Our tempestuous hostess gruffly placed two bowls of chili and two spoons before us on the table and then quickly turned back to the stove. "Times are tough around here, you know. While you party your life away in that fucking palace out in Hollywood, we have to struggle to make ends meet. We only have so many destitute young women around these parts to feed us."

Jamie Lynn eyed the steaming bowls of meaty chili. Her stomach growled loudly in anticipation of food. "Excuse me. I'm actually really hungry," she mumbled apologetically.

I couldn't even recall the last time that I'd eaten and my hunger pangs seemed to overpower my better judgment immediately. I began to hungrily shovel spoonfuls of chili into my mouth with little regard for my suspicions concerning Adrienne's uncharacteristic hospitality. Jamie Lynn quickly followed my lead, and the two of us attacked the meaty mush like a school of starved piranha fish.

Adrienne mumbled to herself as we ate. "Things have been a strange around here since the storms ... those weird red clouds and that stuff comin' down on my garden."

Jamie Lynn paused from her frantic consumption of the meal, looking slightly perplexed.

Adrienne continued her one-sided rant. "The brain jelly shows you things ... terrible, beautiful things."

I felt an overpowering dizziness engulfing me. Jamie Lynn had stopped eating and was simply sitting in her chair, staring down at the table with a look of shock and attempting to keep her eyes open.

Adrienne Matheson turned to face me and I was finally able to get a good look at the old woman, eye to eye. Her pupils were completely dilated—black and schizophrenic. She grinned at us with bloodstained teeth. It was a mad expression—the grin of a complete psychopath. "I'm gonna take real good care of you and your little bitch daughter!"

Jamie Lynn slipped from her chair and fell to the kitchen floor in a drugged stupor.

I observed her with puzzled detachment. "Boy, this chili is really a knockout!" I slurred, as I collapsed onto the floor next to her.

I stared up at the kitchen ceiling, consumed by a feeling of utter incompetence as I faded into unconsciousness. How could I have ever been so foolish?

Weird colors and images swirled about in my head. I fought to regain consciousness, only to repeatedly find myself marooned on an ice drift in the endless strangeness of my own mind. I floated about the galaxy on my magic pumpkin, stopping at the Liquor Barn for a gallon of dream juice cocktail with just a twist of stardust—then a terrible, two-headed clown attempted to sexually assault me in a public restroom wallpapered with medical textbook photos of human sexual organs infected with all manner of venereal diseases.

Dr. Harvey materialized in my cloudy thoughts, looking typically wary of my predicament. "Jamie Lynn is in grave danger, Stanley. You need to make yourself vomit! Do you understand? Make yourself vomit ... think of one of your own books if you have to. That always does the trick for me."

The doctor's image faded and I found myself seated in a darkened theater, the sole audience member in attendance for my Uncle Harrison's crappy ventriloquist act. Harrison laughed at me, affectionately. "Well, well, well. Fell down another manhole, did we?"

His ever-present dummy, Charlie Chuckles, batted his bushy

eyebrows. "*Manhole?* Sounds like a gay bar in San Francisco!"

If I was looking for something to induce vomiting, I needn't have looked any further than my Uncle's act. The only good gags in *his* performances usually came from the audience. My reaction proved to be no exception to that rule, and I suddenly regurgitated a thick stream of vomit onto the theater floor.

My strange visions went black and then I slowly began to regain consciousness. It took me a moment to realize this, for the site that met my eyes was so horrific that I could scarcely believe it was real.

I never realized how terrifying it would be to wake up inside of a bloody cage, but apparently there's a first time for everything. I always thought that I was relatively open to new experiences, but coming out of a drugged stupor inside of a cage in a cannibal's slaughter room was a little bit further into the Twilight Zone than I wanted to journey.

Richard Matheson—or rather, what was left of him—was suspended by the heels with a crossbar that had been rammed through the tendons of his ankles. The nude, decapitated carcass hung upside down, hooked to a block and tackle that was screwed into a beam of the cellar's ceiling. The body had been sliced open down the front, all the way to the groin, and was gutted like a dressed-out deer. Richard's decapitated head stared blankly from a bucket loaded with intestines that sat on the floor beneath the carcass.

This revolting site instantly put a whole new spin on that chili we'd just consumed. Overcome with nausea, I regurgitated onto the floor once more. The purge seemed to clear my head as I gazed around the cellar in horror. More butchered human remains hung from hooks lining the walls of the makeshift kill room.

Drinking in the opulence of the gore-splattered cellar, I saw that our captor had manacled Jamie Lynn to a few lengths of chain bolted to a wall opposite my shiny new cage. The teenager lay slumped on the floor, still unconscious. Our abductor was nowhere to be seen, but the creaking floorboards overhead revealed her current location as the upstairs kitchen. I spat bile and then called out to Jamie Lynn in as loud a volume as I could risk without being heard upstairs.

"Jamie Lynn! Wake up! Jamie Lynn! She'll come back here soon! Wake up!"

The young lady stirred and groaned. Her eyes fluttered. She moaned and tried to lift her arms.

"That's it, girl! We need to wake up before that psycho bitch makes us into a hearty meatloaf that's a snap to prepare and feeds a family of five."

Jamie Lynn raised her eyelids and stared at me. "What happened?" She looked around, slowly realizing that she was manacled to the wall and that we were both in very deep trouble. She spotted Richard Matheson's butchered body and let loose a blood-curdling scream.

"Please try to stay calm, Jamie Lynn!" I pleaded.

"She's a fucking cannibal!" Jamie Lynn thought for a moment and looked like she was about to be ill. "The chili," she muttered and then, seconds later, regurgitated onto the floor."

"She'll never get four Michelin stars," I said, reaching into my coat to retrieve my revolver. The gun was gone. "She got my gun."

"David and the others will come for us won't they?"

"I'm sure they will ... if we don't come out eventually. But by then, it might be too late. If we call for help, that freak might just shoot us in cold blood. Cold blood, just like the stuff splattered all over the walls down here. We'll have to make a play at getting loose. Are you up for that?"

"I'm up for anything if it means getting the fuck out of here alive."

I searched the cage for any sort of weapon, but the effort proved fruitless.

Adrienne's voice came from the blackness of the upper stairwell. "Who's that nibbling at my house?"

The cackling witch descended the cellar stairs, slamming the tip of my cane down on each step as she did so. She paused at the bottom of the stairwell—stared at me—and then grinned her psychotic grin. "I guess this just isn't your lucky day, Stanley."

"Not unless the definition of 'lucky' has changed pretty drastically," I muttered.

"Thanks to you and your mother, we were left high and dry. Richard's drinking got worse and worse. Bills piled up, higher and higher. We had to take in boarders. Richard was always peeping at those little whores. He even drilled holes in the walls so he could watch those little sluts undress!

"But I fixed him, sonny boy! I fixed all of 'em! Just like I'm gonna fix you and this little whore!" The crazy crone struck Jamie Lynn with my cane. The teenager shrieked in pain. The blow drew blood from the laceration it left on her scalp.

My blood boiled. "Leave the kid alone, you crazy witch! I'm the one you have a beef with! No weird cannibal pun intended!"

My adoptive mother spat at me, scowling hatefully. "Finally in a cage, like the little freak that you are!" She walked briskly to the enclosure that imprisoned me and angrily jabbed the cane through the bars of the cage. She poked at me violently, as if she was attempting to pop a jiggling water balloon. The tip of the cane bashed hard against my ribs and then my shoulder and finally against my cheek before I was able to grab hold of the walking stick and pull it out of Adrienne's hand and into the cage.

She cackled at me. "Old gooble gobble wants his gimp stick back!"

The moment Adrienne turned her back to me I pressed a button on the cane's handle and quickly unsheathed a bayonet-sized blade from the walking stick. The concealed cane blade was one of the few tricks I'd learned from Edgar Belmont, my despicable biological father. I hid the blade behind my back and waited for a chance to strike.

Adrienne began to pace madly about the basement, pounding her temples with balled fists and slapping herself violently across the face. "Gotta keep this all a secret! Did awful things to the little slut whore bitches! Gotta just get rid of the evidence! He was a lazy, good for nothin' peeping Tom! Nothin' but a goddamned pervert! Well, I fixed him! I fixed him good! Just like Stanley and his little whore bitch! Gonna fix them too!"

The mad old woman approached a blood-soaked butcher's block and took hold of a meat cleaver. She jerked the blade free with a grunt. Then she turned and walked toward Jamie Lynn, raising the cleaver as if to strike the girl. Jaime Lynn screamed in terror. I quickly followed her lead.

As Adrienne neared the teenager, she was suddenly distracted by the sound of frantic pounding on the front door upstairs. The surprised lunatic turned to glance up the stairwell and Jamie Lynn leapt to action, looping the chains that imprisoned her around the old woman's scrawny neck and pulling them taut in a stranglehold. Adrienne gurgled and gasped for air. Blood began to spill down her chin as Jamie Lynn twisted the chains tighter and tighter.

With the strength of a crazed orangutan, Adrienne stumbled forward, taking Jamie Lynn with her for an impromptu piggyback ride. The bolts holding the chains to the wall jerked free and Adrienne fumbled across the cellar toward the cage with Jamie Lynn straddling her like a murderous barnacle.

I jabbed my blade through the bars of the cage as Adrienne fell forward, landing face-first on the knife. The blade was rammed down her throat as she collapsed. Finally the tip of the knife sliced through the back of the woman's neck and she went completely limp, hissing out a final, bloody breath.

"Holy fuck!" Jamie Lynn yelled.

The cellar door burst open and Solomon, Collins and Dr. Whitlock rushed down the stairs with guns drawn. They looked around the blood-splattered cellar with stunned horror. Collins and Solomon rushed to Jamie Lynn's aid. Collins took the girl in his arms. "You okay, kid?"

Jamie Lynn smiled, obviously glad to see him. "If you can call this okay."

Solomon examined Adrienne's body. "Christ, don't tell me this is your mother."

"Twice removed," I said.

"He wasn't exaggerating about what a crazy bitch she was," Jamie Lynn said.

Solomon rubbed the sides of his mouth. "I guess not."

Dr. Whitlock examined the lock on my cage and then searched through Adrienne's clothing, quickly locating a set of keys in her sweater pocket.

As the doctor freed the two of us, Solomon quickly searched the rest of the house for any further unpleasant surprises.

He returned a few minutes later, holding the pot of human meat chili from the kitchen stove. "The place is clear, but I might suggest that we stick to eating only canned goods during our visit."

Chapter Ten

_____

After tending to our ever-expanding collections of flesh
wounds, we all devoured a simple, but hearty, meal of canned
spinach that tasted as if it had been scooped out of the filter of a dirty
fish tank and a beef stew that might have originally been dog food
preserved with embalming fluid when it was canned back in the year
1872.

Following the feast, we bedded down for a few hours of sleep,
with each man taking a turn standing guard over the house while the
others slept. Solomon woke me for my shift at six pm, shaking me
awake from the depths of my horrible night terrors.

A little food and rest had worked wonders, and I burst out of bed
with the renewed vigor of a man three times my age. My joints felt
as if they were in the early stages of rigor mortis and my flesh was
prickly and sore, as if I'd been napping inside of an iron maiden.

The storm had finally subsided and was replaced by a spooky fog
that hovered about the woods beyond the house, and the unnerving
echoes of thunder far off in the distance. Disconcerting, animalistic
howls and strange wailings echoed from the forest that surrounded
the property.

Beginning my shift as sentry, I mulled over the visions I'd seen in
my night terrors as I paged through Dr. Whitlock's book about the

life and work of Albrect Shiverdecker. The horrible and haunting images in his painting seemed so familiar to me that I experienced something akin to déjà vu when examining them in detail. The devils and demons and tortured souls; the madness and acts of psychotic violence; the vengeful spirits soaring about every which way; the guy who looked just like me being skinned alive by a half-man/half-scorpion monster while laughing devils sawed his arms and legs off—It all seemed so familiar. Examining the look of agony and complete terror on the white-haired, unconventionally handsome, torture victim's face, all I could think was: *Jesus! I'd hate to be that poor idiot!*

Given the fact that Shiverdecker was the same man who conceived the theory of malignant reversal, one would think that his paintings might have included a few more depictions of the malignant forces actually being reversed, and a few *less* depictions of people having their intestines ripped out through their anal cavities.

I paged through the book, desperate to find some image that would actually inspire me to prevent these hellish images from taking place, rather than inspire me to drive off silently into the night—abandoning my colleagues—to take my chances as an LSD-dealing ice cream man. As I thumbed fearfully though the pages of the tome, I was suddenly struck by a painting of the familiar, white-haired man being seduced and made love to by what seemed to be a coven of nubile forest witches—or spirits—clad only in tufts of splendid and seemingly enchanted pubic hair and erect nipples. Nipples that protruded enticingly from the ample breasts that hung in supple abundance beneath their flowing, windswept hair. Dots of white light that seemed to depict a series of musical notes, danced and hovered above the heads of the buxom wood nymphs, as they seduced the strangely familiar, old/young, white-haired man with the erect penis and the gimpy leg. The man was smiling eagerly in each depiction of their impossibly gymnastic sexual trysts. Now this was just the kind of inspiration I was looking for! The man's expression looked as if he was the sole remaining member of the elite squadron known as *Boner Patrol*, and had finally reached his long-sought destination: *Pussy Island*.

I folded down the page of the book for future reference, thinking that I might seek further inspiration in the first floor bathroom of my former parent's house, when I was suddenly distracted by the sound of some oddly hypnotic music emanating from the fog-shrouded forest that surrounded the property. The eerie, woodwind symphony seemed to beckon me forward into the thick of the misty woods that loomed only a few yards from where I now sat on the creaking wooden porch of the house. The music stirred my already extremely blended loins, making my present erection even more erectile, and I shifted the confines of my trousers to accommodate what seemed like a boner the size of the Washington monument.

I was helpless against the lure of the intoxicating harmony, and so, I rose obediently from the wicker porch chair I'd been sitting in and walked, zombie-like, into the misty woods, guided only by the enchanting fantasia that had bewitched me. Beckoned onward by the ever-increasing volume of the sweet music, I forged a precarious path through the fog, braving the strange howls that accompanied the otherworldly melody with their discordant interjections.

As I made my way through the pea soup-thickness of the swirling mists, my mind raced with glorious and terrible thoughts: *Is this my destiny? Will these spirits be helpful to our quest, or are they malignant forces of evil meant to seduce me as some distraction while the demons decimate our numbers? Does "spiritual" sex constitute cheating on Charlotte, even though Shiverdecker's painting seemed to portray this supernatural tryst in a positive light? What if Shiverdecker was taking artistic license and these spirits are not as mouthwateringly voluptuous as he's portrayed them? I mean, these women he painted looked like something out of a Russ Meyer movie, and that's what really invested my interest in this venture to begin with. I didn't get this magical boner just to stumble upon a bunch of second-rate drag queens ... come on! I'm expecting Pam Grier, Tura Satana, Raquel Welch here, not Don Knotts in a fright wig! What if I get some form of weird, supernatural venereal disease from these spirits? Can you even treat something like that? What if I was to get some unearthly form of gonorrhea from these spirits— where my penis leaks ghosts or glowing, green ectoplasm or something bizarre like that? What then? Maybe this is a bad idea.*

Do I even have a choice? I'm just waltzing into the woods for some weird ghost sex like some uncontrollable, paranormal pervert! What the fuck am I doing? What if Shiverdecker was gay and this is some strange gay joke and I stumble upon a bunch of beefy, gay, male spirits all stroking themselves and awaiting my arrival? What if this is all a big supernatural sausage fest? What am I getting myself into here? I didn't sign up for that sort of thing! Hey, who's that really hairy guy over there with the nametag that says "Jerry," pleasuring himself and holding that big black dildo? And why is he wearing a Darth Vadar helmet?

My tumultuous mental turmoil abruptly ceased as I tumbled clumsily over a small boulder and fell face first into a small pool of water at the mouth of a clearing that appeared strangely free of the cloying fog that engulfed the rest of the forest. The freezing chill of the water instantly cleared my head—or, at least seemed to—as I gazed, spellbound, into the faces of four, impossibly beautiful women that gazed down upon me, assembled in a semicircle in the fog-free glade.

One of the women addressed me—her eyes betrayed a sympathetic nature quite uncharacteristic of the familiar words she spoke. "Sythul Kremloch Maccula!"

The words were uttered in the tongue of the horrible Krelsethian witches: the coven of banished witch/gorgons that had occupied the porthole that I had destroyed in the gateway of the Seven Legions of Darkness three years ago—breeders of the Heldethrach demons that now acted as Leland Hull's army of half-demon slaves.

Thanks to my exposure to the vile, poisonous lightening of the Orias nebula, the dialect was now familiar to me and I could converse with these beings without the aide of some antiquated book of witchcraft. I addressed the four witches with a guarded familiarity—as one would address a rock star you'd done lines of cocaine with in the bathroom at Studio 54 and then run into again, two years later, not expecting them to remember you. "Sythul Kremloch Maccula!" I repeated in greeting. "But ... Syhthul Krelseth, insz Shemlach insz fremla Zalu frufrebrack?" I inquired.

The four witches laughed. I took this an encouraging sign. "Zakul

Krelseth Helmach!" the four spirits replied in unison: *You have freed us!* The words rang in my head like the toning of a chapel bell; by destroying the porthole, and their trapped and twisted bodies, I had freed these spirits from their endless torment. Apparently every Orias nebula also had a silver lining.

But hadn't these witches been first imprisoned in their hellish wasteland for their unspeakable crimes against their own kind? Didn't this make my make my erection sort of like having a hard-on for Adolf Hitler? These bitches had committed crimes that would have made Dr. Josef Mengele blush. As my impressive erection began to lose its steam, one of the witches addressed me in broken English, as if she/they had read my thoughts.

"We here now to account for our terrible crimes. To make amends and only do good for our peoples. We here now to seek forgiveness for our unspeakable acts against the Krelsethian. You have destroy the evils within us. All remains now is beauty and love of all things in universe," the witch said in a sweet and very sympathetic voice.

Could this possibly be true? Had I somehow vanquished the evils of their deeds by my actions? Or was this simply some coy seduction to trick me? Was I merely hypnotized by the sweet and powerful siren song that seemed to be emanating from their glowing and somewhat spectacular vaginas that were clearly visible through their sheer and tight-fitting robes?

Another of the witches addressed me. "We know of the evils against which you battle. We know of the horrors you fight against that now plague your world. We know that we must help you. We know that we must now of mind and body join with you to destroy Yarlock the Great Deceiver. With our joining of mind and body you may enter the portholes of the Scorpius Plane to retrieve the Lovejoy codex and its incantations to destroy the portholes of the Legions of Darkness."

"And this joining of mind bodies involves some form of intimate interdimensional sexual contact, during which I would place my interdimensional penis into your interdimensional, singing, alien vaginas?" I inquired, attempting to sound as if I was having some sort of profound revelation. "And of course there are those other interdimensional orifices to explore."

In response to this line of inquiry, the four impossibly beautiful creatures unburdened themselves of their silky garments, revealing the sumptuous curves and astounding feminine glory beneath.

I marveled at their stunning sexuality, slack-jawed, as a stream of saliva dribbled down my chin. "Hmmmm, it appears that you have given me what we call in my world, the human man-boner of mind and body joining. This is an encouraging development."

I could hardly begin to describe what transpired next without a hefty advance story fee from Poontang Parade Magazine. I'm not exaggerating when I say that it felt like I shot a magical rainbow leading to a pot of gold out of my penis.

We ran the gamut of sexual experimentation. The sex was epic and encyclopedic: the Spanish taco sizzler, the Norwegian deep space probe, the Finnish Pretzel, the bipedal Dutch grumbler, the conquistador, Klugman's folly, the Louisiana lobster bib, The Puerto Rican party horn. The experimentation seemed as endless as it was extraordinary; the diplomat, the Swedish oyster bar, the early bird special, the German monkey wrench—nothing was too wild for these ladies. And I was doing this all in the service of the good of the universe!

The Krelsethian witches' restored sexuality seemed to possess a magical collection of healing properties that instantly mended my broken body and spirit—and the longer the sexual marathon continued, the stronger and better I felt. It seemed as if my age had regressed by at least twenty years. Our brief sexual trysts were nearly mystical in their intensity, and during the lovemaking, I often experienced the sensation that I'd been transported to some magical realm where space and time seemed to bend and distort wildly. When the carnal expedition had finally concluded, I felt like a new man, piping-hot and fresh out of the oven.

While gathering my clothing from the forest ground, I caught a glimpse of my reflection in the pool of water that I'd fallen into earlier and was stunned to see that my hair had been restored to it's original sandy brown color, and the lines of wariness had magically melted away from my now-youthful visage like hot, fleshy, butter.

Even the ever-present dark circles beneath my eyes were now gone.

When I instinctively donned my glasses, the lenses seemed blurry and distorted, and it took a few confused moments for me to process the fact that my vision was now magically sharpened to a crisp and clear 20/20 level of clarity that I had never before experienced in my lifetime.

What other strange changes had the Krelsethain lovemaking trysts brought about in my body? Examining my altered and improved physique, I discovered that my body was now sinewy and well toned and that my penis was noticeably longer ... which was going to be difficult to explain to Charlotte, as was the fact that I was now sans a good portion of my annoyingly abundant body hair. It was if I had been run over by a hansom cab and the accident had ended not in bloody tragedy, but with surprising and ironic physical results.

"It's amazing," I stammered. "*Literal* sexual healing!" Suddenly, I thought of my wary, battle-scarred colleagues and was struck by an overwhelming feeling of guilt. "You know, I have some friends back at the house who could also benefit from your healing sexual powers—although I'm not so sure that Jamie Lynn would be game for the girl-on-girl stuff, but you might extend the offer nonetheless."

The creatures spoke in unison, as if with a single voice, "We have attended already to the needs of the Matheson human's companions. They too have been revitalized by our sexual siren song of pussy power."

Relief washed over me. "I cannot thank you enough for these tremendous gifts, especially the Danish wheelbarrow and that mind blowing French moon landing—and let's not forget the Polish mouth handjob."

"That was also a favorite of the human, David Collins," one of the creatures noted.

"Well I can't say that I blame him."

One of the beautiful creatures lovingly caressed my cheek. "This was our debt to you, human Matheson. By this healing we give you powers to travel within the poisonous portholes and not have skull blow apart like smashed melon. You simply now pass though portholes' dimensional barriers as if like they were liquid water of your Earth planet," she explained. "You breathe toxic air only like harmless oxygen of Earth now, without shitting lungs out through asshole like life-sucking, acidic diarrhea."

"Well that's certainly an encouraging advantage! You girls really know how to take care of business."

Again the creatures spoke in unison. "We have much penance to achieve for our terrible crimes."

"Well, I was more than happy to contribute any chance at redemption and as many bodily fluids to your cause that I could offer, ladies. My penis and I are now in *your* debt."

Again, the Krelsethain beings spoke in harmonic unison, "We must leave you now to your fate, human Stanley Matheson. May you triumph against the evils of Yarlock and the hellish Legions of Darkness. Now may you have the proper strength to fight them."

The lovely beings suddenly began to dematerialize as the world around me faded into blackness.

I awoke sometime later, lying on the floor of the downstairs bathroom with my pants around my ankles and a bottle of hand lotion clutched in my right palm. The Shiverdecker book lay beside me, open to the page displaying the glorious paranormal orgy with the Krelsethain witches. As I regained consciousness, I quickly realized that the feeling of youthful vigor had not left my body. Instead, I still felt stronger and healthier than I had in my entire life. The trysts hadn't simply been some masturbatory fantasy, but would most certainly now be for several years to come.

I rose to my feet and gazed into the bathroom mirror. A man at least forty years younger stared back at me. My face and body still looked a fit, forty-eight years old. A drastic change from the previous, worn-out form of the prematurely aged, eighty-six year old man I'd been gazing at for the past three years. My old bullet wounds and surgery scars had even faded away—leaving only vague pinkish hints of their previous existence. The transformation was nothing short of miraculous, and with the sexual visions still fresh in my mind, and the Shiverdecker painting handy to further inspire me, I quickly rubbed one out in glorious celebration of the fabulous gifts that the Krelsethian witches had bestowed upon me.

With this task complete, I buttoned my pants, and with the Shiverdecker book in tow, returned to my place as sentry on the front porch.

Not five minutes later, David Collins walked out onto the porch with a wide and puzzled grin on his face. "I just had the single greatest wet dream that I have ever experienced in my entire life!" he announced happily. "It was absolutely intense! And that Polish mouth handjob was one for the history books! I swear, I feel like I'm twenty years younger!"

And he looked it, too. The difference in Collins's youthful appearance was just as stunning as my own. He gazed at me with a look of utter shock. "Jesus! What happened to you, Matheson? You look like a goddamned college student! What the hell is going on here?"

"Have you looked in the mirror yet?" I asked. I could scarcely contain my own happy grin.

"No ... I, " Collins suddenly bolted for the bathroom. "Holy shit!" I heard him exclaim from down the hall. Seconds later, he walked back onto the porch with a look of stunned joy. The man was flabbergasted." What the hell is this? Some kind of spell?"

"We were visited by a few ghosts from our past, David."

"A demonic spell? But, I feel goddamned great! I mean, better than I have ever felt in my entire life! And that Polish mouth handjob ... I could masturbate again right now just thinking about that! It seemed so damn *real*! I mean, I could *feel* all of it! It's like it wasn't a dream at all. Holy Sythul Kremloch Maccula! Whatever the hell that means!"

"It was no dream, my friend. We've been physically revitalized by the healing sexual powers of the former Krelsethain witches' coven. Their tormented spirits were freed when I destroyed the porthole three years ago at Hull House. This is their way of repaying us."

Our other companions soon joined the discussion, each being

equally astounded by their restored health, youthfulness and feelings of strange euphoria.

"You know, I wouldn't normally go for the girl-on-girl, lesbo action, but in this instance, it was pretty astounding," Jamie Lynn admitted with a pleased grin. The teenager's cheeks were now rosy and her eyes sported a restored and spirited glow that I had not noticed during our previous interactions.

"Well, experimentation is the spice of life," I said.

Jamie Lynn eyed me with surprised glee. "And look at you, you pervert! You look forty years younger, and not all psycho now! They must have run through the entire Kama Sutra on your slutty, old ass!" she teased. "Way to go, ghost pimp!"

Dr. Whitlock's horrible harpoon leg wound had nearly vanished completely, and in its place only a thin, white scar remained. The man's beard had also gone from a snowy gray to jet-black, and he now looked several pounds thinner—with his substantial, middle-age ravaged, belly having receded quite noticeably over the past few hours.

Detective Solomon had gone from rump roast to fillet mignon, and now resembled a thirty-year-old rookie police academy cadet. "Christ! My left index finger even grew back!"

Dr. Whitlock seemed as pleased as he was fascinated by the recent turn of events. "Absolutely incredible ... a supernatural healing process achieved through paranormal sexual intimacy."

David Collins examined his restored body. "My sword wound has practically disappeared ... and my liver even feels healthier. Now, *that* has to be a true Walpurgisnacht miracle if there ever was one!"

Our unexpected repairs and tune-ups at the Krelsethian body shop were certainly a cause for celebration, but we all quickly realized that they offered no guarantee of a victory in our impending showdown with the Legions of Darkness. Even at our strongest, it might all just prove to be like giving a facelift to a boxer whose about to have his hansom visage pummeled into a pile of raw hamburger by an opponent three times his size and strength.

And yet, there was more to our Krelsethian makeover than first met the eye. Our superficial, physical fine-tuning proved quite secondary to the supernatural, intellectual side effects of our paranormal sexual adventures, as Dr. Whitlock was the first to discover when he instinctively re-examined the strange texts penned in the Opus Demonium. "Sythul samareth frelnach greselthrach!" he announced, somewhat boisterously.

"Relfrazn, melezalseth!" Jamie Lynn suddenly interjected in the language of what I somehow quickly recognized as the tongue of the alien Hemyulac race—another breed of extraterrestrials whose vile evildoers had pledged their allegiance to the Legions of Darkness.

"My God," Solomon muttered. "I actually understood that."

"Me too," Collins said, looking completely astounded by his newly acquired comprehension of the strange alien languages of the Seven Legions of Darkness.

"Absolutely astounding," Dr. Whitlock whispered. "Telepathic, linguistic and visual comprehension of extraterrestrial languages achieved through intimate sexual contact."

"May I?" Solomon asked. Gesturing for Dr. Whitlock to pass him the Opus Demonium.

The diminutive doctor addressed him as if coming out of a deep trance. "Oh ... yes, of course."

Dr. Whitlock passed Solomon the book and the detective quickly paged through the tome, examining random pages with joyful awe. "I can understand this. All of these passages that Shemrach Theydarian penned here that previously seemed like a bunch of nonsensical gibberish now seem like nonsensical gibberish that makes sense, in a way that is understandable but still makes no sense! These weird incantations aren't even weird anymore—except for the fact that they're incantations, and were weird to begin with by their very nature—but aside from that, it just seems like a book written by some psychotic nutcase that I can actually understand without actually having to understand what he was trying to say! It's like being able to finally see a forest of insane gibberish through trees whose bark was made up of a diatribe of convoluted nonsense!"

Dr. Whitlock retrieved the Opus Demonium from Solomon's hands with an apologetic tenderness. "This is all a lot for us to take in just now, Detective, but I think we understand the gist of what you're getting at," Whitlock said. "It's a bit like having your skull shucked open like an oyster and having a set of encyclopedias rammed into the orifice and expecting us to make sense of it all. But I think our understanding of these passages will prove advantageous to our quest—I might suggest that we all familiarize ourselves with the incantations and spells of the Opus Demonium before we all go marching so bravely into the belly of the beast we are attempting to disembowel."

It was certainly sound advice, and we all subsequently poured over each word of the demonic manuscripts, soaking in the horrors of the Legions of Darkness like a bloody sponge.

Reading over these horrifying spells and prophecies of sadistic torture with such newfound understanding really brought the terror home to roost. In my case, it happened to roost primarily in my bladder and bowels, offering me yet another very good reason to regret having eaten Adrienne Matheson's chili.

As Dr. Whitlock thumbed slowly through the pages of the tome, he spoke with a gravity that was cautious, but nonetheless tinged with hope that we might yet still triumph over these sadistic forces of evil. "The demons have a dreadful fear of these weapons and incantations, and for very good reason—as we have all witnessed with Stanley's successful use of this strange, demonic annihilation device," he said. "As for these other weapons in our arsenal ... we'll have to just sort them out with the help of Mr. Theydarian's text."

The assemblage of Professor Hiller's strange weapons—crafted by the scholar using the instructions in the Opus Demonium—was as potentially lethal as it was bizarre.

The use of any of these weapons I would not wish upon my worst enemy—unless of course, they were to be wielded against my worst enemy—which made the prospects of anyone, or any *thing* who might stand in our way quite dire, as they might have quite a bit of trouble actually standing in our way, or any way at all, with their intestines dribbling out of their anuses. Obviously, Shemrach Theydarian meant for the human race to play for keeps when he penned his opus—and this collection of strange artillery promised to provide more blood pudding than a Scottish Christmas party.

Solomon examined one of Shiverdecker's paintings in the book of his collected works. "The Krelsethian witches have actually given you the power to enter those portholes?"

"They said that I could pass through them as if the portholes were simply pools of water, and that I could breathe the toxic air as of it were regular oxygen," I said. "The other beings inside the portholes seem to require a human host to enter our world."

"Like parasites," Collins said.

"Yes, in the form of a spiritual and physical possession," Dr. Whitlock said.

"Which is exactly what they used my friends for," Jamie Lynn said.

"Exactly. That's probably the only reason why all of these *human* witches and Satanists were invited to this little party in the first place," I said.

"Leading the sacrificial lambs to the slaughter," Dr. Whitlock said.

"Also exactly, Doc. I'm sure all of these freaky human assholes have been made to think that this celebration is in the service of some great alliance—that they will all soon rule the earth together with the Legions of Darkness as one, big, happy, multi-headed axis of evil," I said. "It's the same old lie that Leland Hull used on his followers when he was the acting Grand Zanndith of the Order of Yarlock the Great Deceiver."

"Sounds like a real asshole convention," Jamie Lynn said. "But, if we have these weapons to fight the demons, then what purpose does your braving the Scorpius Plane to get to the Lovejoy Codex actually serve?"

"I think the Lovejoy Codex will give us the power to destroy the Gateway of the Seven Legions of Darkness. It will close or destroy the portholes that give these beings access to our world for all eternity," I said.

"I believe that is *exactly* what the purpose of the Lovejoy codex is, and why it is so very essential to our quest," Dr. Whitlock said. "Which brings us all now to this enlightening volume: *The Tenets of The Order of Yarlock the Great Deceiver: The Complete Works of L.B. Hull.*" The doctor placed the volume of my great grandfather's demonic texts on the table, laying it across the collection of weapons, and opened the book to a later passage titled: *"Walpurgisnacht And The Great Resurrection Of The Demon From His Slumber In Darkness."*

Dr. Whitlock then read from the pages with dire urgency. *"And on this wondrous night of reckoning there will be a great gathering of souls. And we shall open wide the portholes of the Legions of Darkness to unleash their evils upon the earth, so that we might reign on this planet as hell made flesh."*

"That's the plan alright ... lead the chickens willingly to the chopping block and *wham!* Off with their heads!" I said. "Out with the human souls, in with the demons."

Dr. Whitlock resumed his reading of the passage: *"Following a delightful pre-possession party with live, cookin', hep and with it music that's sure to get those alligators and hoochie coochers in the know doing the jitterbug like nobody's business, we'll get them mugglin' like vipers with a few sticks of tea. Once the fat heads is happy on reefer, the Heldethrach hep cats shall escort them to the happenin' porthole pod hammocks for the killer diller dive to demonsville that will completely flip their wigs."*

Jamie Lynn snickered. "What?"

"Either those are the lyrics to a Cab Calloway song or they're planning to drug their human victims during the Walpurgisnacht celebration to lull them into a state of complacency and then start loading them into the transmutation pods to assure that there is a minimum amount of resistance during the process," Solomon said. "Leland Hull—or Yarlock the Great Deceiver—was obviously trying to channel the language of the 1970s, but was only able to reach about 1946 or so in his search for hip jargon while attempting to foresee these coming events. Hip jargon can be tricky, especially for squares and suits. To a chrome-dome fathead it might all sound like gobbledygook, but to a doll dizzy, ducky shincracker who knows what's buzzin', this baloney is just Swiss cheese out of a pink chimpanzee's anal fez collection."

Jamie Lynn snickered again, "Meaning?"

"Did I say 'anal' or 'annual'?" Solomon inquired.

"Anal," Jamie Lynn said.

"Okay, then scratch that ... this ain't nothin' but a shakedown from the Sicilian pumpkin fart contingent," Solomon said and crossed his arms, as if the matter was finally settled.

The rest of us stared at him, utterly confused.

"Jesus ... I thought I had this! There must be something seriously off with my jargon interpretations these days," Solomon said, looking frustrated. The detective shook his fists at some unseen enemy. "My father was a swing clarinet player, goddamn it!"

Dr. Whitlock patted the detective's arm with compassion. "We get the point, Detective. There's nothing wrong with your interpretation .. in fact, it's spot on."

"Well, for the record, I don't have any idea what *Swiss cheese out of a pink chimpanzee's anal fez collection*, means—just so we're clear on that point," Solomon said."

"Ditto," Jamie Lynn said.

Solomon picked up one of Professor Hiller's strange weapons and scrutinized its design. "And how do we know if the rest of these contraptions will even work?"

"I have a feeling we're about to get the chance to find out," I said. My brain felt the familiar red-hot jolt of demonic telepathy, and I knew that one of our adversaries was close. My mind's eye was assaulted by the usual series of horrid visuals: local towns under siege, the demons running amok, innocent people being roasted alive at the stake, the Boxcar Willie Fan Club grooving to the sounds of the hit tune, *Walbash Cannonball*. I gripped my temples and gritted my teeth. "There's something horrible coming!"

"Arm yourselves! Quickly now!" Dr. Whitlock ordered.

We all took up arms, seizing items from Professor Hiller's bizarre collection of weapons, and rushed out to the front lawn.

There came a terrible, high-pitched shriek from somewhere far above us, drawing our attentions skyward. A full moon shimmered through a clearing in the rumbling storm clouds overhead. It was suddenly eclipsed by a large and frightful shadow. Silhouetted against the glow of the moon was the shape of what looked to be a gargantuan vampire bat. The monster let loose its blood-curdling squeal once more, as it dove—soaring over our heads like some kamikaze crop duster plane. We bolted quickly out of the beast's path, ducking its snapping jaws and nose-diving into the grass of the front lawn.

The horrible bat monster hovered over us, flapping its venous wings and chattering madly. The creature descended, seizing Jamie Lynn by the ankle. The teenager screamed as the monster attempted to ascend with the girl in its clutches. Seconds later, David Collins was upon the beast, leaping onto its back like a crazy cowboy attempting to break a wild stallion. Collins jerked his knife from the sheath on his belt and plunged the blade into the creature's shoulder blades. The bat monster shrieked in pain and released Jamie Lynn from its grasp. The teenager hit the front lawn and rolled over with a gasp as Solomon fired a bullet into the monster's shoulder. The creature flailed wildly, having lost its ability to maintain flight and flopped about on the lawn. David Collins was tossed like a ragdoll into a bush as Solomon continued to pump more bullets into the shrieking beast.

I took aim at the creature with the terrible baby bone weapon and was about to fire upon the thing when Dr. Whitlock spoke up. "Wait, Stanley! Don't destroy it! Not yet!"

The doctor took aim at the flailing beast with another of Professor Hiller's bizarre weapons and then voiced an incantation. "Demonus obitas bindum victus forfitatum grishnu!" he shouted. The incantation prompted his strange weapon to fire a network of fiery red beams that engulfed the monster like a network of constricting tentacles and bound the creature tightly in their grasp. Once incapacitated, the bat monster could only roll about on the grass, hissing and chattering—now helpless to the whims of its angry captors.

David Collins rose to his feet and then nailed the bat monster with a swift kick to the gut. "You just settle down now, bat man!"

As the creature writhed about, bound by its otherworldly manacles, the thing began to change form—its grotesque metamorphosis finally resulted in a completely hairless, humanoid figure with slimy, grey flesh and piercing, red, insect-like eyes that glared up at us with palpable, alien disgust.

Dr. Whitlock approached the creature. "Valcos verminas verbotem?" he inquired of the prisoner, as he placed his foot upon the demon's chest. "Ilsacra deathtu," he hissed and then spat in the demon's face.

The prisoner cackled with wicked delight. "Valcos verminas demonus, optimas verboten humanus!" the demon said, gleefully. "Deathtu humanus! Walpurgisnacht deathtu humanus!" The demon laughed triumphantly, blowing defiant, childish, raspberries at the doctor with its purple, worm-like tongue.

Dr. Whitlock sighed. "Well, we've captured one alive, at least. Perhaps a few of Professor Hiller's special instruments can persuade our prisoner here to be a bit more forthcoming and courteous."

Suddenly, there came a metallic crash from somewhere off in the distance beyond the house. The sound of crunching metal and breaking glass echoed through the forest as we turned our attention to the woods surrounding the property. Next, a great squeal of bending metal screeched in our ears like nails on a chalkboard. Then something huge soared through the air above our heads and came down atop the lawn with a thunderous crash. The battered vehicle instantly resolved any further issues concerning our interrogation of the captured demon when it crushed the creature into a pile a bloody mush.

Deposited in a shallow crater before us, lay the smoking remains of the famous Oscar Meyer "Weiner Mobile," now a mangled pile of frankfurter-shaped metal and plastic.

My heart sank in my chest. "Charlotte!" I screamed and bolted to the wreckage. I searched the smashed cab—there was no sign of Charlotte or Margot. There was also no visible blood splattered about the cab—a detail that I found mildly encouraging.

"Is that the—" Solomon's voice trailed off, sounding shocked and distraught.

Seconds later, a duet of familiar female screams pierced the night air.

"Charlotte!" I shouted. "Margot! It's Stanley! We're here!"

Something large scurried toward us through the trees. We backed away, gathering up our demon slaying weapons. Leaves and branches were torn loose as the creature rampaged through the forest, emitting fearsome roars as it approached. Charlotte and Margot cried out again in terror—their shrieks now only yards away. The tree line exploded, sending branches flying in every direction, as the ghastly beast stepped from the shadows and into the fleeting moonlight. It roared with fury as it laid eyes upon us. The monster was a grotesque hybrid—a sickening sort of arachnid centaur—with the legs, tail and claws of a monstrous, black scorpion and the head and upper torso of Edgar Belmont, my despicable, biological father, would-be murderer and pedophile rapist of my biological mother. The scowling familiarity of the monster's face was unmistakable. The beast held both Charlotte and Margot in its gargantuan claws, clutching the two women tightly around their waists with its ebony pedipalp pinchers. Both women gasped and cried out as they desperately attempted to free themselves.

The Belmont/scorpion monstrosity grinned at me with sadistic satisfaction.

My blood boiled. "You should have stayed out in Hell, where you belong you creepy mother fucker."

The monster cackled with delight. "Surrender the true Opus Demonium, or I will tear your bitches apart like ragdolls, you meddlesome little bastard! Obey, and I will be merciful—defy me, and they die! The choice is yours!"

"I'd think twice about giving *us* orders, you arachnid, rapist, asshole!"

The Belmont scorpion laughed. "Oh really? And why is that, Sonny boy?"

I cringed at the playful reference. "Because, aside from being accountable to the Oscar Meyer Weiner Company for your willful destruction of their beloved, promotional powerhouse, the wiener mobile—you also failed to realize that by asking us to hand over the true Opus Demonium, you are acknowledging that we actually have this legendary tome in our possession!"

The monster scowled. "What the hell are you droning on about now, you pathetic, little idiot? Do you have the book or not? And don't try to pass off one of your shitty books on decorative plate collecting like last time!"

"Oh no, we have the Opus Demonium. You can bet your ass on that, Belmont—or, given your current form—should I say, you can bet your sternate, anus, vesticle and aculeus on that?"

"Give it to me!"

"You sure you want it?"

"Give it to me, you fool! I won't ask you again!"

I eyeballed my colleagues with a raised eyebrow. "Shall we?"

Dr. Whitlock smiled. "If he insists, I believe we should oblige him, Stanley."

Instinctively, the entire group took aim at the monster with our weapons, and—as if we had rehearsed the act many times— suddenly voiced the same dreadful incantation from the Opus Demonium in almost perfect synch: "Demonus valcos verminas verbotem! Demonus tortorum exterminatus!"

A near-blinding array of multi-colored lighting crackled and sizzled as Edgar Belmont's tortured shrieks echoed through the icy night.

To say that Professor Hiller's weapons were effective on the demon would be a drastic understatement. Following our showdown, what remained of the Edgar Belmont scorpion "manster" looked like a bloody used condom full of raisins that had been tied to a dirty, old sock. The pathetic creature begged us to put it out of its terrible misery, but that—unfortunately for the demon—was not in the cards. The ensuing interrogation lasted another brutal hour, during which we utilized every one of Hiller's torture devices repeatedly. In the end, the demon's shriveled, finger puppet-sized head simply fell off due to excessive abuse. We didn't learn much from the creature, aside from the fact that if we tortured it long enough, its head would eventually fall off, but it was somewhat enjoyable doling out some, old-fashioned frontier justice.

Thankfully, Charlotte and Margot had only sustained a few nasty cuts and bruises during their attack, and we were able to administer a bit of makeshift first aid to their wounds. Charlotte was astounded by my appearance. She said that I looked like the same baby-faced weirdo she had first fallen in love with before my mental assault by the Orias nebula had prematurely aged me into the dashing grey fox with a face like an exceptionally attractive, moldy apricot.

I explained our youthful revitalization with an edited, G-Rated version of the magical encounter, in which the Krelsethian witches held our hands and kissed our cheeks to heal our collective wounds.

Satisfied with my strategically abridged explanation, Charlotte caressed my cheek lovingly and planted a passionate kiss on my lips. "I'm so glad you're alive, Stanley!"

"And you too, baby! You shouldn't have risked coming! Either of you! You could have been ripped apart out there," I scolded.

Margot smiled and placed a hand on my cheek. "This was meant to be, Stanley. I know it in my heart. For better or worse, we were meant to face this evil at your side."

"At least this way I can keep an eye on you two," I said.

Next, the ladies received a crash course in advanced and intermediate demon slaying, during which they were shown key passages from the Opus Demonium and The Tenets of Yarlock the Great Deceiver and introduced to the various types of artillery at our disposal. Following their impromptu initiation, we all prepared for the Walpurgisnacht gathering—donning our black hooded robes, applying ritual make-up and strategically planting demon annihilation devices about our persons.

Once prepared for battle, we spent two solid hours spiking the ice cream in the truck with enough LSD to put Timothy Leary in a straight jacket.

Finally, our bizarre party posse rolled out—headed for Hull House and either death or glory. We split into two groups for the drive. Charlotte, Margot, Dr. Whitlock and I rode in the hearse. Collins, Jamie Lynn and Solomon drove behind us in the ice cream truck.

Chapter Eleven

_____

We arrived at the Hull Mansion less than two hours later, and the sight that met our eyes was enough to inspire sheer terror in the most courageous and foolhardy of men. Decapitated human heads lined the spires of the wrought iron gates that surrounded the estate, and the vast crimson/black expanse of the Orias nebula spread out across the sky above the haunted ruins, firing bolts of terrible venous lightening through the heavens in sporadic, nerve jangling, blasts. A squadron of Heldethrach man-demons stood guard at the front gates armed with side arms and scimitars.

"Turtle wax my sphincter," Charlotte mumbled, awestruck by the horrors that awaited us.

"Welcome to Armageddon, baby. I'm sure it only gets worse from here," I said.

A pair of guards approached us as I rolled down the driver's side window to speak with them.

"Who comes for Walpurgisnacht?" one of the guards asked.

"We are the Coven of the Black Sacrament, the eaters of human babies. Yarlock is expecting us. You know how he just loves those baby eaters," I said, picking my teeth dramatically. "Excuse me, I still have some placenta logged between my right maxillary incisor and my right maxillary cuspid."

The first of the Heldethrach guards checked the guest list on his clipboard. "This is affirmative, man-human. You arrive late for party. Every else guest inside already getting happy for porthole transmutation process."

"Oh, well we found an abandoned maternity ward chock-full of crying infants on the way here and just had to stop for a bite to eat," I said.

"And we've brought along a vast assortment of delicious ice cream treats for the Walpurgisnacht celebration," Charlotte added.

The Heldethrach guards' eyes widened. The one standing closest to the car licked his lips. "Ice cream?"

"A veritable rainbow of sweet and frosty treats for the hungry Heldethrach man-demons," Charlotte said.

The two sentries began whispering to each other in excited, but hushed tones.

"I love what you've done with the place," I said, hoping to regain their attention.

"They bring ice cream in whole truck full of ice cream!" one of the two lead guards yelled to their associates assembled at the front gate.

The entire Heldethrach squadron cheered upon hearing the news.

David Collins switched on the ice cream truck's cheerful music and *The Entertainer* tinkled through the misty air, broadcasting through the crackling speakers of the ice cream truck.

The man-demons clapped and danced about, gleefully.

"Man, these freaks *really do* love their ice cream," I muttered.

"How did you know they would react like this?" Charlotte said.

"Dr. Harvey told us, baby," I said.

"You talked to Dr. Harvey? He's alive?"

"Let's just say that he is *literally* here in spirit."

The first Heldethrach guard approached the window again. "You bring ice cream for us and not tell anyone else?"

"Oh no, we brought this delicious ice cream for you Heldethrach soldiers," I explained. "Say, speaking of which I had just spoken, I bet you guys would all appreciate some ice delicious cream about now."

The first guard's expression changed from skepticism to excitement in a matter of seconds. "Yes! We would! We would very much like to eat the ice cream right now!"

"Well, I think the hard-working Heldethrach guardians might deserve a bit of special treatment—given this auspicious occasion—with you guys all standing out here in this fog and all. You guys are really doing a bang-up job, obviously, and, to me, that merits some yummy ice cream for the troops," I said. "I think we can turn a blind eye for the moment while you rally the boys around for some well deserved rewards."

The guard clapped his hands with excitement. "These humans say we can have ice cream before Walpurgisnacht!" he shouted to his fellow guards.

The man-demons rushed to the ice cream truck as Solomon frantically distributed the frosty sweeties to the ravenous crowd, who instantly gobbled down the LSD-laced treats like excited children. Moments later, the first Heldethrach guard blew an alarm whistle and several more Heldethrach mutants rushed from the Hull mansion to join the melee. The vast crowd gathered around the ice cream truck gave me the distinct impression that the entire congregation of Leland Hull's simple-minded minions had converged to collect their delectable and frosty booty.

With our adversaries successfully distracted for the time being, I drove the hearse through the gates of Hull House and parked next to the vast assortment of other guests' vehicles—all of which had been festively decorated with human bones and flesh. As the mutant minions gobbled down their hallucinatory rewards, we armed ourselves to the teeth.

We jogged briskly into the crumbling mansion. The foyer and

halls of the estate had been lit with torches fastened to the walls, and their yellowish/amber glow gave the charred and smoke-blackened interior of Hull House an appropriately hellish ambience that sent a chill up my spine.

From here on out there would be no turning back. I could only hope that I wasn't leading my noble colleagues and loved ones to certain death.

"Okay, ladies and gents, let's crash this bash with our trademark panache, " I said, doing my best to sound cool, calm and collected.

The spiritual vibrations in the house were nearly palpable, buzzing through the atmosphere like a subsonic electrical hum. The hairs on the back of my neck shot up like porcupine quills and my skin turned to chilly gooseflesh.

Margot suddenly swooned, as if overcome by the supernatural forces that surrounded us. Dr. Whitlock quickly took her in his arms before she could faint.

"Harrison?" she whispered, looking slightly dazed.

"Are you alright, Mrs. Donlevy?" Dr. Whitlock asked.

Margot placed her fingertips to her temples. "Yes ... I'm fine. It's just that I sense a presence here that I haven't felt in quite some time."

David Collins exhaled loudly and shook his limbs about, like a boxer limbering up for a big match. "Christ, this place has more spirits packed into it than a discount liquor outlet ... and man, are they ever pissed off. This feels about a thousand times worse than our last visit."

"There's at least one more of the original demons summoned forth on Halloween still at large here tonight. And there's a damn good chance that it might sense my presence—so if my head suddenly falls off of my body, or my intestines squirt out of my eye sockets, one of you might have to pick up the slack," I said. I gazed into Charlotte's eyes for what could be the last time. "I'm sorry, babe."

She hugged me tightly, then kissed me on the lips and released me. "You do what you have to do, baby! You show these motherfuckers who is boss! You are a complete idiot! Do you hear me? And nobody messes with the idiot!"

Margot embraced me and kissed me on the cheek. "Be brave, my sweet boy. I never meant for you to have to experience anything like this."

"I know, Mom. It's not your fault that our tainted gene pool seems to spill out across the earth firing turds in every direction like a shit-filled piñata."

Collins turned to Jamie Lynn. "If I start acting really weird, which is—quite frankly—inevitable under the circumstances, you just hang tough, kid. You stick close to Detective Solomon and Dr. Whitlock."

Jamie Lynn frowned. "I will ... how weird?"

"I'm a spiritual conduit, honey ... so, given what I'm sensing is at work in this place, pretty ape shit crazy is my estimation."

"Okay," she muttered. "But I'll watch your back, regardless."

"I'm counting on it, kid."

Dr. Whitlock lifted a torch from its wall support. "Shall we?"

"We'll take the elevator in the lab. It's down this hallway," I said.

As we turned a corner, a howling spirit soared through the air toward us. We ducked frantically as the banshee flew past and vanished around the corner whence we came.

"It's okay, everybody. It was just a vengeful spirit from beyond the grave." I said, trying to sound reassuring. "It's probably just the ghost of someone brutally murdered in the house ... nothing to freak out about."

We dashed down the hallway to the wall concealing the entrance to the sinister laboratory.

"We'll have to pry the door open," I said, taking a small crow bar from my belt that I'd brought along for just that purpose. I felt along the wall for the edges of the door.

"There!" Solomon said, pointing to the barely discernable outline of the secret entrance.

As I was about to force the crow bar into a crevice in the wall, the door suddenly opened. We froze in terror as a pair of Heldethrach man-demons stepped into the hallway. The two, simple-minded minions stared at us, confused.

"You new entertainment band?" one of them inquired, sounding hopeful.

"Band?" I said.

The second Heldethrach soldier grimaced "Stupid Zog, Claggo and Mushak accidentally kill Peppermint Gang band in green room and make sweet, sweet love to corpses!"

"Music humans only taking smoke break between sets and not ready for kill and dead body sex yet," the first soldier explained. "Still music to play for Walpurgisnacht."

"Yes ... our manager sent us over," I said. "We're the Penis Swashbucklers. We're punk rock. We just played CBGB on the same bill with the Soiled Underpants Merchants and the Chinese Mexicans."

"You've probably heard our big hit, *Skunk Piss X-Ray Glasses*," Charlotte said.

"Yeah, we're busting out all of our big hits tonight ... like this one for example," I said, and then cracked the nearest of the Heldethrach guards across the skull with the crow bar.

With lightning-quick speed, David Collins slashed the throat of the second soldier with his knife. We then quickly dragged the two bodies into the lab and shut the door behind us.

Solomon and I dressed ourselves in the Heldethrach robes and shoved wads of Kleenex up our noses and between our teeth and gums to give us the Neanderthal look or the malformed man-demons. Rubbing our satanic make-up around our faces completed the moronic effect and my trusty brain helmet made a wonderfully gruesome hump on my back when fastened to my shoulder beneath the robe. While Solomon and I donned our new disguises, the others gathered up every scrap of paperwork in the laboratory in case any of it might later prove relevant to Dr. Quinlan's search for an antidote to the Medusa's Uterus plague.

As we were about to descend into the bowels of Hull House, Dr. Harvey's spirit materialized in the laboratory.

Charlotte seemed more relieved than frightened to see our deceased colleague. "Dr. Harvey ... your—"

"Yes ... isn't it delightfully ironic? Your lesser half even conjured me up during a séance the other night," Dr. Harvey said.

"It's good to see you again ... even under these circumstances."

"And you as well, my dear." Dr. Harvey eyed my disguise with a smirk. "I see you've brought Jerry Lewis with you."

"Well, well if it isn't the ghost of flatulence past," I said. "How's the Walpurgisnacht bash going?"

"It's like an Hieronymus Bosch painting down there," Dr. Harvey said. "You should fit right in."

"How's the master of ceremonies tonight?" I said.

"He's got them eating out of the palm of his hand ... literally ... it's quite revolting. One of the Order of the Golden Dragon people just swallowed an entire handful of live maggots."

"Yeah, well that won't be the only thing revolting around here tonight," I said. "These assholes think *they're* raising hell, but they haven't seen anything yet!"

"I must admit, you really rose to the occasion with the LSD-laced ice cream," Dr. Harvey said.

"Chance favors the prepared mind, Doc."

"And the insane one, as well, apparently."

"Their little ice cream social should dose them all with enough LSD to make Ken Kesey piss rainbow-colored Kool-Aid,"

"What can we expect down there, Bernie?" Dr. Whitlock said.

"It's a bit like a carnival being held in the third circle of Hell," Dr. Harvey said. "Yarlock's really pulled out the stops for this little soiree. Right now he's oh-so-modestly discouraging their sycophantic requests for him to dazzled them with a few numbers on the pipe organ."

Meer seconds later, the sound of the subterranean pipe organ echoed through the halls of the mansion. Yarlock was tickling the ivories with a piece from Mussorgsky's *Night on Bald Mountain.*

"He's really laying the Vincent Price vibe on pretty thick this evening," I said.

"And those morons are lapping it up like mother's milk," Dr. Harvey said.

"We'd better get down there while they're all distracted," I said.

"A capital idea," Dr. Whitlock said.

"Watch yourselves. I will be close," Dr. Harvey said, as his visible spirit dissolved into a twinkling, dissipating mist.

"Wait   before we go," Margot whispered, and then extracted Isabella Hull's crystal ball from a leather purse slung over her shoulder. The oracle glowed with an unearthly green light. As we gathered round the orb, a familiar human face suddenly materialized in the emerald mists of the crystal ball: the face of Margot's deceased twin brother, Harrison Hull. "It *is* you!" Margot said. Her radiant smile conveyed delight rather than horror at the sight of her long dead twin.

"I figured your little performance tonight could use a bit of old school showmanship, Sissy," Harrison said. "I thought I might be able to add a little razzle dazzle to this apocalyptic burlesque show in-between the demon conjuring act and the end-of-humankind-as-we-know-it finale."

"I was so scared Harrison—I'm sorry I abandoned you."

"Oh, but you never, did, Sissy" Harrison said. "And now here you are—back in this hellhole again and all ready to right the wrongs of our horribly-tainted bloodline with your weirdo son and his multi-talented troupe of demon-slaying oddballs."

Margot caressed the smooth, glassy face of the oracle. "You were always there to look out for me."

"I still am," Harrison said lovingly. "This broadcast has been brought to you by Dr. Pepper! The official soft drink of the Apocalypse!" the lunatic ghost pronounced, as the crystal ball faded to a dull, frosty/gray sheen.

We packed ourselves into the elevator like cocktail wieners stuffed into a can and descended into the mouth of madness. It was time to act—before any second thoughts could gain a foothold in our frightened minds. We had to strike while the iron was hot and lunging toward our clenched sphincters.

Coming to a halt in the caverns, the elevator door swung open to reveal a scene of such shockingly depraved revelry that it was, at first, hard to believe our own eyes. The Gateways of the Seven Legions of Darkness now resembled an adult-themed amusement park for the sadomasochistic set. The bacchanal was in full swing, and it was obvious from the behavior of the participants that Yarlock's human prey was now doped to the gills with some euphoria-inducing narcotic. The gargantuan porthole windows that lined the cavern walls were now aglow with swirling and colorful mists that revealed eerie, fleeting images of interspecies sexual debauchery and sadistic, human torture, giving them the effect of a collection of drive-in movie theater screens broadcasting snuff films from Satan's own private film collection. Hovering above this shameless debauchery was a swarm of howling spirits that circled about the caverns like angry hornets whose nest had been set alight.

"The vengeful dead of Hull House," Collins said, pointing to the ghostly gaggle. "The spirits of the women that perished here during the attempts to breed the Heldethrach man-demon army. They cry out to us to avenge their deaths."

Despite all of this madness, the stoned revelers ate, drank and made merry, as of they hadn't a care in the world—save for the distinct possibility of contracting a sexually transmitted disease at some point during the evening. The human cattle being subtly herded to their deaths seemed to be having a stone cold blast—the goats being sodomized and fellated were not so enthusiastic, and didn't particularly seem to care for the strange and colorful costumes that they'd been dressed in.

Obviously, this was no run-of-the mill sex orgy—the litany of depravities on display was enough to make the Marque De Sade turn his eyes away in disgust. The lustful crowd writhed and swayed with the throbbing rhythms of the pipe organ as the master of this hellish domain sat with his back to the crowd weaving his musical magic on the organ keys. The vast assortment of extra tentacles and insect legs that slithered and protruded from the sleeves and folds of his robe provided an intricate accompaniment to the primary notes being played by the master's ten to twelve humanoid digits.

I eyed the row of portholes that lined the massive subterranean chamber with dread. The otherworldly fissures now stretched from floor to ceiling of the cavern—their apertures obviously expanded to their maximum capacity to accommodate the great transmigration of souls that would be sent through their demonic passageways during the Walpurgisnacht celebration—nothing remained to block the ingress between man and monster in this hell on earth.

I cleared my throat. "Okay, we should split up ... but not literally. Let's all try to make it out of here in one piece—or, baring that, then *two* pieces that can be surgically reattached."

As we were about to wade strategically into the Walpurgisnacht chaos taking place before us, the devilish master of ceremonies finished his organ number with a dramatic crescendo and turned about on his stool, bowing to a flurry of enthusiastic applause from his willing clergy. The monster rose from his seat and extended his arms and numerous tentacles to the heavens, sucking in the appreciative response like a vampire drinking blood from an artery.

"You're too kind, really," Yarlock said, taking yet another bow. The shapeshifting devil turned back to the keyboards and then played a familiar call to arms on the organ that drew a vast legion of his LSD-dosed Heldethrach soldiers back into his underground lair. The battalion descended the stairwell that led into the subterranean hall from the mansion's wine cellar, now looking mildly confused and unduly distracted by the weird and colorful images being transmitted across the massive porthole windows. Despite obvious efforts to maintain their composure, the man-demons now appeared overwhelmed and highly confused by their surroundings. Some of them pointed at the images dancing across the smooth faces of the portholes with mild horror, while others giggled helplessly as the mind-altered minions descended into the cave.

Yarlock, absorbed in his own magnificence, continued to address his loyal audience as his heavily drugged foot soldiers filed into the writhing throng below. "Children of darkness, tonight we gather in celebration of the dawning of a new age. Together, we shall bring forth from these portholes the masters of a new world, and you—our human vessels—shall be our privileged ambassadors of evil."

The twisting tentacles that extending from Yarlock's crooked spine tapped out a few sinister notes on the keys of the pipe organ keyboard behind him.

Suddenly, there came a great low-pitched hum from somewhere deep within the bowels of the caves below the mansion and, moments later, a gargantuan, pulsating mandible appendage extended from the mysterious black abyss that lay just beyond the porthole chamber. Like some hellish, green/black worm conjured from the darkest pits of Hell, the fleshy, snake-like mechanism emerged from shadows of the subterranean hollow and then came to rest just under the arch leading into the gateway of portholes. The great, flat mouth of the mandible contraption retracted—separating like the fleshy lips of some monstrous, reptilian vagina—and from this strange alien orifice floated row upon row of black, egg-shaped pods. The pods were large, certainly sizeable enough to accommodate a human body, and each hovered above the ornate stone floor of the main cavern in neatly compartmentalized rows. These were obviously the transmutation pods that would carry Yarlock's willing disciples into the horrible worlds that loomed beyond the portholes.

A beautiful woman clad in flowing, black robes and an ornate, spiky headdress stepped from the shadows beyond the pipe organ and approached Yarlock. The ghostly pale beauty had a regal demeanor and an obvious rapport with the evil master of ceremonies, as became obvious when she whispered into his ear. I felt the shocking sting of her telepathic tentacles and suppressed a wince.

The witch was, Yzulyoth—the coven leader of the Hemyulac; the most powerful of all the bloodthirsty villains imprisoned in the porthole worlds. The final demon had reared its, as yet, far from ugly head.

Yarlock nodded at the witch. She turned toward the crowd and took a dramatic step forward. "There is a saboteur in our midst," she warned. "The very same saboteur who destroyed the gateway of the Krelsethian witch coven; a vengeful, misguided psychopath who is driven by insane delusions of grandeur. A crazed, idiotic luddite who would seek to throw a wrench into the wheels of progress that we have set into motion on this auspicious night of celebration."

Mutters of confusion came from the crowd

Suddenly, my image appeared 40 feet high across the misty screens of the six remaining portholes. A loop of repeating images of my demon-slaying handiwork drove home the point of the witch's accusations.

Charlotte muffled a gasp.

"Wow, it's like watching yourself in a drive-in movie," I whispered, impressed my own action-packed scenes of exciting, demon hunting intrigue. "I feel like Bruce Lee or something."

Charlotte gripped my arm tightly. "Shhhh! They'll kill you!"

"Shit, I'm a friggin' badass," I whispered, my eyes riveted to the violent scenes of R-Rated excitement being replayed on the windows of the portholes. I suppressed the urge to cheer my own exploits being replayed for the crowd and somewhat reluctantly returned my attention to the master of ceremonies.

Yarlock paced to and fro, scanning the congregation with his piercing, black eyes. "This wretched vermin carries the stench of the Opus Demonium. He and his assemblage of assassins have infiltrated our ranks in the hope of undermining centuries of work and planning. But this insane little freak of nature has vastly overestimated his chances coming here this evening—and his excruciating death will set an example for any of you who might think to question my intentions."

Yarlock gestured for Yzulyoth to commence her inquisition. The Hemyulac witch descended the steps leading down from the pipe organ stage and walked slowly into the vast throng of revelers.

I shooed my companions away from me. "Spread out! Quickly! Surround her ... and try to keep me covered."

The team dispersed, moving into the crowd as stealthily as possible, as I quickly ducked into the ranks of the hallucinating Heldethrach man-demons. The simple-minded soldiers were all still staring up at the porthole screens, completely mesmerized. They giggled stupidly—lost in the throes of a collective, acid-induced daze.

Yzulyoth approached the squadron of tripped-out foot soldiers with a look of vehement distaste. "Something striking you all as particularly funny this evening?" she asked.

The mutants turned their attention to the Hemyulac witch and began to titter uncontrollably. I backed further into the giggling gaggle of Halflings, keeping my head down.

"Silence Heldethrach scum!" Yzulyoth roared.

The Heldethrach demons cowered before her.

"What the hell is wrong with you?" she demanded, waving her hands before the dilated pupils of their eyes and snapping her fingers to gain their full attention. "Hello? Someone answer me!"

The man-demons persisted in their uncontrollable snickering. "We ate all the funny ice cream," one of the soldiers standing at the front line said.

The witch's eyes narrowed. "*Funny* ice cream?"

"It makes our mind workings act with funny colors and thoughts," another of the man-demons offered.

Yzulyoth gazed up at Yarlock with a scowl. "The interlopers have drugged them!" The witch returned her scornful gaze to the Heldrethrach minions. "This is what we get for breeding you with this pathetic human stock! You are all feeble-minded and weak. Just like the human mothers that ripped their insides apart spewing you forth into this world!"

The mutant hoard stared at the witch, slack-jawed and fearful of incurring her further wrath. Ducking down, I quickly reached beneath my robe and tore my brain helmet from my shoulder so that I might have some meager defense against the witch's inevitable mindscan.

Yzulyoth seethed with contempt. "You would all do well to remember that we could easily breed more of your numbers—should any of you meet with some unfortunate and untimely demise."

"We meant the Hemyulac mistress no disrespect by the eating of the funny ice cream," one of the front line minions said. "It was so sweet and delicious that we could not do but eat the sweet and frosty delights of the ice cream that gives us the funny brain feelings of the mind."

Yzulyoth approached the apologetic foot soldier with a sarcastic grin on her face. "Of course you could not resist ... but I'm afraid the funny ice cream will not prove as sweet and tasty as your untimely death," she muttered.

The cowering man-demon scurried out of the ranks and backed away from the approaching witch. "But ... the funny ice cream ... it made the weird thoughts in our brains!"

The Hemyulac witch stalked toward the fearful foot soldier and extended her spidery fingers. "Heldethrach necronomicus sethlu!" she hissed.

Bolts of radiant, blue electricity shot from the witch's quivering fingertips and engulfed the cowering man-demon. Seconds later, the interbred mutant's body burst violently apart, as if it had been directly hit by some invisible cruise missile, spewing a shower of gore in every direction and eliciting an eruption of gasps and horrified shrieks from the throng gathered in the caverns.

Yzulyoth addressed the now thoroughly terrified crowd with grave authority. "Do not foolishly assume that you have all assembled here of your own free will ... you have each been summoned here for a greater purpose that is far beyond your meager human comprehension!"

The tension that gripped the crowd was almost palpable, as the congregation muttered fearfully amongst themselves. The Hemyulac witch returned her attentions to the battalion of drugged Heldethrach mutants as her eyes began to glow with a fiery, red light. "The saboteur cowers within your ranks ... sniveling and creeping about like the rat that he is."

Crimson-tinted beams of searchlight shot forth from the witch's eyes and began to scan the idiotic infantry that stood quivering before her.

Quickly wiping a glob of the greasepaint mess from my face, I managed to scribble a crude smiley face on the steel interior crown of my bowler hat/brain helmet. I lifted the hat in front of my head just as the witch's telepathic lasers crossed my path. As the extrasensory streams of scarlet doom meet the reflective interior crown of my smiling brain helmet, the horrible rays reflected back into the witch's own eyes with such tremendous force that the impact sent the demon somersaulting backward through the air, end over end until she finally landed face-first on the floor of the caverns, groaning in pain.

The entire cavern went deathly silent.

Yarlock grinned down at the Heldethrach soldiers and then began to applaud with wicked glee. "Kudos ... as I expected, our idiot does not give up without a fight. This is commendable. But, I'm afraid he will pay very dearly for this particular affront."

Yarlock turned to observe Yzolyoth lifting herself from the cavern floor. "I'm sure that the next five minutes of entertainment will be more than sufficient to make up for the premature departure of the Peppermint Gang."

Yzolyoth rose to her feet, gazing about the cavern with now blinded, milky-white eyes. Before the witch could regain her bearings, all hell broke loose.

Collective gasps of horror suddenly rippled through the crowd as their attention was drawn to a terrifying vision now gracing the porthole windows: the putrefying face of my very deceased uncle, Harrison Hull, loomed over the congregation in the sextet of interdimensional gateways, like a schizophrenic Wizard of Oz.

The grotesque ghoul grinned with ghastly glee as his head hovered before a wall of flames. Spiders poured from his eye sockets as blood and squirming maggots poured from his mouth. "Ha ha ha! Foolish Earth humans! I am Meflorp Shlemplor, dark lord of the Scorpius Plane, and you are my prisoners! Do not attempt to escape my evil clutches! You are all about to be slaughtered like pigs! No flesh shall be spared!"

The Heldethrach soldiers shrieked in terror.

"Seize them! Slaughter the humans!" Harrison roared. "Die, you slithering maggots!"

Unlike most of his performances, tonight, Harrison's timing was absolutely brilliant.

The entire crowd erupted in panic, trampling over one another to reach the stairwell leading up into the mansion's wine cellar and out to safety. Both human and Heldethrach fought for purchase on the stairwell with tragic results, as the struggle sent many plummeting to their deaths.

Yarlock stared at them from the pipe organ stage, looking dumbfounded by the chaotic turn of events. "Stop you fools! I command you to stop!"

"I shall feast on your sexual organs with my razor-sharp teeth!" Harrison bellowed at the fleeing crowd.

Solomon rushed forward. "I will stop them master!" he yelled, launching a live grenade into the frantic mob bum-rushing the stairwell and then opening fire on them with a submachine gun.

Yarlock was fuming. The master of ceremonies had lost hold of the reins of his operation and his minions were now running amok, goaded into terror by the horrible warnings of Harrison Hull.

"The earth shall run red with the blood of man, woman and child!" Harrison roared.

I observed several of the Heldethrach soldiers battling over the use of the laboratory elevator, with little headway being made by any of the demonic stooges who seemed incapable of escaping the caverns in any kind of orderly fashion.

"The master commands you to stop!" Jamie Lynn shrieked, riddling the soldiers with machine gun fire.

The image looming on the portholes changed and suddenly Harrison's naked, rotting buttocks appeared forty feet high across the porthole windows.

"Hey, look at me! I'm Yarlock the Great Deceiver!" Harrison said, and then broke wind loudly, firing a spatter of maggots out of his asshole—a gesture of defiance that prompted Charlotte to vomit onto the cavern floor.

Yarlock's jaw dropped. He turned from the portholes, enraged. His eyes met mine and then widened as he spotted the battered bowler hat in my hand. "You!" he hissed. "It's you! You are the idiot!"

I examined the hat briefly and then waved it about, kicking my feet in the air like a vaudeville dancer. As I sashayed across the floor, I slipped on the puddle of Charlotte's vomit and stumbled clumsily into the crack of the rotting, flatulent asshole jiggling around on the Selurach porthole window. I passed through the interdimensional barrier with a loud sucking noise and landed, face-first, on the horrible terrain of the Scorpius Plane. As promised by the Krelsethian witches, I had successfully breached the interdimensional barrier.

I rose to my feet, donned my brain helmet, and turned to gaze out of the porthole window. As I stared out at the caverns, viewing the realm of my own earthly dimension, I saw Yzolyoth turn toward me. Her corneas suddenly cleared of their milky fog, revealing her piercing blue eyes. The Hemyulac witch suddenly cast off her robes and her beautiful body began to change form. The witch took the shape of a seven-foot tall, blue-skinned hermaphrodite demon with gargantuan, fleshy wings, green, razor-sharp teeth and a collection of slithering cobras for hair. The monster smiled at me through the otherworldly barrier, sending an ice-cold chill up my spine. My stomach twisted in knots at the sight of her grotesque, veiny erection. She was obviously aroused at the very thought of ripping me to pieces. It was also obvious that the yellow streak running up my back must be heeded while it was still only a metaphorical concept and not a physical "water sports" sort of deal instigated by the monstrously-endowed devil woman eyeing me through the supernatural egress that I currently faced.

As the creature walked toward the porthole window, grinning its terrible grin, I backed away, trying not to wet my pants. The monster raised its arms and mouthed some kind of incantation—moments later, the beast materialized before me on the Scorpius Plane.

I drew Professor Hiller's bone weapon from beneath my robe and swallowed hard, trying to play the tough guy. "How about a little fire, scarecrow?" I said, my voice cracking with fear.

Yzolyoth hissed at me and took flight with lightening-quick speed as I mumbled my own incantation and fired the weapon. The monster easily dodged the deadly beam as she momentarily vanished from sight.

Seconds later, Dr. Harvey lifted me into the malodorous air and we soared higher and higher above the nightmarish world below.

"I'll really have to get some postcards of this place." I said. "The view from the Great Black Shit Mountain rising over the human flesh rendering plant in Stench Valley is really quite stunning."

"I can drop you there if you like," Dr. Harvey offered. "Just let me gain enough altitude to actually break that thick skull of yours upon impact."

"Unfortunately I'm only here for business rather than pleasure this time. I guess I'll just have to visit the Diarrhea Rapids sometime after the big tourist season."

Dr. Harvey dove to avoid the Hemyulac horror flying after us in hot pursuit. "I always thought David Collins was the man with all of the personal demons to battle, but you seem to have them flying out of your ass these days."

"Must be the new diet. Charlotte has me eating a lot of roughage."

The monster flew by, clawing at my legs. It snatched away a large piece of my robe and thankfully nothing more during the attack.

Dr. Harvey ascended, flying out of Yzolyoth's reach.

I took aim at the beast below us with Hiller's weapon and

screamed another demonic passage from the Opus Demonium. The contraption fired its translucent laser, winging the monster, appropriately enough, on one of its wings.

The demon witch spiraled downward in a deadly nosedive, but then suddenly righted herself before plunging face-first into the rivers of blood and bile below. She soared upward like a ghastly cruise missile regaining its trajectory coordinates and resumed her chase as I frantically attempted to blast her into oblivion with Hiller's weapon.

At this point in the battle, it was quite apparent that Yarlock had reserved the talents of the deadliest of his demons for just this sort of entanglement. The Helyurac witch was not about to disappoint her master by permitting me to slip through her formidable clutches.

"We've got to lose this bitch, Doc. Take us down into the Labyrinth of Terror," I said.

"I'm not so sure that that's such great idea, Stanley."

"Yeah, well hopefully Yzolyoth will feel the same way."

"If you insist," Dr. Harvey said, diving into the labyrinth.

As Dr. Harvey had suggested, I was very soon to regret this act of desperation when the torments of the maze were unleashed in full force upon my person. A swarm of vampire bats flew past my face, snapping at my flesh with their razor-sharp teeth like a school of airborne piranha fish. A fusillade of stinging, red-hot darts shot into my body from every direction as I was propelled through the blood-drenched trenches of the maze. I flailed about, shrieking in agony like a flapping voodoo doll. Jagged shards of glass and metal tore away random chunks of my flesh as Dr. Harvey carried me along, expertly dodging the other horrors that leapt and clawed at me from the crevices and pits of the labyrinth.

"Holy fucking shit this was a terrible idea!" I screamed. "Why did you listen to me? This is a fucking horrible plan!"

"I'd be lying if I didn't admit that I'm enjoying this in some perverse way," Dr. Harvey said.

Yzolyoth maintained her pursuit with dogged persistence, and a complete indifference to the injuries she was incurring during the chase. She was a single-minded and relentless killing machine who would not give up until she had torn me into tiny pieces. Neither would the horrors of the maze. I was trapped between a hard place and a rock, and not necessarily in that order. But there's nothing like a barrage of red-hot needles to your ass and testicles to make one think outside the box.

My epiphany came suddenly: *Shiverdecker's theory of malignant reversal!* The words had come straight from the mouth of Yarlock himself, in a moment of arrogant carelessness. A passage from the Opus Demonium leapt to mind: "Metamorphium beatificarum, revertum, revertum!" I shouted "Malignacium exorcismatius revertum!"

Professor Hiller's weapon suddenly glowed with a brilliant, golden light and fired a rainbow-colored beam from its bony barrel. I waved the rainbow ray in every direction like a urinating demigod spraying beams of joyous, cathartic goodness from the head of its penis. The wondrous powers of the weapon's white magic swept through the hellish, booby-trapped trenches of the labyrinth, instantaneously transforming the tenebrous and terrible landscape into a colorful, flowering wonderland. The jagged stone and steel of the labyrinth were transformed into a leafy, green hedge maze landscaped with thriving rose gardens in full bloom. Swarms of buzzing flies were changed into lazily circling hives of honeybees; chattering vampire bats transformed into singing blue birds and fluttering butterflies. The sweet aroma of roses and honeysuckle replaced the revolting stench of fecal matter. Witnessing the transformation of the maze was not unlike being trapped in a television commercial for air-freshener.

Rosy-cheeked cherubs frolicked about atop pink, cotton candy clouds that now riddled the newly baby blue sky above. An astoundingly handsome centaur graced with the upper torso of an Adonis and the lower body of an Arabian stallion, bolted past below us, expertly twirling a set of candy cane Nunchucks. Hearing the subsequent slapping thud and shriek of agony that followed was all the assurance I needed to know that the centaur had nailed the Hemyulac witch in her big, hairy demon testicles as she soared past him.

Dr. Harvey suddenly ascended, lifting me above the hedge maze so that I might better observe the candy-colored carnage that soon resulted thanks to my handiwork.

Yzulyoth screamed in outrage as a collection of thorny tentacles extended from the rose bushes and ensnared the creature—winding tightly around her limbs. She flapped her wings madly, but could not break free of her entanglements.

As the monster struggled, a plethora of cheerfully cartoonish creatures converged on the demon. Pastel-colored teddy bears gnawed at her ankles as a rabbit wearing a pink top hat and wielding a red umbrella fenced with her whip-like tail. The chubby cherubs descended from their cotton candy clouds and began to tug violently at the demon's wings. A couple of patchwork ragdolls were tossed about like ragdolls as they wrestled with the cobras that slithered about atop the monster's head, while a swarm of winged fairies clawed at her eyes with their sparkling fingernails.

The cherubs ripped the demon's wings from her back with brute force as the centaur bucked his back legs at the creature, snapping ribs and bits of spine. A white unicorn bolted around a corner of the maze and charged at the witch, ramming its horn through her chest. Yzulyoth's still-beating heart was ripped from her body, impaled upon the spire of the bloody unicorn horn.

"Holy shit," I muttered, gazing down with shocked awe as the dying demon spat black blood and finally went limp.

"Bravo, Stanley. Walt Disney is surely turning over in his grave," Dr. Harvey said.

"Let's grab the Lovejoy codex and get the hell out of this blood-soaked wonderland," I said.

Dr. Harvey carried me to the pulpit atop the granodiorite stele, where I retrieved the object of our quest. The Lovejoy codex looked just as it had in the mind of the Selurach witch. I took the tattered section of vellum in hand. The touch of my fingertips seemed to trigger some kind of magical reaction within the codex, and—just as had happened before—the centuries-old hieroglyphics twisted and turned, shimmering with enchanted fire and revealing the hidden incantations of the document. This time the strange words appeared to be spells that would destroy the portholes of Legions of Darkness and vanquish the evil powers of Yarlock the Great Deceiver.

"Well done, Stanley," Dr. Harvey said, sounding almost truly impressed.

"I was wondering ... if you can enter the portholes and lift physical objects ... why the hell didn't you just fly in here and get the codex yourself, Doctor?"

"And deprive King Arthur of pulling Excalibur from the stone?"

"That's not really an answer."

"The Theydarian prophecies specifically state that this was a task to be left in your butter-fingered hands, Stanley. You don't send a ghost to do an idiot's job, as they say."

"As who says?"

"Most of the ghosts say that, actually. It's a little joke we have about the living."

We made our way back to our own world with lightening-quick speed, soaring high above the newly blossoming paradise of the Scorpius Plane.

Bursting from the porthole, Dr. Harvey and I found our colleagues engaged in a fierce battle to the death with the high priest of human extermination and enslavement. Professor Hiller's weapons held Yarlock in temporary bondage, surrounding the monster with searing bolts of enchanted lightening as the team blasted him from all sides. The eater of souls shifted his horrible shape into a variety of abominable manifestations as he writhed and roared in agonized fury. Promptly dealing with the source of my own agonized fury, I jerked the porcupine-like clusters of red-hot needles from my buttocks and testicles and quickly rejoined the squad of demon slayers in their efforts to subdue our malevolent nemesis.

The demented devil raised his twisted claws skyward, invoking his terrible powers of black magic. Moments later, a stone aperture in the cavern's ceiling slid slowly open, and through the shaft poured the poisonous mist of the Orias nebula. Yarlock roared and then inhaled the evils of the cloud—sucking the swirling vapors into his body like a vacuum cleaner. The resulting metamorphosis was as mindboggling as it was grotesque, as a thousand evils churned within the same horrible body, swelling it to massive size.

"He's harnessed the powers of the nebula! These weapons can't restrain him much longer," Dr. Whitlock warned.

Margot tossed her supernatural sidearm to Charlotte, who wielded the second weapon with the skill of a western movie gunfighter, blasting Yarlock with a double-fisted assault of white-hot, supernatural firepower as Margot extracted her crystal ball from a leather satchel slung over her shoulder.

Margot held the oracle aloft, gripping its rounded surface on either side like an otherworldly basketball. "From the realms of the great beyond, I summon the powers of the all-seeing oracle!" she shouted. "Isabella Hull, come forth from the mists of the afterlife and gaze into the eyes of the devil who would have sacrificed you to the Heldethrach demon in order to quench his own insane thirst for power!"

The crystal ball began to glow with an eerie, blue light, as the face of my great grandmother, Isabella Hull, materialized in the sphere. "Leland Hull!" Isabella's spirit cried. "Murderer! Sadist! Inventor of the Puckerbutt Sensations reversible, rubber, fisting mitten! Come forward and be judged by the victims of your terrible crimes! Ilku spiritus maleficarum, ilku spiritus exorcismatus!"

The bloated, shapeshifting monstrosity suddenly began to split into two separate entities, as Leland Hull's human spirit was drawn out of the grotesqueries that churned and twisted before us.

The tormented spirits of the murdered souls that haunted the Hull mansion suddenly cascaded downward, entering David Collins's body one after the other in rapid succession. Seconds after the mass possession, Collins began to levitate, floating a good six feet above the floor of the caverns. His flesh immediately faded to a ghostly, chalk white as his lips turned black and his pupils and teeth glowed with a sickly yellow sheen. Collins cackled and then spoke in an echoing, otherworldly chorus of feminine voices. "Show yourself! Worm! So that we may reap the sweet rewards of your suffering!"

Leland Hull's nude, twisted body was suddenly vomited free from the grotesque, pulsating monster that had previously concealed him. The pathetic, half-human freak slithered about on the cavern floor, with its rubbery arms flapping up and down, as he whipped his maggoty tail about like a mutant rattlesnake. The pitiable warlock scowled at Isabella's face in the crystal ball, wiping yellow puss from his eyes. "You self-righteous bitch! You could never see the bigger picture! I was to reign as the Prince of Darkness in one harmonious joining with the master!"

Margot suddenly cast the oracle to the ground, shattering the crystal ball into hundreds of jagged pieces. Isabella Hull's glowing spirit emerged from the billows of smoke that wafted from the debris, like a genie called forth from a magic lamp.

"Your master has abandoned you, Leland," Isabella said, and then coiled her translucent arms about the quivering warlock in a serpentine vice grip. She then hoisted him aloft.

David Collins descended—looming before the cowering, slime-covered necromancer like an infuriated, supernatural process server prepared to deliver an otherworldly subpoena to the terrified defendant.

"Squirm maggot! Squirm under the boot heel of your cavalcade of sins!" Collins said, intoning the chorus of otherworldly female voices. He then held his weapon outward before him. "Necronimicus vendetatum vengencio necronomicus sacrificium," he said, invoking the fantastic powers of the Opus Demonium once again.

The peculiar firearm twisted and turned—controlled by the white magic of the incantation. Within seconds, the weapon had transformed itself into a ghastly scimitar, its jagged blade reaching nearly five feet in length.

Collins swung the cutlass across Leland's belly, slicing the screaming villain's torso open and spilling a sickening mound of steaming, ebony worms onto the cavern floor. Black blood spewed from the laceration like a freshly tapped geyser of crude oil.

The stunned evildoer gasped and waved his hands about, weakly, muttering a spell under his breath. Collins swung his horrible blade, chopping Leland's hands off at the wrist. Fountains of onyx blood shot from the wounds.

Still the wretch persisted, mumbling his spell between agonized gasps. Finally, Collins raised the sword, and—in one quick swipe—lopped the warlock's head from his body.

With Leland's rein of terror at an end, Isabella's spirit faded into the ether. Moments later, Collins's spiritual inhabitants also shuffled off to greener pastures, leaving the clairvoyant dazed and exhausted, but coherent.

I gazed down at the Lovejoy codex, interpreting the strange instructions now visible upon its surface. I then looked to the monstrous, shifting blob of horror that stood before us and spotted a gapping maw lined with rows of teeth that opened and closed on the creature's lower midsection. The instructions illustrated upon the codex were so simple that even a complete asshole could understand them, and so I consulted Dr. Harvey to make certain that I was interpreting them correctly.

"Is this as obvious as it looks, Doctor?"

Dr. Harvey examined the codex and then spoke to the others with a confident authority that only someone who was dead and had nothing left to lose could muster. "Everyone make your way toward Stanley ... but don't compromise your aim on the monster. Keep firing. We need to gather the weapons together."

Everyone began to move steadily inward, coming closer and closer together like participants in a claustrophobic, otherworldly circle jerk.

"Hold your weapons outward and let them join together," I instructed.

We held our armaments aloft, crisscrossing the barrels of our weapons in a star-shaped formation. Suddenly, Professor Hiller's lethal contraptions began to interlock and shift form—mutating into an octagonal shape like that of some otherworldly crustacean.

Yarlock, roared with utter fury, perhaps sensing that his would-be assassins were finally making some sort of serious headway in our efforts toward his ultimate demise.

We could only gaze upon the final manifestation of the monster slack-jawed and consumed with complete terror—as the creature had now taken a form so utterly horrific that I am at a loss to describe its awe-inspiring ghastliness. If I said that I did not—to some minor, uncontrollably squirty degree—crap my pants in sheer terror, I would be stretching the truth a tad.

Once the weapon had completed its metamorphosis, I took hold of the bizarre contraption and heaved the malignant reversal device into the gapping jaws of the beast's lower orifice.

"It should act like a thermonuclear detonation device filled with the milk of human kindness ... which sounds sort of disgusting, but should actually work like a charm," I said, hoping my assumption was accurate. I examined the Lovejoy codex, as yet another strange passage emerged on the sheet of tattered vellum, glowing blood red against the other texts. "Flurp, blurp, chirp, burp, glurp ... Mervin

Dunlap, blah, blah, blah, gurglesnort, fuck you, you fuckin' fuck lick!" I commanded.

Dr. Whitlock raised a concerned eyebrow. "What?"

"Flurp, blurp, chirp, burp, glurp ... Mervin Dunlap, blah, blah, blah, gurglesnort, fuck you, you fuckin' fuck lick!" I repeated.

"Are you sure that incantation is correct?" Dr. Whitlock said.

I gazed at the codex. "That's what it says. I don't think I would make up something that ridiculous under the circumstances."

"What happens now, Stanley?" Charlotte said.

Before I could answer, Yarlock, the eater of souls, exploded—his twisted mass blowing apart into hundreds of slimy pieces and showering everyone with a splatter of steaming, yellow gore.

"Oh," Charlotte muttered.

Dr. Whitlock placed a slime-drenched hand upon my shoulder.

"You did it, Stanley. By God, you actually did it."

"*We* did it, Doctor. All of us." I said and then passed the Lovejoy codex to Dr. Whitlock.

Whitlock examined the codex with fascination and awe. "It's magnificent," he whispered, reaching in between the folds of his robe and extracting his trusty magnifying glass. He scrutinized the tattered artifact beneath his looking glass. "Absolutely magnificent!"

"We have to close these portholes ... so that no more demonic entities can force their way into our world," I said.

"Will the Lovejoy codex actually do that, Stanley?" Charlotte said.

"We're about to find out, baby," I said.

The portholes swirled with activity as of they were about to burst open and flood our world with their malignant evils.

"You'd better act quickly, Stanley," Dr. Harvey warned. "It looks as if we may have started some sort of chain reaction."

I snatched the codex from Dr. Whitlock's hands and began to read the strange words that glowed atop the vellum cloth. "Shagareth vishtulom olgameth!"

A great rumbling groan echoed through the cavern as the portholes began to close, shrinking in size like the aperture of some great camera lens. The cavern rock closed around them as the portholes shrank smaller and smaller in size.

"Malignant reversal," Dr. Whitlock said.

"Precisely," I said and then returned my attention to the codex. "Kavec shalock mimlep! Kasal, kasal, shalock mimlep! Kresethian, Athvenog, Selurach, Yazalaryat, Urisyazram, Slogarath, Hemyulac! Frobitas entradus un extermitus forbidae, forbidae!"

The portholes slowly vanished into the rock of the cavern walls, leaving not a trace of their former existence. The transmutation pods disappeared into the darkness of the abyss whence they came, as the rocky terrain of the cavern closed around them and sealed shut like a stony doorway.

In the span of a few intense minutes, all traces of the Gateways of the Seven Legions of Darkness had vanished within the subterranean lair. Even Yarlock's horrible pipe organ had submerged and disappeared into the granite that had previously framed its rocky stage-like platform, leaving no trace of its once prominent presence.

I turned to Solomon. "What kind of explosives do we have left in the arsenal, Mort?"

Solomon shook his head, as if clearing his mind of sheer disbelief, and gazed into my eyes with renewed hope. "A dozen grenades, maybe ... I think we've even got a small bazooka with a few missiles."

"We're going to blow this fucking place to kingdom come ... bury these caverns for good. Better safe than sorry. We don't want anybody else ever digging around in here trying to resurrect what once dwelled in these caves," I said.

"You're absolutely right," Margot said. "We should wipe this entire accursed place off the face of the earth."

Jamie Lynn looked to Dr. Harvey's hovering spirit and frowned. "But what about Dr. Harvey? He won't have a house to haunt any longer. Don't ghosts need that sort of shit to live on in the afterlife?"

Dr, Harvey smiled at the teenager. "You needn't worry about my fate, young lady. I am not bound to this place. I am free to roam the strange realms of the afterlife."

"You could always shack up in the haunted rectal suppository factory in Claremont," I suggested.

"How sweet. You're always looking out for my best interests, Stanley," Dr. Harvey said.

Chapter Twelve

_____

We leveled the crumbling ruins of the Hull Mansion with the aid of the bazooka and our small cache of grenades. The only remaining evidence of the horrible Hull Family legacy was a smoking pile of rubble, barely visible beneath the swirling blankets of fog that now filled the void left vacant by the accursed house.

With this task complete, and the Gateways of the Seven Legions of Darkness closed forever, we said our goodbyes to Dr. Harvey, who bid us adieu as his spirit faded into the mysterious realms of the great beyond. Despite our dislike for each other, there was a part of me that was always going to miss the ill-tempted, arrogant bastard. True, it was a very small part—perhaps the knuckle of my right pinky finger or my left nostril—but I did feel a slight twinge of sadness over the doctor's departure. I couldn't help but wonder what adventures the afterlife might hold for him. Would he ever learn to believe in himself, or would part of him always cling to the stubborn notion that he was only a figment of his own limited imagination? Would he mercilessly haunt me when I published a book about the irony of the doctor's strange fate? Would he return from the grave once more to demand residual checks for the book? Only time would tell.

We left the nightmare of Hull House and the Seven Legions of Darkness behind us, returning to retrieve my rented Mercedes for the drive to New York City. There I would connect with Dr. Quinlan, who I could only hope had discovered an antidote for the epidemic of insanity caused by the Death From Medusa's Uterus Plague.

The hoards of afflicted victims still roaming the Eastern region of the United States would certainly make any sort of travel a potentially deadly situation, and my colleagues and I agreed that we all stood a better chance of surviving if we stuck together. And so, we did just that, commandeering the Matheson's Volkswagen van, which allowed us the luxury of a carpool to our final destination.

New York City was like a war zone, its streets teaming with crazies of every stripe; chaos and crime ran rampant—it was almost as if the great metropolis had been completely unaffected by the terrors of the plague. Thankfully, Diseases N' Stuff was still standing, as was Dr. Quinlan, who was excited about her progress with the antidote as well as with the progress she was making with a one act play she'd written about a lonely lighthouse keeper who shares an intimate sexual relationship with an inflatable life vest.

Thanks to our combined efforts, the epidemiologist was able to develop a penicillin-based aerosol spray that all but eliminated the symptoms of psychosis brought on by the alien plague. The only remaining side effect of the contagion was a preference for wearing one's underwear on the outside of the pants with accompanying rainbow-colored suspenders.

The top brass at the Federal Emergency Management Agency determined that the most reasonable way to inoculate the infected portion of the population would be to send out several squads of colorfully-dressed clowns equipped with plastic, novelty lapel flowers that could squirt the antidote into the face of an unsuspecting plague victim. The clowns would invite the infected to take a whiff of their colorful lapel flowers, and then spray the carrier in the face with the anti-psychotic aerosol. The clown squadrons drove across the entire eastern region of the United States crowded into tiny, polka dotted cars—moving from town to town across the infected areas to contain the plague. Though a number of clowns were sexually assaulted and many suffered fatal injuries, the strategy was ultimately successful and the Death From Medusa's Uterus Plague was finally contained.

Epilogue

After developing a strong feeling of camaraderie during our fantastic ordeal, my oddball assemblage of colleagues ultimately chose to continue their association. I may have set the wheels of our strange investigation in motion, but—despite my departure—David Collins, Dr. Whitlock, Detective Solomon and Jamie Lynn Faraday held onto the Opus Demonium and the Lovejoy codex and combined their talents to form a paranormal detective agency that later became the subject of a fictional television program titled: *The Dark Orifice*. Thanks to Solomon's recommendation, his talented nephew, Herman Pinkman was hired as the director of special effects for the popular series.

With our strange work finally complete, I returned to the Poontang Palace in Los Angeles with Charlotte and Margot to convalesce from the injuries I suffered in the Maze of Terror and to begin work on my new book, *Specter Detector: Unraveling the Mysteries of the Paranormal.*

I'd hoped to distance myself from the world of the supernatural indefinitely, but there is now the matter of a strange package I received only yesterday. It contained a battered, leather-bound book and a three-foot spike cast in pure silver. I am reluctant to open the book and have hidden it from Charlotte. There was also a letter addressed to me that had been tucked into the tome, but I stopped reading when I came to the name "Dracula."

The End

Made in the USA
San Bernardino, CA
02 January 2016